PRAISE FOR
HUNGRY RATS

"*Hungry Rats* is an emotional and aesthetic tour de force about deep matters of the human heart. Author Connor Coyne shows why the novel is still the most important medium to write about what matters in a manner that matters."

– JEFFERY ALLEN
Author of *Rails Under My Back,*
Winner of the Heartland Prize for fiction

"Connor Coyne has created a richly imagined world full of surprises for his strange and wonderful characters. This work is wickedly funny and sinfully dark. I found myself both delighted and repulsed, often at the same time!"

– ARLENE MALINOWSKI
Playwright and Performer
Author of *What Does the Sun Sound Like?*

"*Hungry Rats* is an intense, gripping story of a family of outcasts and deviants. In confident, purposeful, evocative prose, Connor Coyne places you in a family where no one is watching out for you, and you had better watch your back."

– LEILA SALES
Author of *Mostly Good Girls*

HUNGRY RATS

MORE BY CONNOR COYNE

CONNORCOYNE.COM
HUNGRYRATS.COM
GOTHICFUNKPRESS.COM

HUNGRY RATS

Connor Coyne

GOTHIC FUNK PRESS

This is a work of fiction.

Contemporary names, characters, and incidents either are the product of the author's imagination or are used fictitiously. Any resemblance to actual persons is entirely coincidental. While sections set in the 19th century are based on historical individuals and primary sources, their thoughts, words, and actions described here are purely fictional.

Published in the United States by the Gothic Funk Press
gothicfunkpress.info

ISBN-13: 978-0-578-06571-7

Printed in the United States of America by Lulu

Edited by **Elisabeth Blair**
elisabethblair.net

Design by **Sam Perkins-Harbin**
forge22.com

10 9 8 7 6 5 4 3 2 1
First Edition

For the women who have raised me and made me:
Jessica, Shannie, Caitlin, Eunice, Georgia, Marion, and Mary.

"Esemplastic. The word is not in Johnson, nor have I met with it elsewhere." Neither have, I. I constructed it myself from the Greek words, *eis en plattein*, to shape into one; because, having to convey a new sense, I thought that a new term would both aid the recollection of my meaning, and prevent its being confounded with the usual import of the word, imagination.

- SAMUEL TAYLOR COLERIDGE

Biographia Literaria

PART ONE:
HUNGRY RATS AND FAT RATS

Chapter 1

Your tender toes never felt such a flood but once. Your tender toes won't never feel —

but then again —

excuse me — you never were an excessive or flagrant girl.

Always well grounded.

Always solid, feet on the ground as they say, and your tender toes never felt such a desperate flood but once. There you stood. At the edge of Lake Michigan. Down on the dunes. Up on the beach. You might as well have stood at the ocean's side, what, the way those slow gray waves rolled in along that midnight shore. Sand black and heavy. Air thick with an afghan fog. Wet like the core of a deadhead log. You never thought yourself sensitive to things like these, but the waves were persuasive. Am I right? Everyone has to have a moment. I am right. Everyone has to breathe.

I know how that weekend must've gone. Nothing new. All recycled. You climbed in the station wagon when Bitty and Betty finished combing their hair. They thought maybe that the Spice Girls would commit suicide and reincarnate themselves in the skin of each twin. And Rodney? Rodney was all dressed up with two diapers: one on his bottom and one on his head. He drooled onto his stubbly chin. These three sat in the back.

Up front sat Mara and Mark, your mom and dad, not talking. You drew them in class sometimes. Your teachers caught you, smiled, and said, "great work, a beautiful drawing." But you knew your parents were easy to draw. Children owned by parents with souls might run into trouble, what with the rending of compassion and all.

You sat in the way back, sideways, seatbelt off, reading the finest of R.L. Stine and Christopher Pike because they were delicious and built from words the depths and drains you plumbed back then. Your brother and sisters screamed and kicked but you prayed to God for peace, and they let you be, and you read on in silence like your sweet Aunt Margaret taught you.

I-69 roped down, loose around Lansing, hooked into the cord of I-94 which ran the rim of Indiana and looped on into Chicago. But halfway down the Michigan coast, your parents left the expressway and drove to the Warren Dunes State Park. They paid five dollars to set up a tent on the parking lot by the beach. It was desert empty out there, and when the engine shut off the only sound was the slipping wind. Even Bitty and Betty quieted up, worn out from their hours of shouting.

"There rats out there?" you asked.

Nobody answered.

The sun began to set behind the lake. You pitched the tent in silence, bending the plastic poles against the wind. You asked your dad for help. He said you'd better not wet the sleeping bag or he'd make you sleep outside. You weighed the tent down using cinder blocks and chunks of asphalt. Your mom made sure the lifeguards had left and pulled off her shirt and bra. Your dad took out the fishing poles and walked off toward the woods. Bitty and Betty and Rodney screamed and ran in circles. You wrapped yourself in your shawl and walked away.

"Meredith! Meredith Malady, where you goin'?" your mom called.
"I'm twelve!" you yelled back. "I'm going for a walk."

...

Each day you'd planned your great escape. Not as a runaway but as a walkaway. A long walk with no looking back. You'd never taken the plunge. Tonight, though, you saw the hopeful lamp of a lighthouse, north, north, and far away, and it pulled on your little heartstrings and drew you away from the camp. A step in the sand. A step in the sand. Crunch. Steps from your mom. Steps from your dad. Bird feathers and seashells. Over the lake, a yellow haze on the horizon.

Chicago?

But the air turned wet and twilight sailed on into night. It was black and purple out on the dunes. A mist steamed up the shore, making for a fog so dense that you lost the lighthouse ahead. The light had left you. It pulled you no longer. Now that you felt cold and alone, you thought: *I'll have to go another time*, and shivered, and turned back.

For ages you crossed great gray stretches of sand. Then, after thousands of footsteps and only halfway home, you heard a splashing sound. A fast and cutting sound that sheared the air just above the gravelly crash of the waves. You went down to the water, looking to find some rusted metal or maybe some floating bottles bumping against each other. Instead, the naked shore went straight out into the lake. Thirty feet out, three things stood, fluttering and translucent dark. They must be lumber stumps, you thought. How did they get out there? But the stumps raised their branches and the branches were arms, and you realized the stumps were people. They wore long black blankets that trailed in the water. The figures stood, a triangle of wet cold quiet. They murmured soft words:

"This direction..." they said.

They stared in searching.

You stared out with them.

You could only guess where the lake met the horizon, but where you guessed you found not darkness but a distant fire. The fog had, if anything, culled the brightest of Chicago's carbon glow from fifty miles away, making it flit and float, flare even, over the black lake, like fingers fanned, like an aurora dancing. The spectacle seemed so alive, so watchful, so very still and yet even approaching, that you knelt on the sand as if you could hide from it. Silly Meredith. You can't hide. Your blood pumped hard. Your eyes stung. A breeze brushed your brow. A wave rolled up and over your sneakers, and the water flooded the seams of your socks and the cracks of your tender toes. You only felt it that once? *So this is why they came out*, you thought. *To testify to the fire.* You wanted to join them. You wanted to throw a blanket over your own shoulder and step out into the lake.

But you feared.

You pulled your shawl a little tighter.

You turned and returned to the camp.

...

This vacation went on for four more days.

Your family sunned and sang and shouted and swam and fought and kicked each other. Betty got Bitty drunk and they built sand castles that Rodney kicked to dust. Your dad caught fish after fish and your mom drank her tea and sighed. You sighed, and each day you walked along the beach, looking for the same seekers. Each night you lay in the tent, packed between your snoring dad and drooling Rodney and listened to the wind hitting the vinyl like fists. Your eyes adjusted. The seams of the tent drew up above you, their lines dismal and utterly different from the shining horizon of the lake at midnight. Your throat clenched and the night seemed to draw out forever.

Finally, you all packed up and went home.

* * * * *

Years passed and other people moved and changed and therefore suffered. You practiced not changing. Not moving. You stood on a trapdoor after all, all day, every day. We all stand on trapdoors. A metaphor of course, not a literal trapdoor. But there you stood. The wood beams creaked awfully. They *wanted* to break. Staying cut your little heart to ribbons, but one step and you might fall through. Only one choice: to live and die here, at your home, with your family. You did your homework, made good grades, and read about ghosts and bloodwet murders. You washed the same dishes you'd washed your whole life and looked out at the same gray skies. You stood, and stood gingerly, spreading your weight as evenly upon the floor as you could.

Two years after the vacation, your family moved across the Eastside, from Jane to Maryland Avenue. At first, you liked the brown shingle house with its porch overhung. The front door opened into a bright living room dappled in green light from the summer sun on the elm out front. A broad arch led back from the living room to the dining room, and off to the right stood doors to the master bedroom, the bathroom, and another bedroom with stairs to the attic. At the back of the dining room, another arch opened onto a tiny kitchen that looked out over the backyard: two stumps, some ragged poplars, and an overgrown sandbox. Stairs from the kitchen descended past the back door and on down to the basement. You smiled the first time you walked through that house.

But the Maladys moved in quickly and completely. Clutter on clutter, empty animal cages, old coupons, broken rocking chairs, broken records, Hamady sacks and beer bottles, all over the porch, the living room, the dining room, even the stairs and the kitchen. Piles of junk covered the grass in the backyard. Your parents claimed the master bedroom, Rodney slept in the attic, and the twins took over the second bedroom. Your parents told you to move into the basement.

"Why do they get the bedroom?" you asked.
"Because you were an accident, and never even wanted," your mom said.
Bitty stuck her tongue out at you.
"I'll get you for this," you said, trying to make your voice hard.

A trapdoor opened. Rodney gave Bitty some raw pork and she ate it because it tasted "real." One month later, she died from the worms. When the pain had set in, she'd been too embarrassed to tell or ask for help, but in the end she looked even more stupid with her lips parted around her buck teeth as she lay shining in her coffin. When 'the twins' lost all meaning as an expression, a bed had opened up and your mom told you to move out of the basement.

A trapdoor opened. After the funeral, Aunt Margaret borrowed Rodney for a visit, then stole him away to California. Your parents sat on the couch.

"If she wants him, she can have him," your mom said.

Two more years. Another trapdoor. Your dad lost his job at the junk yard. He started up as a bouncer at the Vixens, drinking from noon until midnight and working and flirting until dawn. Another year and another trapdoor. The police arrested your mom. She'd spent some cold winter days with the fifteen-year-old neighbor boy. He'd missed school, and that was bad. When your dad called your Aunt Margaret, she said she expected probation. But your mom couldn't stop swearing and screaming throughout her trial. The court psychiatrist found her mentally unsound and your dad signed the papers to lock her away.

Another trapdoor. Three days before your seventeenth birthday, the Vixens fired your dad. Now he drank from noon until noon and slept on the living room couch, twelve feet from his bed. Soon the bottles of MGD and Wild Irish Rose outnumbered the old newspapers, and the whole place stank of dead flies and fermentation. Your throat was perpetually clenched and tight. You hated that house now, and my, but the trapdoors covered the floor.

Looking for solid footing, you moved back into the basement. The room was a small square with white cinder-block walls, but at least it was concrete-grounded. You returned the beer bottles and used the deposit to buy light bulbs. You cut pictures from the piles of magazines and coupons and pasted them on the walls. You lay on your bed and read and thought about doing daring things. Then, your best and only friend, Ashley Fulcrum, the girl you shared three classes with, called and said, "Your birthday was yesterday. I'm taking you out."

* * * * *

Ashley came by at seven. It was warm for early November, and you ran down the porch and jumped into her Sunbird. You raced away with rap crashing through the speakers, and the wind yanked and groped your hair until you'd almost forgotten your whole life. You went to see one of those *Matrix* movies, and you laughed and laughed, almost falling from your seats. Mothers glared at you over the heads of their angry kids, but you didn't care.

Afterwards, Ashley drove you back into town. You found a crumbling bridge in a park near a golf course, arching over a stream and overhung with willows. Ashley brought out a bottle of Jack Daniels. You both stumbled back and forth, your breath puffing, and Ashley talked of the music she'd hear, the movies she'd see, the cars she'd drive, the boys she'd seduce with dirty photos, and the mansions and jewelry they'd buy her in their lustful devotion. "Not only will I do all this, Meredith," she said, "but I'm doing it all in the next year!"

What do you do in conversation with a girl like that?

You repeated some stories about your family. The ghosts and monsters sprouting on the past. You made your tales as lurid as you could. The rats and the pigs and the woods and the flies and the fires. You made her drink these stories like sugar tea and your own tongue thought they tasted sweet. Then you lay down together beneath an old oak in the shadow of the Interstate. A gust rose, and branches briefly grew and flew together for sudden kisses, short seconds, then fell away in a hungry dance. Your mind danced away. You remembered only the mist on Lake Michigan, and your throat unclenched, and you suddenly slept.

...

"Hey, hey, Meredith. Wake up."
Ashley shook you. There was no light.
"It's after midnight. You gotta get home. I can't take you, I gotta get home."
She leaned over you, dark. The sky had clouded over and a fog had drifted in.
Panic. "You can't leave me here!" you said.
"I gotta. I gotta get home now. I'm gonna get it."
"No. I mean. You can't leave me here. I don't even know how to get home from here."
Ashley stood straight. You couldn't read her face from the shadow.
"Okay. Okay fine," she said. "But we've gotta go now. Man, how'd we fall asleep?"
"Don't know," you said.

Ashley started the car, and together you rumbled away from the Westside to the East. She followed the sloping curve of Kearsley Park past the old pavilion and from there onto the forlorn strip of Lewis Street. You sat in silence. You'd unclenched your teeth that night, enraptured by the purity of the dark skies. The warmth that the sun left hovering in the air. The icy breath of the wind and the sharp sting of the whiskey. It all meant to you that Ashley meant what she said, that she *was* your friend and there *were* places on Earth other than the ugly house where you lived. But now she was taking you back. The shadows crowded close. They made themselves into huge beasts and your throat tightened. Something pressed in back there, large and heavy and wet. The pain and strain of breathing brought tears to your eyes. Don't you know that a chestnut in the throat is the sign and seal of those with tentative footing?

"What's wrong?" Ashley asked.

A trapdoor opened. Up ahead, the fog lay thick against the pavement.

"What's that?" Ashley asked.

You'd reached the point where the mile-long strip of bars and party stores crumbled and fell and the houses stood scorched and naked wearing plywood belts, separated by great patches of empty. Where the weeds grew thick and tall.

"What's that?" Ashley asked again, an edge in her voice.

"What?" you asked.

"That."

A garbage bag lay in the street. No, it was several garbage bags stuffed with rotting clothes. No.

"My god!" said Ashley.

A hand and a wrist stuck out from the pile of plastic. A brown hand. A hand wrapped tightly around some shreds of a red-fringed shawl.

The girl lay in fetal position, half in and out of the bag. Hanging strings like nobody's business! Ashley stared. She took her foot from the accelerator and the car slowed as you drew close.

"Is that —" she began.
"Drive," you said.
"But —"
"Drive!"

Ashley turned fast onto Maryland and raced the last two blocks to stop in front of your house. You ran from the car and onto the porch, Ashley right behind you, and slammed open that door. You grabbed the phone and hit 911. Your dad woke on the couch and threw an empty bottle in your direction. It missed and shattered against the wall.
"Yes?" said the man on the phone.
"There's a girl in the street — on Lewis — on the Eastside."
Your dad rolled back to sleep.

You and Ashley were the first to learn of the stabbing death of Maria Puerta. She was two years older than you, but she'd been held back and you shared the same Algebra class. She argued with her teachers and covered her textbooks with postcards from Mexico. She'd followed her brother to a bar on Lewis, and he'd left her there. After that? No one knew. The police interviewed you, but they only gave questions. No answers. It was okay. You didn't have any answers to give either.

You cried that night.

Ashley had taken you home. She'd proven herself a true and loyal friend, and for once you felt "born of pure light," as your Aunt Margaret would have said. But while the leaves had lingered through October, they fell now. You cried for yourself and for the lump in your throat. You opened your eyes and what you saw cut your little heart to ribbons. Cinder block walls and coupon clippings. A basement with a concrete floor. But no. You saw your own personal trapdoor.

"Why do these things always have to happen?" you asked.

That night, as you lay in bed, the fog got thick, and flat clouds hung above the fog, and the rain fell. It drummed on the basement windows. In your dream, the drumming rain rolled together and became waves. In your dream, you stood in the waves.

Chapter 2

It's past midnight.

Don't worry. There's time. I'm willing and able to keep up the prophecies all the way down to the morning sacrifice. Honestly, I should have started at the beginning.

Flint, Michigan grew up near some old Indian battlegrounds. The warriors left their ghosts when they died. The fur traders came and left their ghosts, and so did the lumberjacks. Carriage makers and auto barons. Then, great waves came from Germany, Ireland, England, Hungary, New York, Missouri, Tennessee, and Kentucky. They built cars through the second World War, tore down buildings, and threw up huge pieces of concrete. Sheet metal and train tracks stretched from one end of town to the other and the factories pushed up through each neighborhood like mountains from the early earth. Then, half of the people left. They left their ghosts behind, too.

By the time you were born, the ghosts outnumbered the living. Sitting in the parking lots. Floating on the river and crouching on the runways. Leaning out from up top the radio towers. Their wails cried out like freight trains driven through the night. Your parents and your aunt arrived on a train. When you were born, they named you Meredith, and your ghosts are lumberjack ghosts. They feed on scraps. Do you understand these things?

...

When you were little, you went for a walk with Bitty and Betty along the weedy tracks at Kearsley Park. They shoved you down so you scraped your knees and cried. "Why you cry, Dith?" they asked, and kicked grass and dirt in your face. They taught you that people are predatory things and so you ran from them. You ran into the street and got hit and broke your wrist. You *knew* that a car hit harder than your sister, so why tempt fate? The point, maybe, was that you *could* and *must*. All predators tempt fate, for predation is audacious, and we must prey to live. Predators live and prey dies and people are predatory things. We feed on each other. This is why, wailing in the street, you still threw a rock at Betty's head and sent her to the hospital for stitches. It's why your parents put Nytol in your cans of pop and why they left you all alone at home in the middle of the night. Do you understand all this?

...

Of course, we don't prey all the time, or indiscriminately. Occasionally, we pretend that we aren't of the muck. And so, when guns shot off on Lewis or Franklin, your dad sent you to bed for safety. You listened there in the light of the Jesus nightlight until you settled into sleep. On other nights your mom, with an iced tea in her hand, let you stay up late and read. Sometimes, your Aunt Margaret came by and told you a story.

"Close your eyes, Meredith," she'd say, stifling a yawn. "Lay yourself back, and listen to the Story of Little Red Riding Girl."

"Little Red Riding Girl was a little girl they called that because she dressed up in red until she glowed iridescent. She wore red shoes and red socks and a red dress and red gloves and a red cape flowed down her back. And she had a great-great-grandmother she liked, but the Grandmother got sick. So Little Red had a basket of smoked bacon to take her to eat."

"Now on Little Red's walk through the forest she was noticed by a Big Bad Wolf, and the Big Bad came at Little Red, but she didn't scream because he was a master of disguises. He made himself look like a lumberjack named Little Boy Blue. Now the Big Bad couldn't eat Little Red then and there, because he can never eat you unless you invite him inside first. So Little Blue (who really was Big Bad) said to Little Red, 'Where are you going, Little Red?' She said, 'I'm going to my Grandmother's to give her a basket of smoked bacon to eat because she's sick, and when you're sick you've got to clean your plate.' 'Where does your Grandmother live?' asked Big Bad. 'She lives on the Eastside,' answered Little Red, 'on Jane Street near Lewis.' 'Oh,' said Little Blue. 'Do you want me to kiss you?' 'No!' said Little Red, and stamped her foot so that Big Bad (who was posing as Little Blue) was scared.

"But Big Bad left her and went down to Grandmother's house. And Grandmother, who thought it was Little Blue and not Big Bad, invited him inside. And terrible things happened. Then, who should come knocking upon the door, but Little Red? She came in and Grandmother (who was really Big Bad in disguise) said 'Give me my smoked bacon!' Little Red said, 'Who are you?' and Big Bad said, 'The Devil!' and he climbed out of bed and ate her all up, so Meredith don't you never talk to strangers."

...

Then, there was the time you rode your trike down to the park. You remember that? You understand? When you saw the giant stone pavilion and went on inside? When you opened that rusty door at the corner and the air inside was aboiling with flies? When the sun looked in, and you looked in, and you saw the heaps of discarded meat, chicken fat, hamburger, hogs' heads? When you saw dozens of rats squirming around it, through it, in it, over it, under it, eating it? Do you remember the words your mom recited for you when you got home?

> I have held two kinds of rat,
> one is hungry and one is fat.
> The fat rats roll over onto their backs,
> but the hungry rats sneak and attack.
>
> They run and roll all over the world,
> no rest for boys, no sleep for girls,

in rain and lightning and tornado whirl,
and into the sunrise where the world hurls.

They climb the towering mountain peaks.
They swim the crushing ocean deeps.
And if her children die in heaps
their mother ever onward creeps.

And if you think they're far away
they could come into your house today.
A single one could name you prey
and they outnumber you anyway.

And by the way, I think they're here.
Can't you listen? Don't you hear?
The scrabbling of their feet out there,
the wet of thirst, the sweat of fear?

We swing the axe, we fire guns,
the police and spies, away they run.
The army's lost, they're overrun.
The rats are hot and hungry as the sun.

Maybe you thought you'd use persuasion
but that won't work on this occasion.
The hungry rats don't like oration.
Annihilation is their destination.

And if you think you're with them too,
and that the rats were friends you knew,
I've got a truth to say to you:
They'll eat your eyes before they're through.

You were five.

You never returned for that trike.

You been afraid of rats ever since.

...

My my, Meredith. You've felt besieged in life. Preyed upon. Played out. Drawn down. You aren't a predator. You know this. Even if you did throw that rock, your talent is in lying low. Each day, your throat clenched up. You walked to school up back alleys, past potholes and potheads, Buicks and bailiffs, funeral homes and Bible studies. Each week, you slunk through Kessel's looking for potato chips and cigarettes for your mom, passing cinder blocks and armless clocks and rusted cars and shopping carts, a home to the mold and the moss. You sat back in the farthest corners of your porch and read through the night while white moths circled overhead. The ice cream truck, dust-streaked so its bright sheen turned to vanilla cream, circled the block and sang out the same three-chime song:

Do – be da.

Be do.

Do – be da.

Be do.

Do be do de do be do.

Be da da da dum de dum dum dum.

Ba dum dum dum de dum de dum dum.

Ba dum dum dum. Pum pum pum pum. Ba da da da da da dum.

Be do. Be do. Be do do do.

...

Who knew?

You knew?

You've always known.

You've always understood.

You're nothing but a hungry rat, adrift. Hungry, adrift in the mainstream. Oh, that mainstream. Those trapdoors, flat rafts, and all the hungry rats, roiling on to the end of the world. That mainstream. I'm sure, sure, you understand that one conformity is as good as the next. Right?

I try. I am a very empathetic person, but...still, I wonder what you lock up in that strange brain of yours. You always were a strange girl, tender toes and all.

So, Meredith, that's the middle and beginning of the story. Now we can finally get to the end. That juicy morsel. When you made it to your senior year at Central High School, you didn't plan for college or adventures. Your main goal was a nice bedroom and being friends with Ashley. You always thought a bowling alley would be a fun place to work. Free fries, loud music, and neon lights. Or maybe the public library, for the opposite reasons. That's just fine. It didn't even matter. Just as long as you could take two weeks after graduation to forget who you were, and why you had to be born into such a life.

At least that was the plan before Maria Puerta was murdered.

Chapter 3

The rain fell all night long, increasing before dawn then tapering off. On your way to school that morning, you stopped at the edge of the porch. Diluvianated with rain and river, the Maryland Avenue sewers had choked up. A stinking current moved along the curb. Floating in a pool in front of your house you saw five drowned rats. Their eyes had gone milky white and their yellow teeth stuck out. They turned in slow circles as if adrift in the you-know-what.

You hurried past, caught the bus, and made it to Central. "What happened?" The halls hushed in Maria's wake. "Why Maria?" "Her brother used to run with the Cobras." Eyes followed you. "What did you see, Meredith?" They couldn't ask Ashley; after she let the rumor slip, she'd called in sick. "Meredith, you okay?" the students asked. "You alright?" But they didn't know you, and on other days they might have mocked you. "Meredith, anything I can do to help?" "No, thanks." You felt a cold core in your chest, and you didn't know whether it was anger or remorse. It did make you shake, though. Your throat clenched. You felt for Maria and the loss of all her years. As sign of your sorrow, you rode the Lewis bus home so you could stare at the taped off crime scene.

It rained again that night, and you dreamed of a hulking lumbering. An angry man. He grappled with you and grabbed at your hair, but you slid from between his hairy hands. You woke under your comforter. The black of that basement was blacker than black. Sleet rattled against the windows. Your sheets were wet and sticky with pee. You put them in the washer with your nightdress and underwear and turned on the light. Then you lay down, naked as a blue jay, and clutched your shawl to your chest.

"It takes," you said to the empty room, "it takes my breath away."

You didn't know what you meant by that, but you had inherited the gift of premonition: as you slept, a crime had occurred, horrible and vast.

Strange rumors circled the Eastside the next day.

At school, the police talked to security, security to the teachers, and the teachers to the students. "A man," the students said. "A man was found." "His neighbors found him." "They found him when his dog wouldn't stop barking." "No," they said, "he didn't have a dog. It was the people downstairs. They heard him scream." "No they didn't," they said. "It happened during the night, but he never screamed. They found him in the morning." "How did they find him?" "When they went upstairs to pay their rent." "He was crucified," they said. "No he wasn't." "He was lying on his back with a knife in his chest. But he did have marks and stabs on his hands and feet." "Face up."

So another had been rebaptized. Maria's death, a likely crime of passion. This man's death, a passion play. An inspector pulled you from your last class and took another statement about Maria.
"Do you think they're related?" you asked.
"Do I think what's related?" he said without looking up. Writing notes on a notepad.
"Maria's murder? The man stabbed this morning?"
He looked up. "Why would you say that?"

You turned down his offer for a ride back home. You rode the Lewis bus past the crime scene and walked the rest of the way.

Back home, Betty sat on the floor and drank your dad's beer. He slept on the couch behind her. You turned on the TV to see whether Amos Hammer's murder – what the Flint Journal had called "a bizarre and horrible crime" – had made the evening news. It had. A reporter stood a few feet from a taped-off house. "The puncture wounds on the hands and feet are known as stigmata," she said. "The Flint police are urging anyone with information to contact them." You leaned in. You knew this place. It was on the Eastside. On Lewis Street north of Maryland. Only a half-mile away.

"Too bad," Betty said, and she painted her nails Persian blue.

For the rest of the week, you continued to work on your room. You cut photos and ads from *Parade* and *People* and ran tissue streamers between the light bulb and the wall. You hung Christmas lights in the window wells. On Friday, you called Ashley and asked if she wanted to see a movie, but she was busy. On Saturday, you called her again and she picked you up and drove to Birch Run. The two of you walked from store to store, and Ashley bought herself shoes and sunglasses and a dress. She bought you a pair of earrings, and when you told her that your ears weren't pierced, she paid to have them pierced. Then, on to McDonald's and Cinema Hollywood to see James Bond.

Sunday went by, drizzly and murky, and on Monday another body turned up, this time on the North End. Jimmy Coals, a quiet man, a retired autoworker, lived in his cookie-cutter house alone among the gangs and the turbulence. He had last been seen at a downtown bar the night before. He had had a few drinks and left. Nobody remembered whether he had been with someone. They barely remembered that he had been there at all. The next morning, a neighbor saw Jimmy's door hanging open. The police barred the press from the scene but repeated their request for information. All of the local papers broadcast a "Deadly November."

Down in your basement, the late sun bled through the tissue rainbows and painted your walls in pastel shades. It had been years since you'd graduated from Stine and Pike to Thomas Harris. You not only knew Jeffrey Dahmer and Ted Bundy, but also Belle Gunness and H. H. Holmes. Gary Heidnik and John Norman Collins. None of these monsters came from Flint. Certainly, there were gangs and pimps and bitter ex-shop workers and ex-mayors and even other, more straightforwardly angry souls. Some killed for drugs and money and jealousy, but pleasure seemed peripheral to these crimes. That was fine, perhaps, but where were Flint's poets of murder? Why not kill in symmetry, to make a puzzle? For attention and reputation? Why not? Someone must have had these higher aspirations, and you'd often wondered who he was, and why he was hiding out, restraining himself.

Restraint rarely lasts forever.

Wednesday and Thursday passed in pink sunshine, but Friday shadowed over and fat drops fell, and on Saturday morning, the city made the American spotlight.

20

There, on the screen TV, "Flint, Michigan" appeared in the lower left hand corner. Fox News, national.

"Look at us," said Betty.

Amanda Helmet, a woman from the suburbs had been found eviscerated between her living room and kitchen.
The letter "R" had been smeared in blood on the pearly fine living room wall.
In the hall, "A."
In the kitchen, "T."

"Did it spell 'art' or 'tar' or 'rat'? Or something else?" someone asked a packed press room.

With the story breaking coast-to-coast – poor Flint – starving Flint – nobody notices you except when you writhe – the police were more forthcoming than they had been before. In fact, the stage was crowded with reluctant celebrities: police from Flint and Grand Blanc Township, the Genesee County Sheriff's Department, the Michigan State Police, and the FBI. Flanked by two mayors and police chiefs, the head of the homicide department looked out over the restless crowd. Yes, he explained, Jimmy Coals had suffered from poison and stigmata. Yes, he had been stabbed to death. On examination, dead rats had been found at all three houses. The victims had been poisoned, but not the rats.

"So it spelled 'rat,' then, right?"

Commander Wheatley ignored the question. "If there's anything we can say about all of the homicides, related or unrelated, of the last several weeks, it's that the victims were all alone and unprotected. This includes two slayings on the North Side, which I'll note the press has not covered in such detail. We urge all members of the public to stay alert, to let friends and family members know where you're going and when you will arrive. Don't accept food or drink from someone you don't trust. And, of course, lock your doors and windows and call our tip line if you have any information, or to report any suspicious activity."

You imagined one phone, then several, ringing and ringing, through the day and on into the night. Tips, suspicions, bigotries, and false confessions.

"It seems like we've had to deal with a lot, here, in Flint, in recent years. But we've got each other and we're going to get through this together."

Betty laughed her icy laugh.

"We want you to know that your police and law enforcement are working hard on every lead, and with your help and cooperation, we'll get through this too."

Cut to the anchor.

"Police haven't said if they think her death is related, but skeptics believe that an earlier homicide – a local high-school girl – may have been gang-related, or perhaps a random act of violence." She cut her papers, clearly ready to move on. "Flint *does* have one of the highest crime rates in the nation."

Betty lazily reached out and put on the VCR. Now the Teletubbies stood and smiled as a parade of animals marched by.

Rat. Rat. It made you shiver. You shook as if cold. In the basement below, the furnace coughed into life. You remembered the rats in the pavilion and the words that your mom had recited. You couldn't remember the exact phrasing, but her poem had bitten your mind with its hunger and evocation. Trixie Belden had always started with insight and empathy, and clearly this killer felt something about rats. Might your aversion correspond to his compulsion? Might your fear approximate his rage? You decided to look for the poem.

Up in the attic, Rodney's weary bed and its dust covered electric blanket huddled close to the single window. On top, boxes of your mom's clothes awaited her possible release and return. One-by-twelve planks ran across the naked insulation like catwalks, and in a corner you found three more cardboard boxes. The first held Rodney's toys: building blocks, Hot Wheels, and old cartoons on VHS. The second box held a broken alarm clock, a rhinestone necklace, legal deeds from Wexford and Clare counties, and a photo of an angry and noseless woman with a kerchief on her face and wood chips in her hair. There was certainly a family resemblance, but the picture was so old that the paper had cracked and wilted into a scroll. The third box held books by the dozens! You found *A Picture History of Genesee County*, *Well Do I Remember* by Ann Lethbridge with a green cloth cover and cardboard backing, and a guide to Michigan trees. Beneath these lay a stack of National Geographics and a half-dozen Bibles, all cheap King James editions with red covers and the words of Jesus in red. At the bottom of it all, some S.T. Coleridge and *The Old Farmer's Almanac* from 1958. No sign of the words your mom had recited.

Disappointed, you closed the boxes and went downstairs with Rodney's taped episodes of *Scooby Doo*. Betty had joined your dad in an alcoholic slumber, and you sat beside them in the living room and watched several episodes, always guessing five minutes in who wore the mask and why. You wondered if Flint's rat-and-cross murderer wore a mask as well. You speculated, cataloging kids, neighbors, and family, searching for a man in a three-piece suit with a winning smile and sharp eye teeth. Maybe a staid professional with a brisk walk and a calming voice. A disheveled gardener with red bags under his reddish eyes. But you didn't know anyone like this and you drew no conclusions. You went downstairs. Ashley came over and found you sitting on your bed.

"You heard we made national news. Maybe this'll make us number one for murder again."
"I want to see it," you said. "The house where it happened."
"I'm not driving all the way to Grand Blanc just for that."
"No. The first one. Right near here."
"It's near here?"
"It's north on Lewis."
"I don't like Lewis." She was thinking of Maria.
Trembling with excitement and trying to hide it, you slipped your coat on, clicked off the lights, and left through the back door. Ashley

followed. She stood in your driveway.

"Come on," you said.

She thrust her hands in her pockets and glared.

"Please?" you asked.

Leaves, yellow and red, had fallen into the mud, but their tips reached up from the depths and tossed out copper-colored sparks of light. For a few minutes, everything seemed blindingly bright. Against November-gray days, this rare and true blue sky seemed as sharp as the surface of the sun. You knew you weren't the killer's next target. You were on an adventure.

"Why do you think he did it?" Ashley asked.

"I don't know."

"Why would anyone be so nasty like that? How could anyone get off on that?" You walked. "I mean," she went on, "I get why people murder. Not like, you know, I think it's right or anything. But I get it. If you do it for money then you have something to get from it, and if you do it because someone pissed you off, then you get revenge, right? But this isn't anything like that."

"No. It's not," you said.

"Cause none of them have even been raped. Right? Or robbed. They would have said if they had, right?"

"Serial killers don't kill for normal reasons," you said.

"I don't think rape is normal."

"It is compared to why serial killers kill."

Ashley stared at you, startled. The thought hadn't occurred to her.

"They can act very convincing," you said. "They can have a lot of different reasons, but they're not crazy like normal crazy people. They don't talk to themselves and hallucinate all the time. The dog doesn't tell them to do it and neither does the Devil. They're broken in a different way. They don't feel for other people. For them, killing a person is like killing a fly. So when they want to do these things, when it hits them, they do it. There isn't anything holding them back. Besides that, they're just like us. In every way."

Ashley thought about this. "I think they're perverts. Not perverts for sex maybe. Perverts for blood or something."

"That's exactly what they are."

You walked and great grids of electric wires buzzed above you.

"Thing is," you said. "We all have thoughts like that. We all have days when there's someone we want to – kill or poison or hurt. But we feel for people. We hold ourselves back."

"I could never do something like that."

"I could," you said. "The difference is that I wouldn't."

The silence held for almost a block.

"In fact," you said, "the only way you can know it isn't me is because you think you know me. Unless I'm just acting really well." You burst into villainous laughter. "Or unless it's actually *you*."

The Flint River swung in and cracked the Eastside grid of streets. Several blocks behind you, Maria had lain herself down. Up ahead, Lewis narrowed and broke to the right, and the houses fell aside for the river. You followed the blocks as they dwindled, and the tottering shakeside houses leaned. They frowned. They drooled from their awful gutters that spilled stinking water into the yards and driveways and streets.

"Why isn't there more goodness in the world?" Ashley asked.

"Don't be melodramatic," you said.

The murder house stood taller and larger than all the others on the block and, strangely, the second story was larger than the first. The top half hung – it protruded out past the porch – several feet over the lawn, supported by timbers, twelve-by-twelves, driven into the ground and bolted onto the structure. You couldn't imagine how it had been built in the first place, and the north end had already begun to list, the beams sinking further, too deep, into the soft earth. The river was less than a block away. Yellow police tape wrapped around half of the lawn. It had torn on the other side and the ragged ends fluttered in the wind.

Until that moment, you had thought you wanted to see the house for a visceral thrill. To contemplate different perspectives and angles than your television could give. To ascribe your shivers to the wind. Now, however, you realized that you wanted to see the crime itself. Seeing the house made seeing the crime easier. You walked up the sidewalk, Ashley following, and as the sun shifted behind the trees, it was easier to imagine that it was nighttime. You ducked under the tape to get a better look at the porch. Leaves lay against the doormat. Downstairs, a family sat in their living room, watching their TV. The flickering of the screen danced against their drawn shades. The victim's windows upstairs were dark. The sound of the rain had drummed him to sleep during the last quarter of the game.

Did the killer force entry? The front door, bruised and rusted, stood unbroken. If the killer had repeatedly kicked the door, or had even knocked, the family downstairs would've heard. They'd heard nothing. You walked around the house to the north, where a vacant lot opened onto the street and, ultimately, the flat fields of a large park. Where the second story listed most, the windows had cracked in their frames. Old glass windows. They wouldn't shatter apart if smashed, but the cracks looked weathered and old. Behind the house, the leaves had been raked into neat piles. Amos Hammer was the landlord; he had raked them, most likely. Never bagged them, though. On the south side, a narrow alley separated the house from its neighbor. As you rounded the corner, you saw an enclosed exterior stairway that climbed to the second floor. It was anchored by a gray door, a grimy door, that probably locked on the inside – no deadbolt – and opened inward.

"That's where he got in," you said.

The killer knocked on the door. Waited. Knocked again. The victim didn't answer for several minutes. With the tapping of the rain on the windows, he hadn't realized he had a visitor. When the knocks got louder, the victim slipped on his trousers and a pair of glasses – let's say he was nearsighted – and stumbled down the stairs. He had a terrible pain in his stomach. A doubling-over of the guts. An almost-so-bad-you-can't-walk pain. A gnawing from the inside out. *I have never felt this!* he thought. He opened the side door a crack. "Who is it?" The killer didn't answer. He gave the door a shove. The victim was too stunned to push back. He tripped and fell back against the stairs. The killer had a cook knife and put the blade into the victim's stomach. The victim gasped, coughed twice, then turned and crept back up the stairs, dripping blood onto the wood. The killer entered, shut the door behind him, and followed.

The killer found the victim on his back between the kitchen and the front stairway. He'd made a try for either the phone or the front door, but had collapsed and given up. The killer sat at the kitchen table and watched. Both motionless. Oddly patient. They waited for the bleeding to stop.

It stopped.

The killer cut his marks in the victim and hid his rats and slipped out the way he came. He shut the door behind him. But when did he poison the victim?

"You, you what you doin' here?" asked an old woman.
She stood on the porch of the bungalow next door, leaning on a cane.
"Us?" said Ashley. "Nothing."
"Bullshit nothin', you pokin' roun' where that man died. He dead. He dead so why don't you get gone!"
The rage boiled up. "We said we weren't doin' nothin' you fuckin' whore!" you said.
The woman hurried into her house and slammed the door. Across the street, two dogs, inbred chows with blue eyes, spat barks as they paced in hunger behind a slimpsy fence.
You went still inside.
"Let's go," Ashley said.

One block later.

"I wish I could see that place from the inside," you said. "Look around some. I just – I just really want to know – I know it should freak me out, but it doesn't. I was there when Mom found Bitty dead, so I don't get freaked out."

One block later.

"Ashley," you said. "Do you think I could spend the night tonight?"
"Um," she said, "I was going to go out with Brian Crux. You know, Brian?"
"He went out with Maria, didn't he?"
"No. They were friends, though. Well, he asked me out. To go play pool at the Santa Fe."
"Can I come?"
"No. Sorry."

You walked. Your throat clenched.

"It's kind of a thing between us now," Ashley said. "Brian and me."

"I just... I would like to be somewhere else tonight."

"Oh – I don't know – I – guess you could spend the night anyway. You'll have to put up with my mom. Just ignore her until I get back. Then we can stay up and hang out some more."

"Yeah," you said. You tried not to sound overeager. "I would like that."

"Cool."

* * * * *

Ashley lived in the East Village, just south of the Eastside. She lived on Linwood Avenue near Parkside Drive, and the houses were what you'd expect on streets with such names, from Cape Cods with huge elms out front to stone mansions with surrounding hedges. Ashley's house was among the largest: tall, gothic, half stone and half blackened timber. The lawn had been chemically treated and almost bled onto your shoes as you walked across from the car. Mrs. Fulcrum met you at the door.

"Hi Mom. You remember Meredith, right?"

"Meredith," Mrs. Fulcrum hummed. "From school? Nice to meet you, Meredith."

"Meredith wants to spend the night," Ashley said, "but I already told Brian I'd go out with him tonight. So is it okay if she just stays in the guest room, and I get back not-too-late?"

Mrs. Fulcrum visibly tilted her head, making a point of thinking it over.

"We're playing pool," Ashley said.

"I don't see why not –" said Mrs. Fulcrum. She was unsteady on her feet.

Ashley went upstairs to change.

"This is a gorgeous house," you said. You took off your shoes.

"Thanks," said Mrs. Fulcrum. "I owe you apologies, Meredith. I'm a bit tipsy. I just had a very unsettling experience, so I'm not really making a whole lot of sense right now, to myself or probably to anyone else."

You knew she'd acquired these words, this way of speaking, naturally, through conversation. Not from books. Your envy sharpened.

"So I've been drinking wine. Would you like some?"

"No thanks," you murmured.

You followed her to the kitchen, where she sat on a stool behind the counter and picked up a half-full wine glass. According to the label on the empty bottle, the wine was older than you. A door slammed. Ashley had left.

"I don't know about that girl, Meredith. I don't know," said Mrs. Fulcrum with a cough. "I'm worried she'll become a slut. Mind you, I don't have any real reason to think that, except that she is very much like I was, in every way, right down to the lies she tells me when she steps through the door. Like that she's going to play pool. I'm *sure* that's what she's playing. I could say to her, 'I know that you're lying, because I used to do it myself,' but I'm a bit of a coward and I'd rather not know for sure."

"Oh."

She coughed. "Of course, that's old news, not new news, and who wants to hear old news. Let's see, what's new? I'm sorry the place is such a mess." The kitchen was spotless. "I've had a hectic day, and it just – my mind is spinning and I've been chain-smoking."

You thought her eyes seemed wet, but she turned to look out the window.

"I'm the best thing," she slurred, "the best that girl could hope for. She'll figure it out, someday, I hope before it's too late. This morning the housekeeper came in and told me that she needed Thanksgiving off. You're going to think I'm an old witch, Meredith, for being a bit upset about it, but I did at least let her have the day off. I would be tempted not to, most years, but her mother has diabetes, or a fluttering heart, or some recurrent dementia, or a cyst or something. They don't know about her at all, so she wanted to spend Thanksgiving with her, so I'm thinking, 'How can I say 'no?' It's quite easy, actually, just pronounce the word: 'No.' But I didn't. I told her she could go."

Mrs. Fulcrum sighed. Her long nails rattled on the countertop like the feet of a small animal.

"We have a large family," she went on. "I'm not sure if Ashley has told you that, but we do. I don't suppose – well, hmm, never mind, we have a very large family on both sides. Normally we go to visit them every New Year's and Christmas and Fourth of July. It's more of a pain than you might imagine, because half of them live in New York City and the rest all live in Indianapolis. I love my family, don't get me wrong, but some of them are pretty awful people. They come out here for Thanksgiving and it's a problem finding beds for them and making sure that everyone has enough food. Plus this year we're going to have to do it without the housekeeper, and I don't know how it's all going to come together. Maybe I'll wait until the last minute and call the whole thing off. Has Ashley told you that her father and I are divorced?"

"What? Oh, yes. She told me."

"See what I mean? She lies."

Mrs. Fulcrum stopped to take a long gulp and coughed. She ran the back of her hand along her cheek, casually, dismissively.

"Donald and I aren't divorced. We have a very happy marriage. But that's the same lie I always told at that age. We really are too alike, Ashley and myself. My mother was a housewife, but my father sold all his stock in the Big Three and invested in Arab-owned oil. 'Timing is everything,' as the comedians say. It was a decent bit of stock, so it made a difference. I always lied and said he was a heart surgeon and that they were divorced. It seemed more romantic. 'He heals broken hearts,' and all that. My friends all bought it because he was never home. Are your parents divorced, Meredith?"

"Yes," you said. A lie, but it seemed more romantic.

"See what I'm saying? Oh, I'm not making any sense at all. Ashley's father trades in stock, but he's also got this saxophone habit and he's gone a lot of the time. Right now he's playing in London. He isn't much of a musician, if you ask me, but he's amazing with sound systems and they take him everywhere they go. They use him in the London Philharmonic and even the Chicago Symphony from time to time. He just got back from touring in Japan. He manages their finances for them, you see. Doesn't make much money though. We scrape by on my work. I help coordinate marketing for the Big Three. It's all in SUVs these days, and will be for the next decade at least. Big cars, big profit margins, these are GM's 'road to recovery.' But we don't mind Mr. Fulcrum having his fun. It gives our family a bit of soul. For all its merits, my family is somewhat deficient where soul is concerned."

You went up to the guest room. You sat and read a Reader's Digest. After four hours, Ashley still hadn't returned. You fell asleep. You met the killer in your dreams again. He grabbed your hair and dragged you to dance in crimson light. He spun you and spun you, his dirty long nails digging into your wrists while his features streaked in the spinning spinning. Spinning on constant rotation, like the oldies stations spin old records, so notorious, to be notorious is to be infamous, and the heavy rotation, rotating tires to keep them safe, rolling like SUVs, rotating at high RPMs for speed. So speed built. The next thing you knew, you boarded a plane, a Concorde bracing against the Atlantic and flying you forward for your tour of London.

Chapter 4

Turn your face up.

Turn your face back down.

For every mountain you'll climb, you'll find a slope on the other side.

And every cup of tea you drink – you'll have to let it steep.

You always credited yourself with simple ambitions. Great passions, great pleasures, predicate themselves on the most perilous suspension. The inevitable trapdoor drops the pilgrim into the current of despair. Points of misery. Earthbound tortures. Given their already constant action in your life, you never wondered whether it would be wise to risk more. Someday you'd move away from home, factor out your family. Plant a garden, factor out the street trash. You knew that Linwood and Parkside were outside your reach. You'd never speak as floridly as Mrs. Fulcrum, or even as easily as Ashley.

Your throat clenched up on something large, round, and wet. Your blister chestnut. Your sore swoln. This is the seal and sign of those stranded on trapdoors.

In tenth grade, you told me, you met a boy downtown and told him about your night in the mist on Lake Michigan. "I left them," you said. The words stumbled out of your doubting mouth, like an accidental tripping up the stairs. "I didn't want to, but they scared me." You thought that maybe he would understand.

Semis plowed along Saginaw Street, and as they rolled, they coughed. The coughs gave birth to clouds which joined and made the fog. The boy rolled his cigarettes and smoked them. He handed you one and you took a puff and gave birth to a cloud, and it joined and made the fog. Suddenly you saw smoking not as glamour or as habit, but as cloudbirth. To smoke was to partake of the fog, and you knew that the fog gave you something you needed. You hungered, then. The rain, and oh, the lake.

The boy gave you cigarette after cigarette, but your throat went raw and sore. It wasn't working. The mist of the lake was cool and damp, and the smoke in your mouth was hot and dry. It didn't soothe and pull; it lacerated. In the end, after all you had told him, the boy hadn't seen what you wanted and needed. Some have said, "You can't come back from the dead." They may just as easily have said that only devils and gods make clouds. There was nothing else to do. You took the bus back home.

Your throat clenched.

In eighth grade, you told me once, you borrowed a guitar from the music room. You rode to downtown Flint and entered a shop fronted with a window of wig-wearing severed mannequin heads. You bought a four-dollar pass to the show. There, bands from Kearsley, Carman-Ainsworth, Burton, and Flushing played themselves raw each night. The scarecrow boys and their feline girlfriends twisted and tangled into sudden knots, kicking, punching, and rolling on the stained carpet. Jumping on each other. You sat against the wall to protect the guitar. You knew three chords and strummed them over and over. Did you even know how to tune the strings? No one else noticed you sitting there, and you didn't try to talk to them. Some have said that haste makes waste, and that means that being noticed is the risk of violence and injury. When the show finished, and click-tick, the lights went off and on again, the buses had stopped for the night. The boys and their girls caught their rides, but you walked home under the angry stars.

Your throat clenched. Your water chestnut.

Once, your Aunt Margaret told you about the End Times. She had seen it. "Bagnios and stockades wash 'way in the flood, that river. That mainstream! It feeds the forests and they go to seed and soon they grow big and thorny. Hemlocks and vice, spruces and sin, spires and spears and sharp black needles. The monsters and stars set them aflame, far off at the ends of the Earth, and so our evil feeds the fire. We fuel the furnace that eats us. It's not a normal fire, Meredith. It's the first and only empty fire."

"But then there are also the lumberjacks," she told you.

"They've been given every shortcut and directed to take them all, and they'll be demons to stop the Devil, if that is what it takes. They attack the trees with their saws and axes! Cutting the trees before the fire arrives! Stopping it in its path! Keeping the flames from burning the world! Better a world without trees than a world burned to soot. Better to make Earth a little like Hell than to allow Hell to visit Earth."

"The most beautiful and awful thing, in those days, will be to climb the highest trees and put your hand to your brow. You'll see it. Far off, far, where the world makes a little curve, you'll spy a faint and flickering light, soft orange and all-encompassing. An aurora from the Earth. The fire deep and silent and approaching. It'll burn just over the horizon. It'll feed on the trees. Your breath catches in your chestnut throat."

...

When you were twelve, your family went camping at Warren Dunes State Park, and you went for a walk. The sun went down, but a lighthouse led you forward. You thought you'd run away from home. Then, the fog washed in on woolly gray waves. They seemed to swell to spread their weight. Your chestnut grew until you almost couldn't breathe. It never left your thoughts, really, that chestnut, and it ballooned beautiful whenever you turned to find your way back home. You were short on breath, then, and a little dizzy, when you heard a sound that was not from the wind or the waves. You walked down to the water. Three things stood there, long, wraithlike, wearing heavy blankets. They lifted their arms as if offering sacrifice. They looked out into the glowing distance.

"Will you come in this direction now?" they said, their voices merging low and sweet as honey.

I'll come, you thought.

"Esemplasy," they said.

If you'd had a knife, you might have sliced your throat and ripped out the chestnut. You'd have flung it to the sand and clasped your hands over your bleeding neck to breathe beyond obstructions and blocks. You wanted to join these strangers in the water. They knew that water washes away. They understood.

"Raise the oceans to quench them," they said.

I can't, you thought, and walked away, you throat aching.

...

Back at the camp, your mom sat on the asphalt looking out toward the lake.
"Fuckin' hate that fog," she said as you approached. "Fuckin' hate camping. You know what we could buy with the money this all costs?"
You shook your head. She shook hers.
"Where you been?" she asked.
"Walking."
"You been out walkin' a long time."

She coughed.

"Well, sit down. We been worried about you. An' quiet up so you don't wake nobody."

She watched. You sat down beside her. You both studied the darkness.

"Meredith, Meredith," she said. "Meredith, Michigan."

She coughed.

"Don't think I love you," she said. "Don't think."

She paused.

She sighed.

"Still," she said, "you're the one I like best. Too bad you were born last of 'em or I might not have hated all – this," and she waved her hand. A vast movement. It took in you and your family, the sand, the stars, and the entire universe. Everything that she despised, because she despised everything.

She pulled in her pocket. She palmed a flask of Old Overholt and gave you a bolt. It burned in your throat, a familiar fire. She smiled a little. She laughed, almost.

"Meredith, Meredith," she said, and ran her hand fondly down your back. "I wish you were never born, none of you. I mean it."

She waited. You didn't speak.

"I don't say it to be hard or cruel. I don't. I just – look, don't you never talk to strangers, Meredith. And don't go with them and be with them. And make sure you don't get pregnant. I swear, Meredith, you'll think you'll love your babies awhile, but then some time passes, just a little time, and you'll see what they do to your life! But you still do it – give it all up, just so these screaming, shitting little things can live!"

Her voice was low and cautious, an attempted calm and soothing sound. But she put her hand on your knees, and her fingers and nails felt skeletal.

"I – hate all my children," she said.

You thought for a moment.

"That's all right Mom," you said. "We don't like you either. It's 'either' by the way, not 'neither.' White trash say 'neither.' We call it a double negative. And all that about not talking to strangers? Hell, Aunt Margaret told us that years ago. She told us in her stories. You know, we wish you'd just die so we could live with her."

You expected her to slap you. Instead, she looked away, drew her knees up to her chin, and shuddered.

"And you know what else she said?" you said.
"Get the fuck in that tent!"

Water chestnuts multiplied and clustered in your neck.

Do not boast about tomorrow, for you do not know what a day may bring. Someone, I'm quite sure, said that.

* * * * *

One morning, in twelfth grade, you woke up in the Fulcrums' guest bedroom. You'd wet the bed. You stood at the door and listened to the house beyond. It was silent. You ran downstairs and grabbed a trash bag, then ran back to the room and stuffed the sheets and your underwear inside. You put on your jeans and shirt. You hurried to the bathroom, pumped some soap onto a washcloth and rubbed it into the mattress pad. You wiped it clean and as dry as you could, and put the washcloth into the trash bag, tied it off and dropped the sack in your backpack. Then you hurried to the linen closet, found a new set of sheets, and dressed the bed.

When you'd finished, you knocked on Ashley's bedroom door. She wasn't there. You went inside and looked out the window onto the street. An old man poured mulch over a frosted flowerbed. The sun washed warm between the tree branches. Where was Ashley?

You went downstairs, put on your shoes, and stepped outside. It was warm. You found yourself walking on Linwood, then Parkside, past the brick mansions until you came to Court Street. You followed the yawning lawns of the college until you came to Franklin, then followed Franklin past the East Village houses with their tastefully arrayed garden displays. You crossed Longway and passed the

Eastside shacks and bungalows with their dirt-streaked siding and muddy tractor ruts. You came to Maryland and found your house and went inside.

Lunch was on: macaroni and cheese. But Betty had used the powder cheese for her corn chips when the salsa ran out, so lunch was just macaroni. You ate and went to your room. You sat there and thought for a long time.

When Ashley finally called, you took the phone and stretched the cord to the bathroom for privacy.

"You left," she said.

"What was I supposed to do?" you asked. "There was nobody there." You burst into tears.

"Hey, wait, wait, what's wrong?"

"I was – I was just worried for you." *Were* you worried? You hadn't felt aware of any worry, only the same old isolation. "I just – I just wanted someone around."

"You were *worried* about me? Why?"

"Because –"

"It didn't have to do with Brian, did it?"

"No, the killer. And you and –"

"Meredith, you really have to not freak out about this. I mean, yeah, it's creepy, and we've got to be careful and serious, I guess, but what, did you think it was Brian?"

"No, but Tracey Paules –"

"Brian was over at my place when the second thing happened. It probably isn't even someone from around here. It's probably some freak from Bloomfield Hills or Grosse Point or something. He comes up here because he thinks nobody cares about people in Flint. And of course he's right, so it's worth the drive. Think about it."

"I didn't think it was Brian." You had stopped crying.

"Okay. Seriously, Meredith, just relax a little. It's my senior year. I want to have some fun."

"Did you have fun? Last night?"

"Yeah," she said. "How did you get home?"

"I walked."

"That's a long walk. I was going to have you stay for lunch."

"I already ate. Thanks. But do you think – I could spend the night again tonight?"

Silence.

"I don't – I don't think my mom would like it, Meredith. Maybe next weekend?"
"I'm going to run away from home."
"Not yet. You should finish school first."

When you came out of the bathroom, Betty saw your red and puffy eyes. "Baby," she said.

Back in your room, the walls glowed with cutouts and Christmas lights, and the few remaining spots of exposed wall gleamed white around flowers and fireworks you'd drawn in with highlighter. You put the Fulcrums' sheets in the washer. Why, you wondered, had you cried? Was it really worry for Ashley? So much had been taken from you, and she *was* your best friend. You claimed this one thing, so now you, once again, had something to lose. You nodded, and breathed out. It all made sense: a typical trapdoor. But something else nagged and tugged at the back of your throat. No, there was more. In your peripheral vision. Or standing behind you, watching. Someone, you sensed, was playing with you. Someone *studied* you.

You knelt under your bed and dragged out an old box full of papers you'd put together. Mementos from class, "A" homework assignments, book reports, photos, and your grade school recorder. You sat on your bed and played it. After three low notes, there was a flash in the window wells and thunder shook the house. You threw the recorder down.

The next morning brought news of another murder, just south of Flint, in Burton. The front door had been left open. When the mail carrier looked into the living room, he saw Candi Grim and her two children sitting in front of the television together with their throats neatly slit. Their palms and feet were marked and at their feet lay dead rats.

The press conference was more-of-the-same, but everyone read between the lines. The killer, they assumed, had seen the earlier news report. After all, the commander had said that "the victims were all alone and unprotected." If this wasn't a reply, than what was? The Journal announced that a "Serial Killer Terrorizes Genesee County" while the Free Press claimed that "Flint's Rat Man Strikes Again!"

The Rat Man.

So now he had a name.

There was, however, a bright spot. Seven-year-old Amalee Grim had, it seemed, survived the attack. She remained in critical condition, and she could not speak. Her remaining family sat at her bedside at Hurley Hospital, and the police hoped that when she recovered a little, she could give a good description of the attacker.

"C'mon Meredith," your dad said. "Margaret says your mom's been signed out, and we got to go pick her up. I've had too many to drive right now."
"Where's she going to live?"
"She's coming back here."
"Why?"
"Margaret don't want her. That boy's mom don't want her. Who else is going to have her? Hell, it's good enough your aunt's coming up to help. I didn't expect that much from her since she made off with Rodney."

You said nothing for the whole drive. When your dad returned to the car with your mom, she was silent too. You pulled out onto the street.

"You ain't sleepin' in my bed," said your dad.
She was surprised. "Why not?"
"I don't want you makin' it dirty."
"Oh, come on, Mark, you know that's all behind me."
"You mean it was in your behind. Look, I don't care. I don't want your filthy stuff in my bed. I don't want your filthy self in my house. The deed's in your name, you bought it, that's why you get to stay, but you got to know I don't want nothin' to do with you no more."

"Yeah, you're better you fat fucking faggot! Eighteen and fifteen is such a difference. At least you only heard about mine. I caught you three fucking times!"

"At least mine were legal —"

"Shut the fuck up. Twenty bucks don't make it legal! That fifteen-year-old, you want to know, he was his first time with me, but he was better than you ever were and bigger and —"

"I'm fucking sick of you and your shit! Your whole family's all fucking fucked up, an' I'd give anything, anything to get you out of my life and this — I'd give — You all perverted an' shit, an' your sister actin' like she's Jesus, but then she robs her family of their son across state lines. An' your parents tryin' to kill us — bathin' in pig blood so they look young. You didn't even tell me 'bout that shit by the time we got married. I had to ask, 'hey, did it look like some people were murdered in the bathtub?' Fuckin' freaks. You pass your infection on to my kids. Rodney's dumb as fuck, Betty's mean as fuck, Bitty nasty as fuck, sick as fuck, oh, I forgot, dead as fuck, an' now Meredith cries all day like she wants to slit her fuckin' wrists! Why I get stuck with people like that?"

What if you had just jumped into the air? What would that have done to your trapdoor?

"Because," your mom said, "you're just like a fucking lumberjack, and you didn't never tell me that you fucking faggot."

Because it was already creaking.

...

When you got home, your dad walked straight to the fridge for his Irish Rose. Your mom stormed between the attic and her bedroom, unpacking the boxes of her clothes. Betty smoked up on the porch, smiling at the whole parade, and you went down to your room. You listened to the radio and waited. You knew what you were waiting for. You didn't have to *do* anything to make the trapdoors snap open beneath you. They groaned and squealed on their own, regardless. They might fall open anyway, so why *not* take a chance? Why *not* try life? Why accept the solitude and torment? Why not... *hope* a little? The sun went down. The shouting stopped. When the lights shut off and the footsteps ceased, you turned the radio off.

It was time to run away.

With tell-tale-heart care you crept around your room. You tucked books, clothes, deodorant, your toothbrush, your shawl, and your hairbrush into your backpack. You added the Fulcrums' folded sheets. You said goodbye to your basement, with all of your drawings and decorations. They had almost made you happy on your trapdoor, but now you were ready to step off. Upstairs, you heard your dad vomiting in the bathroom. You found his wallet by the television and took out a couple of twenties. You took his handgun from beneath the couch. You opened the back door and stepped out into the night.

I'm doing it, I'm doing it! you thought. You carefully crept along the side of the house until you reached the porch, then hurried down the sidewalk as fast as you could.

A few blocks later, you stepped into a parking lot strewn with glass and paper. Yellow light rained down from the carbon street lamps, and the only sound was the buzzing of the wires overhead. *I'm out here with him*, you thought. *Somewhere – right now – he's doing his work.*

You continued, step by step, into the shadows at the edge of the lot. *I have to get to the mall*, you thought. *It's outside the city. I can find a corner to sleep in tonight, and then I'll go further tomorrow.*

You went one more block and heard, in the distance, a squeal of tires. A dog barked, and you heard its teeth bared in the sound of its frothy mouth. A chain dragged fast across the dark ground. You were three miles from the mall and the night felt cold and hollow around you.

He could be anywhere, you thought.

Maybe tomorrow morning?

You counted out of the moments slowly, while your heart raced ahead.

...

Tomorrow then.

You hurried back to the house on Maryland, slipping through your back door. Your dad was still vomiting. You kept his money in your pocket but you hid the gun under your bed, in case you woke beneath a Big Bad or a Little Blue. You lay down without undressing. You buried yourself beneath the covers.

Chapter 5

The next morning, you sat up with light streaming through the windows.

I'm doing this, you thought. *I'm doing this differently than I ever intended.* Within you, something stirred. Something woke.

You shouldered your backpack and went upstairs. Your mom sat on the couch. Betty was singing Usher in the shower. Through the crack in the bedroom door, you saw your dad tangled in blankets and pillows. He must've slept with your mom after all... You stood in the archway between the living and dining rooms, then crossed to the front door. You turned to face your mom and gave a little wave.

"Meredith!" she said. "Where you goin'?"
"Away."
"When you gettin' back?"
"I'm not."

Her face was a flat mask. The shower ran in the background. Then, for the briefest moment, her mask cracked and you saw a softness beneath.

"Good," she said. The mask was back.

Two blocks later, you felt something large pushing in at the back of your clenched throat. So you hacked and coughed and bled up a slashed and swollen water chestnut, bleached and rotten from all the years. You gummed it up until it split and oozed brown sap, and spat it out into the street, and as you wiped the drool from your mouth, it was gone. Burning inside as if you were drunk, you laughed. The sun was out and the grass was licked with frost. High above, the blue on blue cascaded through the crystal thin air and burned inside your lungs.

You walked to Ashley's house and knocked on the door. She answered. Her face seemed gray, and she was barefoot.

"Ashley! I have to ask about – what's wrong?"
"They canceled school today. Didn't you hear on the news?"
"No, I didn't see it."
"The killer – the Rat Man – he killed Mr. Catgut."
"Mr. Catgut – I had him last year," you said. Cold waves rolled in on you. "He was going to take over Model UN." But you couldn't – didn't – feel sorrow. It was too much, too soon. "He was..." You had to ride out the immensity of your escape before you could acknowledge the loss of Mr. Catgut. You stopped speaking.

Ashley took a step backward into her house.

"He said," she said, "he said he'd write my recommendation for U of M – and it was – he can't – what I mean is – he was the only one who'd write for me. He was the only teacher I liked." She was crying.
"Everyone liked Mr. Catgut," you said.
"He always let us eat lunch in his classroom!" She was shrieking.
"He read to us from *The Iliad*."

Ashley led you into the living room and stood in a corner, forcing herself to breathe slowly. You sat on the couch and waited. After several minutes passed, Ashley told you, in short gasps, how Mr.

Catgut had been killed. He lived a mile from the school in a restored Victorian in Carriage Town. That neighborhood – one of the oldest in Flint – had seen the shift from lumber to autos. It had emptied and burned through the twentieth century until stalwarts like Mr. Catgut had moved in to reclaim it. He had followed the directions from the news, locking his doors and windows. By morning, he sat on his couch, bleeding from his throat and his belly. There were rats, of course. Mr. Retch made the discovery when he stopped by to take Mr. Catgut to a morning meeting.

"What were you going to ask me?" said Ashley, wiping her nose with her sleeve.
"Nothing," you said. "I should go." But where would you go?
"Why did you come over?"
"I left home."
"You left?"
"I ran away. "
"Where are you going to go?"
You smiled. "I don't know yet. I don't have anywhere *to* go."
"You can stay here. For tonight. I'd say longer, but I know my mom wouldn't let me. She sucks."
"Thanks, Ashley. That's better than I'd hoped for."

...

You sat at the mahogany table. One room away, Ashley boiled some soup on the stove.

"I guess I *am* glad you got away from there," she said. "They weren't good for you. I mean, I know I said to stay there through graduation, but now I think – I think anywhere else would be better."
You watched her through the crystal glasses and crimson-hued candle stands.
"I'm glad we're friends, Ashley. I'm glad we're best friends. I mean, you are my best friend. I trust you."
"Thanks, Meredith!" she said. "You're a good friend too."

She carried out two bowls of chicken noodle soup. You felt her watching you as you leaned over the bowl and breathed the steam deep. You thought it smelled of comfort. What you'd always hoped home would smell like.

...

That afternoon, you took another walk. You walked through the community college and watched the students with their books get in their cars and drive home for the evening. You passed Whittier Middle School, and saw some black boys playing basketball. A public housing high rise – the tallest building in the neighborhood – reached long and lonely over the parks below. A cold breeze cut in from the west, but even this late in the year, cooling units hung from the windows, eight, nine, ten stories high. Every road, it seemed, was named for one of the suburbs and ran off toward the wilderness. You followed one until it reached the expressway. From there, crooked side streets chased grand old mansions whose facades seemed painted with dust. These furtive paths dead-ended against a stream, but a small footbridge parted the trees and broke into a broad park. The city was easy enough – straightforward on a map – but on foot it seemed a labyrinth. In the park you saw tennis courts and a playground and a huge oak in the middle of a large field. No people. Nobody comes out to play in the cold of mid-November.

You sat down on a swing and kicked off. When the swing rolled back, you had no choice; you had to look at the oak, its skeleton branches reaching like a tyrant over the park, the neighborhood, and all that brown grass. When the swing swung forward, you could forget the tree. You turned your face up and drank in the cloudless sky. You imagined it was spring, when people filled the park and kites sailed out from the hills. But when the swing rolled back, spring receded. You had no choice. You saw what you saw.

Eventually, you stopped swinging and crossed onto the field between the playground and the oak. When you reached the middle of the open space, you lay down on your back and wrapped your arms around yourself to keep warm. Now, *you* controlled your view and looked up into the blue radiation. The blue *was* radiation. Scattered sunlight. Mr. Catgut had told you this, even though he had taught Social Studies. The radiation rained and poured itself out even on the clearest days.

When you woke, the sun had set. The radiation had diminished as well and now it shimmered a deepening purple. You rolled onto your belly and found yourself looking at the oak again. It was much closer now. It stretched over a hundred feet into the air and blocked your view. You wished someone would cut it down. Why *did* it bother you, that tree? What did it mean? What did you feel? You weren't sure, other than that it felt an intrusion. An unfair obstruction, and therefore, an abomination. A relic that should have been dead. Again, you felt the strange sensation of being watched. Of being noticed. It felt like a gentle tugging at the back of your brain. You looked over your shoulder, but the park was still empty. Not a soul in sight. Then again, it was dark now, so who really knew? Your back ached. You walked the last few blocks back to Ashley's.

...

Ashley stood in the door when you arrived.

"We almost ate without you," she said. She hesitated for a moment. "By the way, my parents aren't divorced. Sorry, I made a mistake when I told you that. My dad's just gone a lot."

Two minutes later, you all sat at the table with cuts of salmon and lemon wedges and three massive glasses of wine. Mr. Fulcrum drank a beer.

"I'm sorry we can't have you longer, Meredith," Mrs. Fulcrum said as you ate. "I really wish we could. But we don't want to get involved – I mean, we don't want to get between you and your parents. If you ever formally clear things up with them, I mean, if you ever come to – if they ever say that you can go then you're welcome to stay a bit longer."

You smiled. You knew how to resolve this. "They don't mind that I'm gone. They're glad I'm gone. They – don't dislike me. Or my sister or brother. They just get annoyed because we get in their way and keep them from doing the things they want to do. It's like when my sister died. They were sad that she died. But they were happy that she had left. So they're happy that I left, too."

To your surprise, Mrs. Fulcrum didn't respond for several moments.

"Well," she said, "Ashley was saying that she may have found a place where you can stay for the next few weeks."

"Really?"

"With Brian," Ashley said. "I called and asked him while you were out today. He says it's okay."

"But I don't know Brian."

"You have to stay *some*where," Mrs. Fulcrum said.

"What are you worried about?" Ashley said. "This way you and Brian and I can all hang out."

You waited a moment, thinking. You didn't want to stay with Brian. But you didn't want to go home, either. Brian's, then.

"I'm sorry. That sounds good. Thanks, Ashley."

You cut yourself a slice of salmon.

"I know you all think I'm a runaway. But I told my mom that I was going. She knows I left. She could find me if she wanted to. And I'll do better without them anyway. I'm more of a walkaway. And Mr. Fulcrum, how was your tour? Of London?"

Ashley and Mr. Fulcrum turned to you with more attention than you thought the question warranted. Mrs. Fulcrum smiled at her plate and quietly tapped her napkin with her fork.

"I like London," Mr. Fulcrum said, "Yes. There are plenty of British there."

...

Later that night, you lay on a sleeping bag beside Ashley's bed. You had asked to sleep in her room, even though you worried about wetting the bedding. You couldn't stay away or alone, not yet. Ashley lay in bed in the light of the television, and after several minutes of gentle sounds — shifting positions, adjusting the pillows — she rolled over to look down at you.

"How did you know about my dad's tour?" she asked.

"Your mom told me about it the other night when I was over here and you were out with Brian."

"You didn't tell me that she told you."

"I know," you said. "I should have."

You closed your eyes.

Something felt wrong in that moment. You realized that you should say more, that you should tell Ashley again that she was your very best friend. But you'd already told her that once today. Her reply, that you were her *good* friend, wasn't lost on you. You didn't hold that against her. You weren't angry that she had lied to you about her parents. You weren't angry that you were going to be living at an unfamiliar boy's house. You'd left home for less than a day, but already the simplicity of your choice had seemed to erode. Did your throat clench? You tried not to think about it.

"I'm sorry." You mouthed the words.

You opened your eyes. Ashley had turned off the TV. She was a black shape on her black bed, but you saw her silhouette clearly. There was a coldness in her, a marble hardness in the moments between her blinking, her measures of silent exhalation. You studied the tiny hairs on her arms and knew that her breath was soft and damp, like new life. Still, she seemed unreal now, a little too bright. Small lights shone all around her, and you realized that Ashley's walls and ceiling were covered in glow-in-the-dark stars. You pretended that the stars were real, that the walls had the same hue as the blue and purple sky. The same radiation. Then, an imaginary version of yourself, a girl six inches tall, crawled out of you. She pressed herself into a corner and slid up the wall to the ceiling. She looked down at you. She turned to look at Ashley. Then she reached out her tiny hands and slipped her fingers under the nearest star. She began to swing from star to star and held on tight so she wouldn't fall. If she did she'd spiral up and up and lose herself in the blue. We lose our grip and slip sometimes and rise into the sky serene. When we fall up we forget who we are, and that's how we lose ourselves, dizzy, in dreams.

Chapter 6

That night, the seraphim and cherubim enspiraled your mind and beat back the bitter dreams. As the sun rose over the frosted horizon, you heard Ashley's voice and you opened on up to the morning.

"We got to hurry!" she said. "We'll be late to school."

She lurched through the room with a toothbrush in her fist, looking for her books and homework. You stood and stretched and yawned and smiled and scratched your back and went into the bathroom. You smiled at the the mirror. One day had passed and you were still free. You rinsed your face and the water felt as fresh and cold as the Muskegon. You took the clean linens from your backpack and left them in the closet. You wrapped your shawl around your neck. You were ready.

...

At school, Brian Crux glared at you when he met you in the hall. He lifted your hand and when you opened your fist he pressed a key into your palm.

"Thanks," you said.
"There's a cat," he said. "My mom wants to meet you. You should stop by now."

* * * * *

You left Central and a few minutes later you'd crossed the expressway. You passed through downtown and entered the industrial area just south of the river. The Hole, I think they call it. There was no neighborhood there anymore; half of the homes and factories had been torn down and half of the remaining houses sat empty. Brian's lay with the weeds beside the river, a two-story brick bungalow with chipping brown trim. You'd never seen a lonelier place in your life. But the river was there for company, at least, and its quiet gurgling reassured you. You knocked and Brian's mother came to the door with her lips curled around a cigar.

"You Meredith?"

You nodded.

"You on drugs?"

"No." You laughed.

"You lyin'?"

"I never am," you said. A little sharp tone there.

"Come on."

She led you around the house, pointing out her bedroom, as well as Barney's and Trey's, two of Brian's friends who also lived there. Although four people stayed in the house, it still seemed too large for them all, as if it overpowered them with the size of its needs. Weeds choked the backyard. Some of the hideous 70s wallpaper had been stripped, but nothing had been repainted or redone. A round length of pipe stuck out of the house and over the driveway as an improvised spigot. Brian's mom showed you your own room, a bare-walled second-story room with a hospital bed and a window looking over the river.

"I'm gonna subdivide the place, but I ain't got nobody to go in and do it for me yet. I ain't got a lot of room here, so I suggest you find somewhere else to stay asap." So she didn't want you either. "But I'll keep you for a week at least." She hesitated a moment. "Maria used to stay in this room when she was over."

"Maria Puerta?"

"You need food?"

"Do you mean –"

"You got money for food?"

You didn't want to give this woman your money. "No, I –"

"Do dishes, clean some, pay for your food that way then. Watch out for the cat. The cat hates us. I hate that damn cat. What's your last name, Meredith?"

"Malady."

She confirmed your parents' number, their address and names, and suggested you get a move on back to school.

* * * * *

Back downtown, on Saginaw Street, cars moved north and south, kicking out exhaust, and students passed between classes at U of M. They crossed on tubular glass walkways that connected the buildings several stories up. You didn't feel like going back to school, and since no one seemed to care, you went to the university library instead. It was a strange, prismatic space. A crescented atrium opened at the back, and three floors of polished mahogany and burnished chrome faced an unfolding bank of windows. These opened to the north, but the sun shone in, reflected from a building across the river. The metallic curves of the room threw the light at odd angles and made faint rainbows against the stacks. As the sun moved down the sky, the rainbows gleamed and rose and faded away. Each windowside desk had its own set of lamps and its own set of sturdy wood chairs. *This is what learning is supposed to feel like,* you thought. You decided to stay awhile, and maybe learn a bit more about the Rat Man.

You built piles of books.

The Blank Slate. The Modern Denial of Human Nature. Killer Among Us: Public Reactions to Serial Murder. Portrait of a Killer: Jack the Ripper – Case Closed. Man into Wolf. The Mismeasure of Man. Little Red Riding Hood Uncloaked. You read all of these. Sort of. You opened one, and when a sentence bored you, you opened the next. When you'd went through them all, you started at the beginning again, and as the library prepared to close at nine, you ripped the bar codes from the dust jackets and slid the books into your backpack.

You performed an act of faith. You slipped your key to the house on Maryland from its keychain, slid it to the center of the bare table, and turned and walked away.

A librarian met you at the door.
"Are you looking to fill any jobs?" you asked.
"Well, we're always looking for people to help with shelving. Are you a student?"
"I will be soon."
She looked you up and down.
"When you get here, see if you can get Work-Study, and when you know come talk to us."

You walked back to Brian's in the dark. He wasn't home, and neither was Barney or Trey or the mother, or even the cat. The only sign that anyone lived in the big old house was a dirty litter box and a sinkful of dishes and scummy water. After cleaning and heating up some leftovers, as you lay down bed to reread *The Mismeasure of Man*. It had been a good day. One of the best days. The fresh air and the reading had exhausted your store of mysteries. As for passing a night alone in a haunted house... it wasn't any worse than your old home. For the second night, you did not dream.

* * * * *

At school the next morning, suspicion echoed in the hallway gossip, and the kids quietly drew in their notebooks and stared out windows. Flint had come back to front pages nationwide with the slaughter of the Grim family and Mr. Catgut. His own classroom lights were out, and a sheet had been taped to the door directing his students to other teachers. Below, dozens of cards, flowers, and a couple teddy bears. A dog-eared copy of *The Iliad*. As you stood there, you wondered whether someone walking past would expect to find you crying. You didn't feel like crying. You still felt nothing but exaltation at having run away. There was little room left in your heart for your murdered favorite teacher.

Later that night, as the river guzzled by outside your window and the occasional car thudded over the potholes, causing headlight beams to bounce up and down the ruins of the Hole, you fell asleep with *Case Closed* open on your chest. Ghosts haunted the landscape, but you didn't dream. You'd escaped your family, and the cherubim protected you in light and darkness, the third night.

* * * * *

On Thursday, your mind finally returned to the living, and you caught Ashley talking to Brian at her locker. He smiled.

"Hi, Meredith. How do you like the house?"
"It's all right," you said. "Where've *you* been."
Brian shrugged nonchalantly, but you didn't care.

"Ashley," you said, "what are you doing after school today?"

She smiled for a moment. "Hey Meredith, can we talk after lunch?"

"Sure," you said.

At your next class, you sat in the back and drew geometry. You wrote wire lines from the toes of your notebook up to its brow, then traced over the light blue horizontal bars. You'd made a mesh cage. You wrote me into a little box in the lower-right-hand corner. You wrote you into the upper-left-hand corner. "Rat Man," you wrote at the center. You began filling in the page with tiny rats and crosses. Soon you'd filled in every box, and you were separated from me by rodents and the Rat Man.

When you caught up with Ashley in your Government class, she sat still, smiling and opening her eyes wide.

"I think we're going to go somewhere special and far away tonight," she said, her voice shaking with excitement.

"We are?" you said.

"I mean Brian and me. He asked me for gas money!"

"Oh. That's great."

"How're things going for you?"

"Okay. Actually, I've been really good. Brian's mom is kind of strange —"

"I know. She's cool though, if you talk to her... she smokes those big cigars —"

"— and she leaves me alone, and that's nice. Everyone leaves me alone. Only I can only stay there for a week. Then I have to see where I can go."

"What are you going to do?"

"I guess I'll see if I can get into foster care."

"I don't know anything about that. Do you think you'll get in fast?"

"I don't know anyone who has. They got too many cases. It's messed up."

"It can't be more messed up than your house was," she said.

"I'll tell them about that bottle my dad threw at my head... if you were asked, would you say that happened?"

"Sure."

"Maybe we can say it hit me. I don't care. I'll tell them about my mom and the neighbor and how Bitty died. Maybe that'll get things to go a bit faster."

"Can I just say, I'm really glad that you got out of there? I'm not trying to judge, but your family's about the most fucked up I know. I always thought the thing with your sister dying was fucked... I mean, even back in junior high when I first heard about it. And then your aunt kidnapped your brother –"

"My aunt's fine. She's a good backup plan. It's too bad your mom doesn't like me, or I could stay with you and not even have to do the foster care thing."

"It's not that – my mom. She makes people think she's a wonderful person who wants to help. But she's not. She doesn't want to put herself out."

You nodded, but you already understood this.

Ashley noticed the long silence. "I'm not lying," she said, defensive, her voice edged.

"I didn't say you were," you said.

"Don't think I'm lying, Meredith. I would love for you to stay with me. I really would. You know we have enough space. I hate my parents."

"Not as much as I hate mine."

But your hate was as numb as your grief for Mr. Catgut.

* * * * *

You'd started to enjoy walking from school to Brian's house, and that day you decided to take a longer route. You walked through an older neighborhood that rubbed up against downtown. That place with the Victorian spaces: giant mansions and small brick factories. That's right: Carriage Town. You stood on the sidewalk, looking up at Mr. Catgut's house. Flowers and stuffed bears covered the porch, in blatant defiance of the police tape. Evidently, Flint had other problems and couldn't spare all of her cruisers to monitor crime scenes, even for *this* sensational case. The sun had started moving down the sky, and punctured the knit lace curtains with bullets of light. Heavy shadows fell inside, but no lights lit up behind the dark windows.

...

A few blocks farther on, you found a coffee shop in a plain, one-story brick building. Wild-looking plants hung against the windows. You went inside. The scent of cinnamon spiced the air. A tall man swiped a rag across a glass and added it to a stack.

"Hi!" he asked. "What can I start for you?"

His shop was bright and open. It was crowded and it welcomed you. You realized that while you wouldn't give Brian's mom your money for food, you'd happily pay this man for coffee. It was something in the tone of asking. Your money... your right to say "yes" and "no."

"Something fancy," you said.

He smiled and set to work.

He made you a cappuccino, and you sat down at a table by the window and looked out. Across the street lay vacant lots, and behind, more vacant lots. The setting sun seemed to expand in the sky, then dispersed into small fires as it plunged behind the hills and the skeletal trees. Blocks and blocks had been demolished. You could see a mile and farther. Clouds moved down the sky. It was a stream, a torrent, a mainstream that made a mere mirror of the river below. You looked out and let the occasion of movement distract you, and once it caught you it enthralled you. Once in its thrall, you were lost. Lost your hope and lost your comfort... because there ain't no hope that lasts past seven in such a story of movement as this!

After all, Flint was the birthplace of the auto industry, and almost of the automobile. You didn't understand the way cars worked, no, not really, but you knew that they moved by a belly-deep metal plunging and oscillation with the visible result of speed. Motion happened because these things were made to move. Because the motion of their organs caused movement. Flint fueled locomotion and her ghosts have defined themselves through motion. Do you understand?

Let me explain: Many misunderstand ghosts.

You don't become a ghost when you die. You make a ghost whenever you leave. Now no ghost can leave, and no ghost can abandon itself, so it's a *profound* frustration to be a ghost stuck in a town defined by motion... abandoned like the ghosts of Flint or Meredith. Don't you understand?

Let me explain.

Ghosts sit in every parking lot. They float over the river and crouch on the tarmacs. They lean out from high, high on the radio towers and their wails sound like freight trains driven through the night. Do you understand, Meredith? Do you understand? Every ghost in this city is obsessed with movement. They're trapped on that mainstream and can't stop that motion. But motion saturates them. Flint is flotsam.

Let me explain!

When the Indian warriors came, they fought each other for control of the river and of movement. Many died and their families buried them in mounds. They left their ghosts.

When the white settlers came with their thick brows and hair all over, they took the river to found a ford and trading post. Then *they* controlled movement. Traders moved up the river, down the river... they left *their* ghosts, and the place started to get a bit crowded now. But now the lumberjacks came.

The lumberjacks?

Yes! And when they came, they drank cheap whiskey and hacked their way clear from Ypsilanti to the straits. The only place they didn't log off was upstate, near Clare, where the rivers weren't deep or wide enough to move timber. Then the trains moved in, and the lumberjacks logged off Clare and Harrison and Meredith. But here when the jacks stripped Genesee County of its wood, and its leafy trees pickled in the Flint River, many grateful New England families rolled west in wagons and carts built from the forests of Michigan. Flint was now the grounded source of momentum, and the lumberjacks left, and you couldn't throw a wooden plank nowhere in that drafty closet without clocking a ghost on its skull!

There's a song about it all, in fact.

"Some men love to roam,
over the dark something foam,
something something wild and free.

But a chosen band
in a forest land
and a life in the woods for me."

It didn't last forever.

When the last tree had fallen, the mills and slips were rearranged and re-outfitted and lumber came in from other states and snapped and twisted and burned and rejoined until it'd all been made into carriages. Flint sold them with horse and harness, and mansions sprouted out of Carriage Town, and Flint caused movement. The workers left their ghosts with mouths warped into woody Os, dead and dry like cut hickory, and packed and pressed into thick tight piles.

And then the cars came along. At last! Flint's moment had arrived, for now the city caused the motion of millions, and millions needed Flint to move between New York and California. Flint was important, and people arrived and left by the thousands, and the streets grew so tight with the ghosts, living in the cracks, packed among the dust, and standing on each others' shoulders, that the brick surfaces broke down and needed to be repaved.

But by the time the streets were repaved, the jobs and the people had left.

They left their ghosts.

Behold! The streets are broken once more. They aren't important anymore. They do not cause movement or motion. They are not used, and the ghosts outnumber the living ten-to-one, sitting, waiting, decaying. Yes, but they wait and they decay. They decay... Flint drifts on the mainstream, desolate and dead. Deaths are the scraps left for the ghosts. Your ghosts are lumberjack ghosts. They retired from jobbing and sold drinks in Harrison and Meredith. Do you understand?

You finished your cappuccino. A pleasant milky warmth hung in your throat.

Let me explain...

You looked outside and saw the ghosts. Where were your cherubim? Where were your seraphim? Why had you stopped and started to wonder? You sat miles from the grime of Franklin, and you reclined a long way from the gross of Lewis. This city might be sad, but you'd left the Eastside. So where had your comfort gone? You weren't afraid of the Rat Man. Little Red Riding Girl had some chompers of her own, and if she ever met Little Boy Blue, she knew how to handle him. Who the fuck was the Big Bad Wolf? Who the hell were werewolves? You had it all in your veins. Who really looked up at the moon and ripped a boy's leg off of his body? Who really ate hearts fresh from the chest and devoured the brain of his son? You smiled. The Rat Man? Fuck the Rat Man. You'd seen live rats in the pavilion at the park and you'd seen dead rats in the gutters outside your house. You knew all about rats. You knew how to handle them too.

Moreover, just 'cause, just, just because you resisted temptation, that don't mean, it... didn't mean you couldn't have poisoned and burned and buried your folks if you chose to. Just 'cause these thoughts, they, they stayed your happy fantasies and they became nothing more, no, that don't mean that, once you decided, once you resolved, you'd flinch and forget how to carry through. No! If you ever met the Rat Man you knew exactly how you'd handle him. You'd poison him and kill him and turn him inside out. You'd weave his pieces through the streets of Flint. He'd make a nice path to take to find his victims' souls and their discarded shoes. Those who'd need to feed would feed. Those who wanted the credit would take it. But you would have done the deed. There are, after all, two kinds of rats, and it's only a matter of time if you know what I mean. You bit down on your index finger, on the knuckle. Now, you tasted your blood. An unpleasant metallic bite.

Do you understand?

I think you do.

Where had your comfort gone?

I can't tell you, because I don't know.

* * * * *

Back at Brian's, the house was empty. You did the stinky dishes. You cleaned the litter box. You called Ashley. The phone rang ten times. Mrs. Fulcrum answered.

"Hello?" she asked, sounding cross.

"Hi, may I please speak to Ashley?"

"She's not here. Is this Meredith?"

"Yeah."

"She's out with Brian. We're not expecting her until late – if at all. Why don't you talk to her at school tomorrow?"

"But –"

She hung up.

You decided that it didn't matter. *If Brian is the Rat Man, then he'll kill them all, and I don't care if he does!*

That night you snuck out of the house, a delicate process of stomping out through the front door, since the lights were all out and nobody was home. You quickly walked west along Kearsley Street, staring into the block long shadows. The Westside factories gave way to towering houses and mansions, beautiful once but now worn and overgrown, and these gave way to aluminum-sided bungalows. They stood apart, like little islands, bleary and cold in midnight floodlights that shone as bright as the fat waning moon. Finally, you reached a restaurant at the city limits and spent most of your money eating ice cream and coneys and drinking coffee after coffee. You sat there for hours reading *Killer Among Us*. You knew why you'd left Brian's house. You hoped to meet the Rat Man. You imagined the moment, vivid and fresh. You didn't fear it. You hungered for it.

Walking home along Second, you passed Hall Street and a factory and reached a place where there weren't any street lights. The Rat Man watched you pass. He was tall and hairy and very muscular, though easily in his fifties. This was different from his usual MO, but you were alone together, and how could he pass up on a seventeen year old, clueless in the streets at night?

"You," he said.
"Fuck off," you said.
"Did you just say –"
"Fuck off motherfucker."

He had become accustomed to fear in his victims. You knew because you'd read of Glatman and Gacy, who sniffed and snuffled and licked their chops over even an ounce of fear. The Rat Man was one of these. He'd grown discontented with TV and the movies. He wanted to witness an immediate and accurate fear, a fear that he himself caused. He knelt in orgasmic contortions, thinking that the girl on the street feared that she would be dead soon, that he was her sad "the end," and that her fears were correct.

But you buried your teeth in his head. You cracked him and wrecked him, and when he was paralyzed, you chewed him up. You slit his wrists and slit his throat. You sent him to Hell in a leaky rowboat. All week, your joy had known no bounds, but where had your comfort gone?

No more comfort.

When you got back to Brian's, after three, you passed quickly through the hollow rooms and curled up under your covers. Laying there, sweet and warm and apparently innocent, you dreamed up more encounters with the Rat Man, on Saginaw, on Corunna, on Pierson and Dort and Maryland. On each street of the city you met him, and each time you killed him, you freed the Earth from a terrible burden. The whole world was beautiful, and you were the most beautiful of them all. The cherubim flew in a sphere around you, but they no longer shielded you from nightmares. Like turbines, they drove your dreams. Their wings whirred in a high pitched whine. They really flew that fast.

My dear, when we danced, we diamondbacked.

We did it with a touch, no need for spitting.
As a carousel, the world is spinning, spinning.
I don't think they get it.

Don't think they're listening.

Chapter 7

That whine.

Those fists on the bedroom door.

"Meredith!" yelled Brian's mom. "You gotta pack your stuff."

The next morning was your unexpected last at Brian's house. He hunched over a bowl of Cheerios while his mom explained her regrets.

"I gotta get it subdivided, and your room's coming in two. Plaster and paint."
"I could sleep on the couch?"
"What couch?"
There was no couch.
"Where should I go?" you said.
"You talked to the social worker?"
"No."
"Your parents kick you out?"
"No."
"Well, it doesn't sound too good for you, but you might well try. Social services is out of that flat stony brick thing on Saginaw. That ugly building —"
"What if they don't take me?"

"I guess then it's back to your parents."

You repacked your backpack, and it was so full that you had to carry most of your books in your arms. You had wet the bed that night, of course, and threw the wet clothes and sheets in a dumpster as you left. A few minutes later, though, you trudged back and fished them all out and tied them up in a discarded garbage bag. You hated the thought, but you might need them soon, if you ended up sleeping in some parking lot corner. As you walked toward downtown, you wondered why the wind was blowing from the east. Then you thought, *I'm going to catch the Rat Man.*

You suspected that, ultimately, you were his most attentive fan and harshest non-professional critic. You both had a history with rats. You'd staked out the scene of his first major crime and went on to study every article, story, and rumor about him. You knew about Clarice Starling and Kay Scarpetta. The police had clearly made no progress, nor the FBI. Why not Meredith Malady?

At the Genesee County Administrative Building you met with a social worker, Ms. Leavings. She advised you that you'd have to return home. You told her about your dad throwing the beer bottle at you, citing Ashley as a witness, and she frowned. Then you dropped the bomb about Bitty's death. "When did this happen?" she asked. It had happened three years earlier. "But you weren't taken into protective custody at the time?" She sat and thought for several moments. You shook your head. She frowned and shook her head. "It's been too long, and anyway, the system is overburdened," she said. "Maybe you have a case here, but there's not much the state could do for months. Given your age, you're almost an adult as is."

Running away had been a risk, and now, for the first time, you felt the consequences pressing in.

"Can I get you a drink of water?" Ms. Leavings asked.

You shook your head. You rubbed your brow. You noticed your hand was shaking. *I won't react, I won't react,* you told yourself. But you started to feel overwhelmed.

"Do you have any friends or family you could stay with for the next year?" Ms. Leavings' voice sounded like it was coming down a long tunnel, hollow and round.

You looked up. "I have an aunt," you said, "in California."

"Better weather than here!" she said, smiling.

"I'm not sure she'll want me... and I'm not sure my parents would want me to go either."

"I thought you said they didn't care that you had run away."

"They don't." It sounded strange to you, too. "But I *do* think they would care if I moved in with my aunt." Why? They hadn't cared when she'd abducted Rodney. Was it because he had ADHD and was retarded?

"If you aren't going back to your parents' residence, you'll have to find a place to stay."

"I know," you said. "I can do that. I can find a place." You weren't sure you could, but it was all you could say. Your mind was set. You *weren't* going back. You'd decided that you'd rather die than spend another night in that house.

Ms. Leavings pressed you. "Could you stay with a friend, perhaps?" You had one friend and she didn't want you. "Or you could stay at a boarding house." You were out of money. "Only if you're desperate." *Maybe I could hitch a ride down South, where it's warmer...* "I know of one, actually," said Ms. Leavings. "It's on the South End. It's not bad. I think it's close to a bus."

You told her you'd think it over and let her know by that evening. You left, steeling yourself away from anxiety about that night; you had to catch the Rat Man. After wandering aimlessly down Saginaw Street for several blocks, you found yourself outside the old Halo Burger, a stucco building with a Mission style brick roof. Painted gnomes grinned in from a mural across the alleyway. You went inside and spent the last of your money on a burger and fries. You sat in a booth near the window. "Now then," you said, "the Rat Man!" None of your accumulated evidence seemed to connect, so you started counting and writing lists on your napkin:

Mr. Catgut. 1.
The Family on the South End. 3.
The Grand Blanc Woman. 1.

The North End Autoworker. 1.

The Eastside Autoworker. 1.

$1 + 1 + 1 + 3 + 1 = 7$ victims.

$1 + 1 = 2. + 1 = 3. 3 + 3 = 6. 3 + 3 + 1 = 7.$ *Is he killing in increments of three?*

...

$1 + 1 = 2. 2 + 1 = 3. 3 + 1 = 4.$ *Not six. Not likely. Not much there. Okay.*

This way of thinking wasn't getting you anywhere.

Mr. Catgut died. Cats hunt rats. The cat was devoured by rats. The Autoworker – no.

This way of thinking wasn't getting you anywhere.

...

All of the victims were stabbed and sliced and then crossed on their hands and feet. There's a reference to rats, definitely. There's also a reference to crucifixion. To Christ? Because the stabbings are worse and worse, more extreme each time. But no. Because the worst was Mrs. Helmet, the Grand Blanc woman. The numbers aren't right. The numbers aren't, right?

What made your analysis different from any of the others? How could you deduce what trained detectives – what the F.B.I. – with all of their tools and experience and access to the crime scenes failed to deduce? What endowed you with wisdom? You were just a girl who stood on trapdoors.

...

You had Maria Puerta. You knew Maria Puerta. You'd shared classes with her. You'd shared the same neighborhood. She'd dated Brian Crux – you were sure of it – and she'd been killed within blocks of the first autoworker. She'd been stabbed and he'd been stabbed. Was that a difference in your analysis? That you couldn't accept that Maria wasn't involved? You didn't know the Rat Man's ritual victims, but you knew — you felt sure — his first victim.

Maria Puerta.

$1 + 1 + 1 + 1 + 3 + 1 = 8.$ *Do the killer's ambitions escalate with each crime?* Half of his murders occurred during his last two outings. But the Grim family was an exception, and most people assumed that this was a response to the press conference. A way to defy the police, to taunt them, to shove the public toward a panic. Most serial killers *do* escalate. You knew this. *But eight homicides in one month? Now that's one crazy escalation.* $1 + 1 = 2. \ 2 + 1 = 3. \ 3 + 1 = 4. \ 4 + 3 = 7. \ 7 + 1 = 8. \ - 1 = 7.$ Amalee Grim survived in the hospital. She wasn't a murder victim, not yet at least. *Okay.* Did this way of thinking begin to get you somewhere?

...

Ghosts fill Flint to its brim. Ghosts in the trees and the ramshacks and the gulleymaws and the subplasm. Flint is filled with rats. So many rats that when the city floods the sewers flood, and rats rise to the surface. Maybe the Rat Man lives in the sewers with the rats. Nobody could live in those sewers but a literal rat. Not a cat or a Rat Man. No, this way of thinking didn't get you nowhere!

You finished your hamburger.

Did the Rat Man kill Maria Puerta? He did. You shivered a moment. You felt an exhilaration and a fear that was not strictly academic, because now her murder put you literally in contact with the killer. You and Ashley saw Maria first. You had been the first to see her since she'd been killed. *Ashley and I have an alibi. Nobody else does. Two people are definitely innocent. Some billion people are suspects.* Then again, you'd been asleep at the park beforehand, and Ashley had access to a car. *Maybe Ashley did it.*

Maybe Dad did it. Maybe Betty did it. Maybe the ghost of Bitty did it.

...

Flint is filled with ghosts... Your head hurt.

...

The Rat Man has wanted to kill for a long time, you thought. *But he never has. He finds a girl, young, pretty, walking home at night on the Eastside. Who's going to help her? Who will even see what happens? There aren't any houses out there, just weeds and trees and empty shacks. He does it. It's easy. He has a knife. He stabs her dead. Drives away. Goes home. He has built up his courage now and knows he can kill without getting caught. Years of hunger crowd in on him. The need to prey. He must prey on life. Predators live and prey dies and people are predatory. Deaths are the scraps that are left for the ghosts. So the Rat Man preys so that he can thrive. To take blood. And anyway, Maria was wearing a blood red shawl that night.* Again, you shivered. *I wear a shawl sometimes*, you thought. *The red shawl that Aunt Margaret gave me, that she was given by her grandma. Maria was about my height and build. Maria could have been me.* Now you shivered and shook, remembering the dagger glance your mom had given when you put on that shawl after Bitty's funeral.

You moved on to your other, more comfortable, connection to the Rat Man: *I fear rats*, you thought. *The Rat Man and me. The killer hates rats. The killer fears rats? Rats attract the killer? When the killer gets home, he crawls into bed. He wraps himself up and tries to forget killing Maria. The wideness of her eyes. The moving of her blood. And the next morning, he gets up, and goes out, and...*

...

He sees drowned rats! Floating in the gutter. Where the sewer backed up with river water.

...

He lives near the river! He saw the rats on the same morning that I did! The sewers backed up outside his house and when he woke he saw the rats! It turned something in him. He wanted to prey, and now he'll prey until he's caught. You can't satisfy a hungry rat! The hungry rats will always attack! They feed on the fat rats. And the ghosts? When we leave, we leave ghosts, and there are ghosts everywhere in Flint. Ghosts and fat rats and hungry rats and monsters and the mainstream and – wait! Clear your head, Meredith! you thought. *You're letting you go to your head. Settle down. Stick to what you know. The Rat Man lives near the river.*

Where else would he have seen the rats? The investigators will have checked the pet stores and labs and... they haven't said if the rats they found were like pet rats or sewer rats. They'll keep that to themselves. You couldn't know for sure, but you wrote a note to yourself to call the tip line and tell them about the rats you saw in the gutters. It *felt* right... you *believed* that he lived near the river.

...

Now. How does he get his rats?

The gutters aren't that deep. He wouldn't find more than a few at a time.

...

The rain?

You thought you knew...

...

You counted backwards in case you were mistaken.

1 + 1 + 1 + 1 + 1 incidents = 6 dead. Yes. It did rain before each murder. A rain before each murder would make the river flood, the sewers back up. The rats rise to the surface and that's how the Rat Man finds his supply. And his hunger.

But wait... $1 + 1 + 1 + 1 + 1 + 1 = 7$. *No. It didn't rain before Maria died. It rained afterward. What does that mean?*

You took another breath, to still your soul, and added a note to tell the police about the rain before the five ritual murders. A wind brushed your brow. The windows of the restaurant did not fit perfectly, just like the cracked windows in the home of the Rat Man's Eastside victim. In both places, a steady draft. Maybe tiny idiosyncrasies and flaws played a decisive role. Maybe you were wrong about everything. Maybe you shook. Maybe you shivered in ecstasy. In esemplasy. Maybe you shuddered like a swimmer in the deep ocean, knowing that nothing but your power of will kept you above the dark and crushing below. Maybe your power of will alone kept you from the truth.

Now you flinched, unlike John Douglas, and did not solve the mystery.

You tried again. You clenched your teeth and rotated yourself into the mist. You held your breath and shut your eyes against the bright skies "serene" and "radioactive" as Mr. Catgut might have said. You reached deep into your gut. You called upon the fires. You called upon the November rain to clear your brain of fog. You called upon the oak tree. To find the familiar flaw that unraveled the mystery of its knotty bark like the knots in Mrs. Helmet's intestines, or the blood trickling from Mr. Catgut's neck and down across his chest. To grant you a pure vision.

All you saw were incoherent numbers and shapes.

You opened your eyes. You let your breath out, and it sounded hard and fast, like the rush of a breeze. You'd lost track of how long you'd held it, and several other diners – homeless, probably – turned and looked at you. You smiled. What else were you supposed to do? Hide your amusement? You looked just as nasty and crazy as they did. You stepped out into the morning.

I guess it takes more than determination, you thought.

"Where should I go?" you asked the street. But objects are only objects, Meredith. Silly Meredith. They can't answer. You began to doubt the existence of ghosts. You could go to the U of M library... but you'd stolen the books you wanted. You could go to the coffee shop... but you'd spent your last dollar. Besides, these tricks seemed like stalling. They had helped you to chart your path, but by Friday they were well-worn dead ends. You wanted to fight something directly, head on. Even an ordinary day sounded like a nice change of pace. You decided to go to school.

* * * * *

Math.

"Meredith," whispered a girl who never talked to you, "Ashley Fulcrum says you left your home."
"Yeah."
"Where you stayin'?"
"I don't know. Around."
"I was just sayin', we was all freaked out for you 'cause – you know – 'cause of the Rat Man."
"I'm not scared of the Rat Man," you said.
"But he –"
"He always kills people who are ready for him. They're in for the night, safe at home with their their doors locked." You smiled. "You're in more danger from him than me. I'm just a girl on the street."
"You know he's the most wanted right now. In the state."
"I don't care so much – whether or not they catch him."

You didn't know why you said it. No, that's not true. You said it because you wanted to shock them. You didn't know why you wanted to shock them. Something about navigating their confusion, maybe, but your thoughts were all tangled. Regardless, it worked. Once you said those words, you heard thoughts echoing off the creaking floor and falling from the fan turning overhead. It was really the sound of held breath, which makes softer sounds audible. The kids hunched over their notebooks, but their invisible eyes turned and fixed on you. Even the substitute, reading the lesson plan at his desk, stopped moving his eyes across the page. They were all thinking about Mr.

Catgut, you knew. You thought of Maria Puerta.

"Hey Meredith," the girl whispered, "is it true your mama let your aunt run off with your brother?"
You nodded.
"Why?"
"'Cause she didn't want him."
"Why?"
"Because he's retarded and she's a dumb bitch."
"Ha!" The girl laughed. "An' then your sister killed herself?"
"It was an accident."
"What kinda accident?"
"She ate bad meat. She didn't go for help. Why you askin' me all this?"
"We was just wonderin' 'cause we heard—"
"Who is we?! Where is we?!"

You heard your pitch and volume go up. You hadn't meant to lose control. Now the kids stopped pretending, and they openly stared at you. So you stood and answered them:

"What the fuck! Is this what Mr. Catgut left? Yeah, my house is fucked up. So are half of yours! So shut the fuck up! Shut the fuck up!"

You expected the teacher to stand up, to hurry over, to send you to the office. He only stared, like the other kids, with interest and without shame.

"It was your friend Ashley told us all this," said the girl, her cheeks pinking a little. "She wanted to say herself, but you're too much. You scare her."

"Oh," you said. The world seemed to settle around you, and you couldn't imagine that you'd been screaming a moment ago. "Then I guess she's a bitch too." You looked at the sub. "I'm leaving now." You walked into the aisle and toward the front of the room. "I'm going to go." You stopped at the door. You left.

Chapter 8

And now for some tenderness.

"Ashley you fucking bitch, what the fuck you talkin' trash 'bout me for? What the fuck you bitch!"

She stood at her locker, and, from her looks, she'd had a day almost as awful as yours. There were bags under her eyes and her shoulders slumped, but she turned toward you with a sad smile.

"Meredith?" she said.
"You heard me!"

Around you, kids were laughing. Ashley took your wrist. "Shh!" She pulled you along the hall to the vestibule at the front of the building. A few kids watched, coming and going from their classes. You started to shout, but Ashley looked at you with meaning, and you shut up. She pretended to make small talk until the halls cleared and the bell rang. Then, she opened an inconspicuous door that led into a dark stairway, spiraling up as if in a castle. You entered and climbed several steps so that Ashley could fit inside. Central High is honeycombed with places like this; there is a neglected radio recording room, and an entire gym hides above the ceiling panels of one wing, unknown to most of the kids in their science classes below. Following the spiral of those particular stairs to the top, you emerged from a turret one hundred feet high, with all of the city sprawled at your feet, a quilt of skeletal tree branches. But pigeons nest up there, and sometimes they dive on students that climb too high. You sat down on the dusty stairs.

"What is this, Meredith?" Ashley's voice echoed up from beneath you. You'd never heard her sound so tired. "You can't act like that," she said. "People are all weird since Mr. Catgut died."
"Why you talkin' shit about me?"
"What do you mean?"

You told her what the girl had said.

"Meredith," she said. "I did tell some people – a couple – what was up with you, but only because I thought I could help you find a place to stay next week."

"I need a place to stay now!"

"Not for a few nights –"

"Brian's mom kicked me out."

"She did?" A little laugh. "Well, I guess I'm not surprised. I broke up with Brian yesterday."

"You did?"

"Yeah. It turns out that our special date wasn't special at all. I thought he was going to take us to a club in Royal Oak or something. He just wanted to lie in the back of his old pickup and look at the stars."

"That sounds really sweet, actually."

"Yeah, well... it wasn't. It turns out that Brian isn't a very nice person. Not at all. I should have thought him through more."

"What do you mean?"

"You know," she said. Her voice sounded flat and irritated.

"Anyway, you didn't ask me. If you could tell."

"I'm sorry," She didn't sound sorry.

"You haven't been around much," you said.

A pause. "I'm not a bitch."

"I know. I'm sorry," you said.

For a moment, neither of you spoke or moved. You actually wondered if she'd left somehow. If you'd imagined the whole conversation. You held out your hand and put it on her shoulder. It shook, gently.

"Ashley," you said. "You know last Tuesday? The first day I went to stay at Brian's? I went to the library downtown. The one at U of M. I was there all day, and then I asked about getting a job with them. They asked if I was a student there. So I said, 'soon.' I just said it like that, but I realized I meant it. I even left my house key there. I'm serious about not going back to my parents'. I want to go to college. And I'm thinking now – I don't even want to go in Flint. Lansing maybe? Or Detroit? I don't know, it doesn't seem far enough. If I could, I'd go in a different country. I could learn the language. It would be perfect. Somewhere warm and sunny. Maybe Mexico. Maybe I'll just get a bus ticket and ride it as far as it goes."

"Don't do that."

"I'm serious, Ashley. I mean it. It isn't worth it, right? Isn't it? Sin is a wicked lamp, but how do I see where I'm going? I could see about moving in with my aunt. But that's not enough. I want to get rid – I want to get rid of all of them. I want to get rid of all of this. What I mean is – I mean –"

"Don't go –"

"But I need to go," you said.

"Please don't –"

"Hey, it's just – a world of plastic rocking horses."

"I, I... I don't even know what you're talking about, Meredith!" You were surprised to hear her voice wet and catch in her throat. "You're not making any sense!"

You weren't quite sure what you meant, either.

"Things I heard somewhere –" you mumbled.

"Meredith. You know you aren't alone in all this. You know you can count on me."

"Oh, don't say that! I am alone! My problems are mine... Ashley? Are you afraid of me?"

Another pause.

Her cutting laugh. "For real, Meredith?" She laughed.

"Ashley, I think I can figure out who the Rat Man is."

You told her about the rats and the river and the rain. It seemed to lift her spirits momentarily.

"That is weird," she said. "You don't think the cops know?"

"I hope they know. I hope they could figure that much out. They haven't said it, though. I'm sure they know something about the rats. But the rain? It's been raining a lot – too much for this time of year. It should be snowing. When the rain stops, will the murders stop too? Because then we'll know for sure. But then again – maybe he can't stop himself by now. Maybe he'll just keep going because he's too hungry now – too hungry to stop –"

"You know, I really don't want to talk about this right now. I just don't feel like talking at all anymore."

It was so hard to get a read on her, and the darkness made it almost impossible.

"I know," you said. "I know."

"We should get back to class."

You sighed. "I can't. I have to go and find a place to sleep tonight."

You heard Ashley's hands in her pockets. She put some money into your hand.

"What's this?" you asked.

"Maybe a hundred? I don't know. It's what I have. You know my parents are loaded. They'll give me more. But you have to go back to class. You can't blow it now. Especially if you want to go off to college after you bring down the Rat Man."

"I'm sorry, Ashley."

"What for? I mean, I know you are."

The door gave a squeal as she pushed it open. In a sliver of light, she flashed the quickest silver smile and disappeared.

* * * * *

Maybe Ashley was willing to forgive and forget, but the students wouldn't forget your storm down the hall, and they wouldn't forgive your comment about Mr. Catgut. You went from class to class, and notes about you went behind your back and the teachers pretended not to notice. When teens walk their sneakers squeak and when they squeak they slide and when they slide they turn heads on giraffe-long necks. When teens glare you down, it's so genuine that even the bitterest Benjamite must come to terms with and do penance to such obstinate sincerity. Nobody loves like a teenager loves, and nothing is as hateful distilled as the hate in teenage eyes. Those eyes drip with angry tears, an ichor ink.

You wanted to put a Sharpie through their eyes.

Mr. Catgut would've noticed the notes.

He would have stopped them!

When the last bell finally rang, you sat at your desk awhile, letting the school empty. Then you shouldered your backpack and moved out into the cool night. You took your time on the walk downtown and tried to confront your situation head on. *Ten days ago I was reborn*, you thought. You'd walked out on a sidewalk of trapdoors with thorny trees rising high to either side; the left and the right. You'd walked the ways of pins and needles. But *you'd* been pure and young and had made choices as a newborn. These choices had brought about changes. The first were warm and wet like the wash of your birth. Angels swam in your wake. You had woken. From a room full of stars to dreamless sleep to dark dreams, you had walked through the city discovering libraries and rivers and promise. If this new path, this new life you had chosen, if it was genuine, then you owed it to yourself to follow truth to its source. And so other thoughts had followed at coffee shops and coney islands and shadowed streets alone at night. A man, a murderer in a matter of movement was in motion again. You had sensed his ponderous weight pushing down, his nose to the ground, waiting for the rats to rise again. You had been alone at Brian's for hours and hours, days and days, and you had had plenty of time to think of the deeds, and your thoughts had brought you out at night. With your mind cleared and your eyes full of the world, you'd finally obtained ample capacity for awful truths. You'd opened your imagination and heart and let the Rat Man in. Now, the angels flew near the Earth and dove upon the ignorant. Above you, the screaming stars. Below you, tunnels a turmoil with the movement of rats. Before you, a tearing mainstream, a burning horizon, and a boarding house, somewhere out on the edge of town.

You entered the Genesee County Administration Building and waited in line for a long time until you finally met Ms. Leavings.

"Where did you say that boarding house was?"

It was on a side street, adjacent to Windiate Park, off Atherton Road on the South End. You didn't know the area well.

The sun was sinking fast when you caught a bus running south and stared out as the buildings flew by. You passed the monolithic

Masonic Temple and City Hall, with its narrow windows framed and arrayed in blue and gray like deceiving cell blocks. Then I-69 slithered beneath you, and you crossed into a land of used car dealerships, broken-down gentlemens clubs, Chinese buffets, and auto body shops. Another couple of miles. You passed a school and a church and suddenly the Great Lakes Tech Center, cold with huge planes of bricks and glass. The structure blazed with white lights like a massive landed space ship.

It was twilight when you got off the bus and started walking in search of Windiate Park. Ms. Leavings hadn't given very good directions. She'd told you to take the bus to Atherton and walk alongside the park on Saginaw Street. There *was* no park on Saginaw, but on Atherton you saw a dark lawn sloping away behind an unmarked chain-link fence, and you followed it, looking for a sign. After several blocks, you saw sand traps in the distance. *This isn't Windiate Park at all, this is a golf course.*

You continued onward, hoping against hope to see the park float into view. A half hour after you'd left the bus, you reached Dort Highway. The light turned red. The haloed glow of chain restaurants shone out at you from between the vaster shadows of shuttered strip malls. You turned around to look behind you, the way you came. The final greasy streaks of sunlight had faded completely from the sky. You knew you'd missed the mark and had gone too far. But you had no one to answer to, and something in the thicker darkness ahead drew you on. Maybe it was the wide and empty, cold and looming, and hiding – what?

What was it that escaped you here that you might capture out there?

The Rat Man, perhaps?

The light turned green.

You crossed Dort and moved on. The asphalt began to break into chunks, the modest houses you'd passed dropped away, and moldy shacks hobbled and huddled across weedy reedies that stuck up and saturated like wumpty stumps.

This was still the city, however.

"Rat Man, you out there?" you asked.

He didn't answer.

...

You moved on.

You walked along a dusty harrowing where the houses and shacks fell away completely. There, tacked upon a telephone pole that sprung a molten magma viscous from the street, splintered and stripped dead hung a sign: "Illegal Drug Area. No Loitering." With a syringe crossed out upon its breast. "By Order of the City of Flint." The sign hung twelve feet off the ground, safer than you were. Looking past the pole into the brush, lights winked deep, deep and drums rumpummed out and beat down the death watch.

This was still the city, however.

"Rat Man, you out there?" you asked.

He didn't answer.

...

You moved on.

Now, you'd really reached the brink of brinks.

On your left a crack-assed black stop spat and scratched by Reedy Weedy went Loco Pogo in the Furnsie Pern of a Loobledy Pop. It rusted and skewed the bulb, which illuminated jack shit. Still your Nocturnum have poked and pried about the Starsy Warsies long enough, and now in that spectral shower, that radiation rain, you made out the shuttered hulk of some abandoned plaza, some shattered shock, some spattered spark, some Greasy Peasy where children had once waited in the wumbles to get their hidey eyesies checked for concussions, cataracts, stigmatas. Some Lumbi Pumbies got all hitched up for the Corndog Catmaw flame-broiled over authentic pitch butch and shaken down the suntan. And some Hogledy Puggles went all Zeitgeist and shut the whole Shabam Shabang Shazoozoozoo down, a Delphi, indelible, delectable, table balanced on four legmen of the apocalypse.

Soon, every city on Earth will look just like this, all crack-assed among the weedy reedies, and so the sentence ran on and on and on and on and on.

It was still the city.

"Rat Man, you out there?"

He didn't answer.

And then you knew he wouldn't answer because his work had been done for him here, or if he had been involved, it had happened long ago. No, the Rat Man would've commenced his gnawing further inland, along the arteries, where people and civilization strived, groping and grasping. Rat Men had no use for the thing that lay before you and to your left at that moment. It was abandoned, after all, completely abandoned, except for you, Meredith, who happened at that moment to be standing there on that brink of brinks and revelationizing around and about the whole morass.

You turned and walked back the way you came.

You found a drug store back on Dort and asked about Windiate Park. The woman behind the counter didn't know, but she looked it up on the map in the phone book, and so you learned that the park was just a block from the intersection where you had left the bus.

When you finally arrived, you found out that the boarding house was for men only, an important detail that Ms. Leavings had forgotten. The proprietor had a weak smile and watery eyes, and when you invoked (at his prompting) Jesus Christ as your only savior, he agreed to let you stay.

"The bathroom's communal," he said. "S'don' watcha pisser!"

You went to your room. It was bigger than a bread box, barely, with a view of the park, black as soot. You dropped off your backpack and returned to the lobby. You found a quarter and called Ashley. She wasn't home, but you weren't surprised. *I'm not sitting here,* you thought. You went back to your room, put on the single skirt you'd thought to pack, put on sparkling enchantment with improvised makeup, and headed out toward Dort again.

After all, it was just, what, eight o'clock? After all, you were, what, a senior? Clubs stayed open far into the night. South Dort was the red-light district and you knew you'd find dance floors and someone to let you in. There, you'd lay your arms on some fine jacket or other and smile endearing and secure drinks for the evening, a hit of this, a bit of that – this was your second childhood after all; why not capture it? Why not capture all that you had missed the first time around, now that you suspected it wasn't really worth missing? There, sauced and stoned and practically pureed, you'd make your way to the dance floor and fling and toss and saunter and sauté, just like they do in the movies, and you'd move and move. After all, life could be spectacular and spectacularly miserable at times, so why not allow yourself your pedestrial allotment of empyreal ecstasy?

To your pleasant surprise, it happened almost exactly like that.

Your control never faltered, and yet, in the shimmering electronics discreetly mixed in with the top 40 radio hits, you never felt a slave to control. You met a chubby girl from Carman-Ainsworth, and she told you that her boyfriend had just dumped her, and she'd been planning all night to come to this purple poppy preptastic club with its Chippendalish bouncers and five-dollar gin ebonics, and she wasn't going to fuckin' change her find for him! Your eyes rolled around in your head like marbles, this being your first radical libation revolution, and you fixed her in your vision and your heart palpitated and you wondered – *She seems so alive and determined!*

Why could I never be like that? you thought.

And then you realized that you *were* like that.

At that point, you had to go to the bathroom, all swank and pearly like the toilets in *The Shining*, but here the violetine ambiance shone throughout, and you stared in the mirror, apprehending your live and 'termination – on returning to the bar, you found mirrors all around and admired yourself in each and every one – on returning to the dance floor you found the beats as thick as a dream and danced as long as you had arms to fling and hips to careen.

The night could've moved in a more drastic direction, but you chose for it not to, and obediently, it complied.

At four o'clock, the club closed. You called a cab, rode back to Windiate Park, and found the boarding house. As your eyes drifted shut, another answer descended upon you, drifting down like a sheet of paper. It was your notebook paper, drawn like a cage, filled with crosses and rats, with you and me and the Rat Man between us.

You slept until ten the next morning.

Chapter 9

When you woke, the ceiling above you seemed close at first and then far away. For some reason it made you think of a belfry, even though there was nothing too church-like in the cream-colored trim and bone white spread. This was your first hangover. A weak light trickled in from between the shades and seemed bright. Bells chimed, and something fluttered in the space in between. What fluttered? Your shawl, its tips drifting in an imperceptible breeze. And also the words of a poem. They trickled through your mind, and you fixed on occasional phrases: "hungry rats," "won't work on this occasion," "the world hurls." You couldn't remember much else. That poem held the final answer, you knew. It told your story. The time had arrived for resolution.

Of the rough hundred dollars Ashley had given you, seventy had covered your room for the week, twenty had gone for drinks and the cab the night before, and you still had ten. You went out to the lobby and the manager made change for you. You found the pay phone outside the back door and called Ashley. Mrs. Fulcrum picked up.

You spoke. "Hello, may I —"

She hung up. You waited a moment. You called again. Mrs. Fulcrum picked up the phone.

"Ashley, please, Mrs. Fulcrum," you said as fast and clearly as you could.
"She's out."
"Do you know when she'll be back?"
"I'll have her call you back."
"Tell her I know about the Rat —"

She hung up.

You slammed the receiver against its cradle and swore. Some boys playing soccer down in the park turned their heads in your direction, then returned to their game. Their yellow and green shirts sported flags of Brazil and flashed bright against the gray sky. The clouds above hung heavy and low.

You stood and thought.

You called Ashley again. You got her answering machine.
"Ashley," you said, "sorry to bother you all at home. It's Meredith. I just wanted to tell you that I know about it."
You hung up.

You took the last quarter from your pocket and held it against the coin slot. You took several deep breaths. You put the quarter into the slot and dialed the house on Maryland.

"Hello?" the voice on the other end reminded you of your mom's, but softer, gentler, and very empathetic.
"Aunt Margaret?"
"Yes it is! I was hoping I'd hear from you!"
"What are you doing there?"
"Your dad, he told me he told you that I was coming, but it's like bitter honey that you're not home. I came to help your mom settle back in. And there's something else. I brought Rodney home to you."

Someone murmured in the background.

"Is Dad there?" you asked.
"Uh-huh."
"Is Betty?"
"Yes."
"Don't tell them this, but you can tell Mom if you get the chance to. I'm staying at a boarding house right now. Aunt Margaret, I don't know if you've watched the news, but there's a killer on the loose around here."
She chuckled politely. "It's Flint, heart, nothing new about —"
"He's a serial killer. He killed two people near our house. He left rats at the crime scenes. Now, listen. I think he has to be near the river, because the sewers back up whenever it rains. And he's killing when it

rains. And Aunt Margaret – there's a poem about it – about the Hungry Rats and the Fat Rats? I remember it from when I was little. Mom told me. I can't quite figure it out, but this all has something to do with us. It's strange, but I know it has something to do with our family and those lumberjack stories. Maybe in a not direct way. I don't know. I know I want you to be safe. And I want Mom to be safe. And Rodney. And Betty, and Dad too, as long as they don't have anything to do with it. So just tell Mom about this when you get a chance, and try to stay safe, and leave the city when you can. Go back to California!"

"This all sounds a little silly, Meredith. You should come home now." You heard the anxiety running fast beneath her calm and measured words.

"Maybe it is silly."

"Why don't you come home? I can come and pick you up."

"I'm not doing that. You're the only one I like in that family. And you'll leave again. Maybe Rodney can have my room."

"But Meredith –"

"Mag!" You heard your mom's shriek, gravelly and ferocious in the background. "Get the fuck off that fucking phone right now!"

"I'm going to hang up now," you said, "but I'll call as soon as I know something else. Good bye. I love you."

The words played awkwardly on your lips. You mouth wasn't used to the taste of such a saying. You hung up. You looked at the sky.

It's going to rain, you thought. I'm missing something, but I almost have it. I almost have it. I just need one last piece. The final connection.

You had nine dollars left.

...

You crossed the park and entered the neighborhood. It was built of small houses, clean yards, modest aspirations. You crossed Pengelly Road and thought it was a funny name. Somehow, you found yourself back at Saginaw Street and turned south. You walked. For ten minutes you passed the Tech Center, then left Flint entirely and entered Burton, where the Grim family had met their end – or at least their abridgment. For a while, looking down each street you passed, the long banks and shelves of houses stretched out as far as you could see. Then side streets turned to dirt, broke off with dead ends, and finally ceased altogether. You passed a bowling alley. You passed a roller skating rink. The sky grew darker even as the sun climbed. An hour later, you entered Grand Blanc, and the teenagers with their hundred-dollar haircuts and shiny leather jackets stared at you. *They aren't angry*, you thought. *They're curious.* They didn't know who you were. You found a Big Boy and sat down at a booth. You ordered a cup of coffee.

For a few minutes, you watched a soap play out silently across the television in the corner. Then you opened your backpack. You'd brought two books with you, seemingly unrelated. *Little Red Riding Hood Uncloaked* and a collection of student poetry from U of M titled *The Post*. You read them with intention. You read to make the last connection. Why, then, had your evidence file become ever more broad and incidental? What did small cakes and a pat of butter really say about the Rat Man, and how might you weave a greater truth from some student's "turgid tapestries of the heart?"

Your Aunt Margaret had said you sounded "silly" and you knew that you were grasping at straws. You wondered if your earlier revelations counted for anything at all. You couldn't divide the first four murders into a shape suggesting numerical continuity or symmetry. The rats: what if the killer had raised them on his own, pack by pack? You didn't know. All of your guesses were guesses. Maria's shawl: many girls wear shawls. The notebook: what could that even mean? And as for the rain, you felt that your guess was close to the mark. But couldn't the timing have been a coincidence?

It *had* rained a lot that month.

Outside, the sun began to make its way down, and the clouds grew even darker.

I'm walking down a path in a forest, you thought. *It's not that I don't know where I am. I have a map in my mind. I have all the necessary information. What I need is orientation. Maybe I'll climb a tree, in order to get my bearings. That perspective – the ability to rotate the pieces into place – it may be all that I need.*

"Hiya sweetie," said your waitress. She was swaying and dirty blonde, in her forties but trying hard for her thirties with a slightly forced smile. "If you won't order something to eat, we'll have to ask you to leave."

You decided not to leave until you'd found the path again.

"I'll get a slice of the key lime pie," you said. "And some fries."

For hours you sat and read and reached, and the sky went from gray to blue to black. Occasionally, a drop landed on the eaves and rolled down your window. You tried not to notice. You kept your eyes on your book, but after a while you weren't reading. You turned the pages automatically, but your thoughts had moved in other directions. You looked for other landmarks. *After all,* you thought, *I wouldn't feel so sure I could figure this out if I can't figure it out. Right? I have the rain, I have the rats, I have the shawl and the fire burning on the horizon. I've discovered all of the abstractions. All that is left is to render the concrete.*

Where was the concrete?

It was in those cinder blocks you had used to weigh down the tent. It hadn't rained on that first night, that fatal and turning night. There had been fog. There had been both fog and rain on the night that Maria Puerta was murdered. Tonight, rain would fall. Tonight, no fog. Still, for some reason, Warren Dunes stood out in your mind as a clear dividing line, not in the career of the Rat Man, but in your own life. It hadn't marked a division between happiness and misery exactly, or even between comfort and distress. Something had happened there, a coincidence perhaps, that prompted the incremental disintegration of your life.

That falling open of the trapdoors.

Your family moved to the house on Maryland Avenue.

Bitty died.

Your Aunt Margaret kidnapped Rodney.

You mom was institutionalized.

Your dad lost his job.

Maria Puerta died.

Where was the concrete?

You felt dumb and literal, but all you saw when you thought of concrete was the cinder block you had set against the tent. A path from the tent led to the beach, and the sun moved down the sky to the lake.

...

After you arrived, you left on a walk, and as you walked, the beach diminished slowly before you. The wind scattered the sands like the sparks of sun riding the crests of waves. To your right, the tall grass joined the sand and dirt and rose toward the flowing summits of steep dunes. To your left, the lake slid away toward the horizon. The sun finally sank and vanished. The pale white beacon of a distant lighthouse drew you forward. You wanted to reach the lighthouse and you wanted to run away. But the late waves pulled in a watery mist that canceled out the beacon. With such an immensity of darkness before you, what could you do but turn back?

As you rippled back, however, across the knotted paths linking regions where humans lay – that night, interstices truly putrid-empty and heart-wretched – you heard a splashing to your right that was more than the waves on the beach. You walked down to the water, expecting to find driftwood or some bottles banging together. Three things stood in the water, hovering, fluttering, indistinct, and translucent dark. They wore blankets on their backs. The blankets were so long they trailed in the water.

You'd thought of this moment often, and it was easy to recall both your longing and your anxiety. But what questions *specifically* had you asked as you watched them? What words had echoed through your brain? Where were they from? Why did they do this so far from the park? Why did they carry blankets? Why did they stand in the lake? Why did they look out over the water?

Chicago.

Back at the Big Boy in Grand Blanc, the evening news had come on, and you read the captions as they announced the breaking story: Amalee Grim had recovered and had spoken to the police. She'd given them a detailed description of the Rat Man. A sketch was expected within the hour. You imagined yourself cinematically, in profile, taking a step forward into the water. You'd answered one question, and so had moved closer.

The three didn't face the lake out of reverence to the water. They faced it because they could see Chicago. Not the Sears Tower, not the John Hancock – those hundred stories and more were not enough to render them visible across fifty miles of shallow water. No, the people in the water saw Chicago as a yellow haze that hovered on the edge. At Warren Dunes, dispersed by fog upon the treeless plane of the lake, the view could never have been clearer. It seemed a fire broad and deep and silent and approaching. An aurora from the Earth.

But you didn't join the people in the lake. You feared them. You were only twelve. You thought they might hurt you if they heard you. You backed away and returned to the park and your family. Your mom sat outside the tent.

"Fuckin' hate that fog," she said as you approached. "Fuckin' hate camping. You know what we could buy with the money this all costs?"
You shook your head.
"Where you been?" she asked.
"Walking."

And then she apologized again, again, and then she told you again, again that she hated her children more than she loved them. Her eyes were wide this time, however – no rage – and she meant what she said. She told you that her family had been cursed since before she was born. There was evil in her. Murdered cities and devil lumberjacks. Pig farmers. But your father had been a traveling Bible salesman and had seduced her and she had gotten pregnant. Her parents had threatened to kill them both, so your mom and her sister and Mr. Malady had fled on a train to Flint. He'd gotten a job at a junk yard and your aunt had become a secretary, but your mom had gotten the worst job of all. She could barely read and she couldn't count. Her hands were sore and broken and the teeth were already falling out of her mouth. So she stayed in those Eastside shacks, and multiplied, and raised her children with hate and resentment.

"This is my last amicable bone," she said. "I'm warning you," she said. "I don't say it to be hard or cruel. I don't. I just – look, don't you never talk to strangers, Meredith. Don't you go with them, and don't you be with them, and don't you have no children. I – hate all my children," she said.

And you thought for a moment. Did you take another step into the lake?

"That's all right Mom," you said. "We don't like you either. It's 'either' by the way, not 'neither.' White trash say 'neither.' And all that about not talking to strangers? Hell, Aunt Margaret told us that years ago. You know, we wish you'd just die so we could live with her instead."

You expected her to slap you. She looked away, drew her knees up to her chin, and shuddered. Did you take another step?

"And you know what else she said?"
"Get the fuck in that tent!"
"She said that there's two kinds of rats. Hungry Rats and Fat Rats. But a rat that is hungry cannot be filled up. He always wants to eat. That's what we are. That's what you were all along, and why I am made like that! A hungry rat! And I eat and eat and eat and I can't stop because I can't!"

Your hand slipped and you knocked over the coffee mug. Your waitress glared at you over her shoulder. It didn't matter though. You knew who had really told you the poem, and what it all meant. You stood with the three in the lake and you understood them and their purpose. You communed with them. "I'm sorry," you said. Your voice shook. The waitress shook her head. You nodded. You took the last of the money that Ashley had given you and set it on the table. On the television overhead, the anchor prepared to report on the Rat Man, with a detailed sketch based on Amalee's description. You didn't need to see it, though. You didn't need to wait. You knew who the Rat Man was. You wrapped your red shawl around your shoulders. You stepped out into the night.

Chapter 10

You walked. You did not run. You did not attempt to catch a bus or flag down a car. You didn't think of calling for help; this was your cult, your clan, your war. This was your moment, your mission. And so you walked, and walked as quickly as you could. As you understood it, there were three scenarios. You could get back before, and that would be the best. You could arrive after, which would be a loss for your family, though you would live and resolve the issue. Or, you could arrive during. You didn't want to arrive during.

You followed Saginaw Street north out of Grand Blanc, and soon the brick storefronts and condos were replaced by open grass and factories. After about twenty minutes, you turned onto the barren stretch of Dort and made straight for the Eastside. The rain began to fall, first in spots and drops. The drops became a drum roll and finally rolled out as sheets that swept down the highway, plastering your shawl to your shoulders and your jeans to your thighs. It was a cold rain. The air would continue to cool over the next several hours, and the rain would become snow and ice to blanket the trees like the crystal glaze that used to freeze the monstered forests of Northern

89

Michigan.

Now the trees and farmhouses were replaced by motels and strip malls. You entered Flint again, an hour after you'd turned onto Dort. You passed Atherton where you'd found the wumpty wumps that the Rat Man knew but didn't acknowledge. Its trees had been cut. Twenty minutes passed. You passed the preptastic club where you had drunk and danced as if you could change your life forever. It shone a cold and violent violet among those rickety latter-day bagnios. Twenty minutes further. You reached Court Street. You easily could have followed it to Linwood and tiptoed into Ashley's room without Mrs. Fulcrum knowing. There, you'd hide from bleak, vast things with starry eyes and fleshy breath, and nothing nothing nothing holding them back as they blazed across the horizon with their rotten teeth in their heads. Ten minutes. You were back on the Eastside. Twenty minutes. You were on Maryland. Ten minutes. You were a block from home. Two minutes. You were home.

Just six days — not even a week — since you'd walked away and promised yourself that you'd never return, you stood in the wet driveway as the rain subsided to snow. The windows sat cracked in the horrible house, all of their backgrounds black like ink. In there, you knew, bleak, vast things gibbered and hid and watched and waited for you to step inside.

I don't have my door key, you thought. *I left it at the library. The door is usually locked! Maybe I can't go inside!* You felt a moment's rush of hope.

But the back door was unlocked.

Chapter 11

The hinges of the storm door made a single squeak as you pulled it open, but you managed to keep it from rattling. You could not avoid the wooden pant of the back door as it scraped against its molding. Then, you took a slow step inside and closed both of the doors behind you.

At first, you thought of shouting to warn your family, but the darkness and silence of the house had taken you off guard. It wore you down, tricked you into secret complicity, docility, weakness, like a swaying cobra charms his prey. Like a woman once mixed poison into whiskey in a yellow clay cup, ha! It tricked you into vulnerability. You knew that whatever was in that house knew that you were there, didn't you, you thought that, yes. And yet you remained silent. You chose to stay when you could have run away. No posturing this night, no, none of that. You felt enthralled with the power. Like your imaginary girl who had met the Rat Man on the street, you feared that you would be dead soon and you feared that your fears were correct. You hoped that by keeping silent you might be mistaken. Maybe it wasn't aware you were there. Maybe it was preoccupied. Or maybe it wasn't there itself.

You knelt.

Made yourself wait.

Counted to ten in your head.

Gripped your shoelace and pulled.

The wet lace went taut and with a slippery slide and a graceful glide and the tiniest tide of tension it slipped: Tsh-sip. It was almost silent, except for the tap of the tape-wrapped lace as it fell against the linoleum. You counted to ten in your head and undid your other lace. Tsh-sip.

You took off one shoe.

Its rubber tip tapped against the molding. You took off the other shoe. A joint in your ankle cracked. You slowly stood and climbed to the kitchen.

You knew the sink was full of dishes. You smelled them sitting in standing water. You knew that the floor was covered with newspapers and magazines and pots and pans and boxes. Probing with your foot, one inch, one inch, one inch, one, you made your way farther. To the doorway. Into the dining room. Into the living room. You listened to hear your dad breathing on the couch as he slept, but there was no sound. You smelled something rich and damp. It stung in the air like wet and rancid copper. You reached the front door. You turned so that your back was pressed against the wall. You put your right hand on the door knob and your left hand on the light switch.

You turned on the light.

After you stabbed your dad, you turned on the light switch, am I right? Just to see what it looked like? It was a hollow mess, the circle hole you had cut in his belly, a little concave and ragged on the sides, sere from blade chafing, and already drying a bit on the edges. And inside, the putrid and sticky mess where you'd made his ropes into ribbons. It was like he had a second mouth, even bigger than his first. Fewer teeth and more cavities, and crosses across his palms!

Or you didn't stab him. There are at least two versions. I know which one I'm going to tell.

At any rate, your dad was dead.

A bloody steak knife lay at the foot of the bed. You grabbed it and held it up before the shadows. Then you realized what you were doing and dropped the knife. It was too late. You picked it up again. You breathed breathed breathed and composed yourself, then sidled to the master bedroom. You turned on the light, and there lay your mom, almost mermaidlike, the way the bed sheets enwrapped her legs and pinned them together. She lay on her back with her feet on the bed and her shoulders and head on the floor. Her arms were splayed above her like a ballerina's and her blue nightie bunched up around her, red. A meat cleaver stuck out of her belly, and you saw the dangling crosses on her palms.

As I see it, you killed your dad without even waking him. If your mom woke when you entered her room, it was probably because she thought you were your dad. Or maybe she woke in great pain because the poison was finally moving within her, slowing the rest of her juices down. Ethylene glycol, that is. Antifreeze. It must have tasted like the sweet tea she made, back when you were young. A little plump and oozy? I wouldn't know. I've never tried it. But maybe you mixed the poison in her tea. Was it the same poison you used on Bitty?

At any rate, yes yes, your mom was dead.

You took the knife and went to the other bedroom and turned on its lights. There, of course, sat Betty against the wall beneath the window. The very fringe of her hair would have been just visible from the driveway. She had scissors in her belly and crosses on her hands. She'd been in the midst of escape, and *must*, therefore, have heard you killing your mom. Maybe your mom had called out for help and wheezed and spluttered as she died. Betty woke up and shut her door and fumbled with the window latch. It was only a short drop to the driveway. She couldn't open the window, though. Your dad had painted it shut. And maybe Betty didn't struggle much in the first place – if the poison had worked within her. If she'd been struggling with the window, you would have stabbed her in the back. She wasn't stabbed in the back. She was stabbed in her flower-tender plump redneck's tummy. You probably found her in this position when you opened the door. You slapped her feeble protesting hands away and then you stabbed and stabbed.

...

Am I correct in this?

...

But am I correct? I might be wrong. I'm quite empathetic, but I might misinterpret. Because, after all, Betty does sleep pretty heavily, especially if she's high and poisoned. Maybe she was already dead from the poison. Taking no chances after Amalee lived? That would be fair enough! So maybe you just dragged dead Betty from her bed, shoved her up under the window as if she had been making an effort to escape, and stuck her body there. Cross. Cross. All done now.

Why would you do it like that? Search me... I don't need to know! Heavens, I don't know!

At any rate, Betty was dead.

You vomited, but just for appearances.

Or maybe it was a real, a genuine horror. You hated your family. You told everyone. But this?! You had to see this?! The bloody pieces of your tribe, your soul, your skin, your threads, your people come in from the Wilderness. This of all nightmares the worst alone. Or maybe not alone.

There are no rats, you thought. *She hasn't placed the rats yet,* you thought. *She's out getting rats. She's coming back!*

So you ran through the rooms making noise like a New Orleans jazz band and lurched toward the back! No, the front! No, the back door, and in a second you'd be out in front of the house, in the street, waving your hands and screaming screaming screaming for help after all! But first, something seemed absolutely essential, more important even than getting out, and it was in your bedroom. Your dad's handgun. You'd put the thing under your bed before you left. And you banged through the dining room and crashed through the kitchen and ran down the stairs and into the basement and inside your room you lay on your belly and put your whole arm under the bed.

You remembered exactly where you'd left it.

You found it.

But it was all wrong. You shrieked and pulled your hand back, because instead of a metal handle your hands had brushed against something wet and stiff. Something you knew had fur and whiskers and white eyes and yellow teeth, if only there had been some light.

"Let there be light," I said, and turned on the light.

Oh, it was the cliché of clichés, I know, but how could I resist?

"Get up," I said.

You stood. What else could you do?

"Turn around," I said.

You turned around. Since you'd been expecting me, you weren't surprised to see me pointing the gun at your chest with no hesitation, no nervousness. Both of us calm, composed, keeping a cool head in an electrical storm.

"Sit down," I said.

You sat on your bed, facing me. You opened your mouth. Shut it. Then, for a moment, something animated within you, in your eyes, as if your hate could fly from you across the room and strike my soul and strike me dead. I recognized this fire. It's all genetic, you know. It's all in the blood and you get it from me. I get it from *him* and *her. Don't think I don't.*

"Where's Rodney?" you asked.
"Don't worry about that," I answered. "He's safe from you."

Then I saw that you were barefoot.

"So," I said, "you spent all that time, when you first got here, taking off your shoes? It must have taken you five minutes to take them off! You were very quiet. I wouldn't have heard you if I hadn't been standing ten feet below you. You really spent most of the time since you've gotten home taking off your shoes. Are your feet cold? It's been raining terribly out. Did you walk all the way here in the rain? Oh your poor toes, all white and wet. Wrinkled like a prune! Ha!"

And sad toes.

And tender toes.

They never felt such a flood but once.
No, no, I am certain, and surely your tender toes never felt such a flood as that but once. The flood of the rain is not the same as the flood of the waves, but after all: fire is fire, wood is wood, and water is water."

You didn't want to speak.

So I spoke.

And I told you a little long story, Meredith, because I've been keeping an eye on you, and you've been very clever to figure this all out. That poem, that old poem, I know it by heart, and I was visiting when you ran home without your trike. *I* told you the poem. I know the true story of the Big Bad Wolf. I didn't need to repeat these tonight, really, you understand, but they're my favorites. They're your history. Your family tree. Ha! Trees. Yes, a line of lumberjacks, a passel of trapdoors, the hungry rats and the fat. Our stories: the mainstream and the fire. Gifts from your great-great-great-grandparents. And now I think we've covered everything. Your fingerprints on the knife, motive, means, family history, and a character witness in me.

Who is the Rat Man, really?

PART TWO:
HUNGRY RATS AT THE DEVIL'S RANCH

Chapter 1

Rats. Flies and squirrels. What? Enough.

...

I had... let me envision. I have... Where's the whiskey? The whiskey! I can't see a damned thing. Mag? Maggie?

...

I see you now.

I couldn't see you. Bob let the damned fire go out.

I was dreaming, God damn it. It's the damned whiskey. He took the damned whiskey.

With just a bit of rum or whiskey, I wouldn't have these damned dreams. My eye, Mag, it was a monstrous dream, and it mostly applied to you. I don't reckon that I was involved at all.

...

You were alone here. In the cabin. It was daylight outside. It was the summer time. It was the Sabbath day. You moved about, breathing and cleaning, scraping and rearranging the pots and knives, and every so often the door swung open and the soot blew from the stove. You thought it was the wind, but I knew it wasn't the wind. No, it wasn't the wind that stirred you to trembling. It was what else breathed the wind. No, the wind does not blow from all directions at once. The sound you heard was a storm of ghosts. They encircled. They were hunting for scraps. Hunting for you. Through the rest of ninety-one to ninety-two.

Where's the whiskey?

You went to the door and threw it open. You saw trees, their leaves waving overhead. I wondered where you had gone, because this forest had been reduced to slashings a decade ago. You yourself did not perceive the strangeness of this mutatis mutandis, this abominatory dislocation, and perhaps you had no time to notice. The ghosts were hard upon you, of course, just out of your sight, riding the mainstream, afraid of the fire. You heard them coming and you ran from the cottage. You ran as fast as your legs could carry you and went deeper and deeper into the woods.

You arrived in Meredith. It looked just like it does now, except it was surrounded by trees and the tracks had been pulled up. You saw an opera house.

Now who in Meredith is going to go to an opera?

You went from door to door, banging and calling out, but nobody answered. Nobody lived there anymore. You gave up and walked back to the Devil's Ranch... the Devil's Ranch was there. You found a chair on the front porch and sat down and leaned back against the wall. The rushing sound resumed. This time, though, it wasn't the ghosts. It was the fire. The ancient fire. It had been coming, slowly, for a long time, years even, and it finally found Meredith, hidden in the deep. You watched the flames leap from building to building, and you knew there was no way to escape. When it started to burn you, ha! Mag, it was just like little rats crawling on your body and biting you with their teeth.

Well, you know they won't be biting your nose.

...

It wasn't my favorite dream.

...

Although it's almost preferable to waking up in these circumstances. It's what, January? If Bob keeps swindling us of our whiskey, I won't live until March. How is a man to keep himself warm? But how is your blanket, Mag? Mine is fine against the cold, but it doesn't make much good against that wind.

And then... that's not the wind. Those are the ghosts chilling my bones. They're running out there in the blizzard. Cobden and Frankie and the Roscommon shanty boy. The others. Even though they can't bite me with their teeth, they can blow right through me and freeze my blood, and that's how they'll kill me.

When I was a boy, back in York State...

This is a hard night, Mag. We'll need some warmth soon, some fire and some whiskey, some coffee. Some whiskey. I've never felt so cold, even stumping in the winter. I feel so cold I don't feel cold. Many more nights like tonight will emphatically kill us.

When I was a boy, back in Buffalo, I watched the Grand Army march out on its way to Tennessee and Virginia. You know I don't pray much, but each night I prayed that the war would go on just six, five, four more years so that I could join up. It's a heathen thing to say, but it's true that we take strength from each enemy we kill. It's a heathen thing to say, God damn it, but that was something the pagans understood, why they conquered Judah three times, why they conquered the Roman Empire. At the end of things, sin offerings and conversions are just spit, blood, and words. A false password, a malodorous pass. A belief in God I just might testify, but don't believe those lies and rumors that forgiving your opponent heaps coals upon his head. A kiss is a kiss and a coal is a coal. I wanted to slit rebel throats.

The war ended before I got my growth, of course. I could have joined up and gone and fought Indians, but I didn't want to march and I didn't want to take orders from ignorant men. I wanted to lead. I still want to lead, but leading takes money and I was haywire. That was why I went to Toledo. Chicago. When I heard that shanty boys working for Deaslee and Gerrish were making over forty a month, that sounded like a lot of money. I went up, but I should have kept moving west.

They never did keep me on for a river drive, and most of the time I ended up swamping and clearing dead horse. No great riches there. Nothing for it. I made my way. I ran from limb to limb and swung the axe and trimmed a trunk faster than any man. While the others banged their dulcimers, sang their songs, did their stomps, I read. I read the newspapers and the Bible and all of the company statements. I went to their Lyceum, and I learned everything the Chautauqua had to teach. I set up games. I brought the cocks. I took bets from those sons of bastards and I wrung them dry. They were... rags in my hands. I made my thirty into forty and fifty, and down in the Catacombs I made my fifty into sixty and seventy, just by staying on my feet. Three floors or nine circles of Hell? Who can say in such a horrid place, and yet a man in the gutter cannot complain. I was "the devil who doesn't give up the fight," because when they fought I fought them, and at the end of a fight it was their blood on my hands. And when they slept I fought them, and at the end of the night it was their cause in my hands. *I am Jim Carr*, I thought. I am Jim Carr, two sounds. My name sounds like sledges falling. The weight.

If a man gains strength in prevailing over his enemies, then I have the power of many men, and that's what they learned when I got to Harrison. But Meredith! Damn that name! Damn that name! God dammit, the whiskey! Mag, I am a man who cannot move. Give me matter and motion and I will build you a universe. Give me fifty filthy things, the whole shebang, and I will crush them close together in my fist. Everything is important, but now I cannot move!

...

If I have the power of many men, then I will bear us out of here, and we'll run from both the ghosts and the fire, and leave Meredith. Damnation on that name, Mag. We'll go up north, where they're still cutting. We'll open a new Devil's Ranch. And by the time they've logged off the state, we'll have cleared one hundred thousand. We'll peg out of this land. We'll go to the Olympic. We'll drink that Spanish whiskey. We'll master the tricks of those Masons and Papists and learn their secrets of long life. We'll ride in a carriage carved from a single tree and gilt with gold. We'll build our house of iron and hemlock, no white pine, and the Corrigan House will look like a wanigan. You'll wear a shawl of spiders' silk dyed with the blood of thirty-three virgins. We'll buy girls of the first water and we'll send them around the world. They'll go to India, where they wear rubies in their skulls, and to the Chinese, who bind their wives' feet with twine, and to the Ethiopians, with their studded pendulum cocks. The sun will never set on the Ranch girls' saturnizing. And when we've cleared one million million we'll make ourselves into kings and gods. Gods, Mag. Omnia possimus omnes. Esemplasy. We will do this. We will consume the world. My teeth hurt for it.

"The difference is in the allotment of all power."

But I don't want to die, Maggie.

Oh, don't let me die.

Chapter 2

You must die, my husband sweet.

But not yet. I must die. One of us may die tonight. We cannot die tonight. If we can keep talking, telling stories, wakeful, breath full, we might live.

I don't want to die.

I say: "To die is to offer up your life." You say: "To live is to kill your enemies, to take on their lives, and so take on their strength." I say: "Well then, what does that mean?" Here's what it means: People are predatory. Death is giving up, lying down. It's letting those still shades, sad fronds branchstuck close in above you. The last thing you'll ever see. The sharp and snowy air, the last thing you'll ever smell. Your own blood, throatfalling, wet and weeping, the last thing you'll ever taste. That is what it is, and it sounds like a sweet sadness, like sugarwater, but the Devil you say! It is really bitter like quinine. Fuck cunts! It's shit scraps, and it's what the ghosts feed on! The fucking ghosts! I don't want to be devoured by ghosts, and I don't want to die.

Can you hear the wind running in circles?

The sleet taps the walls, and the tapping is from the ghosts' fingernails. They see us, and they see that there may be some death for feeding soon. The tapping is only the sleet. This isn't your dream. I cannot run. I wish that the snow was rain.

Once, after a rain, there was snow. The ice was slick on the tree limbs and the forest floor. The world was gray and blue like the surface of the moon, and giant mushrooms sprouted as big as a man, and white caverns yawned beneath the ancient tree trunks. The air was spiced with pine and ice water, and the world was silent, silent, except for the deer, the crush.

Once, a boy and girl knew love in the jaws of a blizzard. They kissed with lips ice-wet and blood-warm. They never left each other ever, forever.

Once, in a town known for its goodbyes, an old woman calved for the thirteenth time. Five had died along the way, and three turned tricks, and the rest were farmers and shanty boys. The youngest child, a daughter, tricked to keep her mother in health and whiskey and grub, and while the other children went away on the winds and gave up their ghosts, this girl remained at her mother's side because her mother threatened murder, and said she knew a hambone who would do the deed easy and cheap.

Now Jim Carr may say he's never been as cold as he is tonight, but the girl has been this cold before. She's been in a cold so cold that the aurora froze and fell to the Earth. It broke branches as it fell, crashing down like fallen angels and lying there like a shattered chandelier. It was so cold that the pines got frostbite and their needles fell off like frozen fingers. The girl's shanty john abandoned her deep in the forest. He left her dead drunk in a wooden shelter without even a bed of straw to lay on. The walls didn't reach all the way to the ground and she could see the branches ticking together through the holes in the ceiling. The full moon and the wet wind and the dry snow screamed across her skin. Frozen slopes. Her tits became brittle sticks. Her toes became icy mountains. She fell asleep there and the snow came and lay like a pall upon her. She slept so deep, her blood moved so slow, that she didn't wake when a starving shrew began to devour her nose. People and rats are predatory things. The shrew would have to destroy the girl to survive. It ate and it ate.

But near dawn another shanty boy came through the woods, and he discovered the girl as white as the snow she lay in. "Haloo! What is this here?" piped his little prick. "Just a noseless girl," he said in return. Now this man had a soul so small that it could spend a lifetime crossing the back of a bedbug and never make it to the other side. But the hoot owls started hooting, and he knew in his heart that if there was one and only one for kindness in his life, it was her. He chased the shrew away and covered the girl with his scarf and mackinaw. He tore down the wall of the shelter and made it into a fire. He pressed his body against hers to give his warmth, and while it was like sleeping with a blue corpse, her shape warmed the last love left in him to life.

The next morning, when the shanty boy woke, the girl was crying and cupping her hands over her hollow hole of a nose. The boy recited her a poem:

> I've beheld two kinds of rat
> one is hungry and one is fat
> the fat rats lie upon their backs
> the hungry rats eat and attack
>
> and if you think you're friends with them
> and that you share with them in sin
> here's the truth: they'll eat your tongue
> and when they're done, they've only begun

"It is very wise," she said. "Where did you hear it?"
"A German shanty boy," he answered. "Off the boat. From far away. I didn't say it first, but I understood it best."
He roused the fire and left then, but that night he returned with a new outfit for the girl. He brought her a white petticoat and white

stockings and black shoes and red gloves and a red dress and a red shawl for her shoulders. He presented her with a red silk handkerchief, fringed with lace, to tie across her nose as a veil.

"You have," he said, "a nose like chopped pork, but I've never seen a pair of lips so cold and firm, and I've never in my life known a soul like yours. What is your name?"

"Because you brought me this shawl, I am your Little Red Riding Girl."

"Little Red," he said.

"What is your name?" she asked.

"Because I gave you my mackinaw, I am cold, and I am your Little Shanty Boy Blue."

"Little Blue," she said.

We stayed awake through the night that night. The temperature rose and the snow fell, and after midnight the snow became rain. The fog drifted in. As winter's cathedral melted around us, we watched. We saw petty spirits and sprites and atomys and ash. The warmer wind blew the sylphs in and imprisoned them in ice against the tree bark. The Frost King stomped his feet and riled the snowflakes and the raindrops. Now and then, a branch broke and made a footfall in the snow. The pixies and the pine combs. The singing raccoons and the dancing bears. Frozen fish and dewdrops. You dipped your hand in a puddle and wiped your mustache slick and wet. The fog cleared and the sky opened up. I took your hands in mine. You took my life in your hands and I took yours in return. We trembled with what we were becoming. All the rage and the song.

"Now," I said. "We're going to look up. Are you ready to look up?"

We looked up.

While creatures and charms and protections and talismans cradled the ground, the sky was angry and heavy with monsters among the stars. I saw a monster with a tongue of steel that rolled into a tube. With its tube tongue, it pierced the belly and sucked the intestines out from end to end, and next the stomach, the lungs and the throat, and left its prey a sack of empty skin. You saw a monster with hair of tiny swinging axes that aimed, always, for the eyes. Its teeth were shaving razors, and it ate your face but left your skull and the rest of your body intact. I saw a monster that seeded like a plump red cherry in our stomachs, spread to our livers and spleens, and swelled, and finally sprouted grass and weeds from our skin. When its roots had drawn all the water and life from us, it turned to dust and disappeared. I saw monsters that were all mouths and teeth flying apart to laugh and cackle and flying together to embed themselves in the knuckles and knees, the elbows, the cuticles. We both saw, I think, behind it all, the fire -- beating, bleating, bleeding away. Its pupil dilated to swallow us up, and when we were in its wide expanse, we froze and disappeared. It killed us in the night. It was a strange fire. The first and only empty fire.

You explained that you wanted to become one of the most powerful men in the state. You'd worked in molding, meat-packing, and lumbering, and had finally made enough boodle to open your own saloon and bagnio. You had set your stake on Harrison, the county seat in the biggest county for logging. The rails had opened the town to lumbering for the first time, and the government wouldn't put up the funds to build a jail or pay for incarcerations. Which meant that Little Blue could cut corners. You knew shanty boys. You didn't, however, know how to run a bagnio.

I explained my own state, in which I felt nearly powerless, having been raised a slut by a jade, the equivocal slave to my mother, who had whored out her daughters from the time they were nine. I had thought of leaving, of stepping down and walking out. But girls who flew off most often landed in new and strange bagnios. Most often, the newcomers died first. But my mother kept a cabinet apothecary, which meant that Little Red could cut corners. I simply had to deal with that hambone. Also, I knew how to run a bagnio.

We both knew, I believe, that this was our last and only chance to relinquish our course. We both knew that we must fix our faces forward, must bind our necks with cords if necessary to keep our gaze level and firm. Even a shrug henceforth would have been a great danger, and repentance was out of the question. For just a moment, it was sad to let go of our souls in the snow, leaving them to freeze and die somewhere in the heart of the forest – but predators prey. We never gave voice to the question. The sky had given our answer.

Now: onward.

Your Little Blue met my Little Red. We merged and became a monster vast, the Big Bad Wolf, who is not consumed but who consumes. Who lopes and roves as it follows the mainstream. The next day, I returned to my mother, while you took the iron horse up to Harrison. We bided our time. Then, one day, my mother got very sick. She puked Red Eye and blood and shat uncontrollably and her cunny burned with a fire. Her eyes became glass and sparkle. A day later, she dropped like a stone. The hambone vanished. Some said he'd left town. No one knew where the body was buried. I put on the red outfit my Little Blue had gotten me. I rode up to Harrison. You met me there. You wrapped your arm around my waist and led me on up the hill.

"Misfortune nursed me as her child,
And loved me fondly, too;
I would have had a broken heart,
Had it not been for you.
Kind words were whispered softly sweet,
But glad I could not be,
Until I found that you had been
A faithful friend to me."

Chapter 3

I'll tell you about myself, Mag:

> "Oh Jim, One Almighty is, from whom
> All things proceed, and down to him return,
> If not detour'd from evil's path, created all
> Such to demention, one first matter all,
> Endewed with various forms, various degrees
> Of substance, and, in things that live, of life."

...

You are the one with true muscle, Mag. I have the strength in my arms and legs, but you have the strength of your breath. I am deliberate and decisive in my plans, but you are the furnace that puts life in my fingers. You are the breath that animates me. If I hadn't met you in that shack by Farwell, I may have kept moving west instead of courting ruin and disaster in Meredith. Who would have known my conquests, and what would they have gained me? You are Trophonius and I am Agamedes. Without you, Mag, I am the teeth without the jaw.

I have heard that men in New York City pursue progressions and inventions and innovations for inspirational sums. They'll give bully jack to a gentleman who attempts to make a carriage without horses. Hell, or a dentist who sculpts a faster cutting saw blade, put into the mills with engines and fires. Every galoot knows that landlooker Charlie Eddy was selling one hundred thousand parcels of white pine by the dozen in the seventies. It'll be decades before that's worth the paper of the deed, they said. But those insatiable mills sped up, and the narrow-gauge railways came in, and for a few years those parcels were worth a thousand times the pulp they gave. Eddy ought to have taken those thousands and put them into a philosopher's skull. If his dreams had become of flesh and blood, of wood and steel, of stone and wood, then those nickels would have become dollars. A thousand nickels become a thousand dollars. A million nickels... well, we live in a world of wooden rocking horses. But I never had enough nickels to get started.

...

One must evaluate the extent and virility of the resources to which one has recourse. I know a little of shipping – how quickly a product moves in and out of a town, and that it moves as well by train as by ship. I know a little of meat-packing – how to slit a mammal from neck to the belly, and that a knife moves as well across a man as it does a pig. I know shanty boys. I know how a man who dies at forty looks at women when he's thirty, and how much her chasms and key holes mean to his bridges and keys. I know how little his money means to him. I know how much he is willing to give for a little feminine balm to bend soft the aches and blades of the shanty camps and widow-makers crushing his brains into meat and mess, the sawmills tearing his flesh into shreds and strings. I know this. Don't think I'm not umbrageous, Mag. I have the star's anger that I have this knowledge, this experience, and not the prerogative of putting nickels into philosophers' skulls in New York City, or of selling saws and magical carriages.

Instead, I took the knowledge that I do have and I wrung from it what I could, like a wet rag in my hand. Those shanty boys didn't care about lace curtains or gas lamps, so I put up a big shack of whatever short stuff got chopped to scoot so that even the pirates didn't want it. I piled it up on that big hill outside the town so those sheriffs didn't feel they had to come around, and that way I could make the place as crowded and dark as I wanted. You know what I did about the girls. We saved a lot of money with that.

But it was impossible, Mag.

We made a great monster, yes, but others were greater still. When their mechanical forces came together against us, when they leveled with guns and munitions, how could we stand against them? I can still see that tally book, God damn it, as if it were branded upon my eyes. We got the place built giving credit to those shanty boys, and that was something. I still had to featherbed some of the push to go for a walk when their dinky locomotives rolled through town. That set us back. Sheriff Cramer was graciously accommodating. He never came by unless someone with better eyes threatened to come on his heels. He spoke for us to the newspapers. The expenditure on his part, however, was nearly prohibitive, as were the judges, the journalists, the Harrison and Meredith "Corrigan Club" with their cigars and British gin. Even the girls cost more than I thought. Edith got sick that time, and none of the girls would eat horse meat for months. There was the help: Henry Jones, Oliver Gosine, all of the others. So much help, but we needed it all to keep the crumbs from running away. Even the damn pan boy cost us more than we thought! I remember one night he was running in to scrub up after Frankie and her john. Frankie asked him how much he made.

"Two dollars a week," he said, even though I had told him that wasn't common knowledge.

Frankie came running out, Hellfire in her eyes, and she yelled down at me that she was the lady, the mistress, and she couldn't conceive of lying with the shanty boys while the pan boy earned almost as much as she. I thrashed that pan boy, but I still had to start giving Frankie extra dispensations.

I still can see that God damn tally book. Branded. When both Harrison and Meredith were open, we took in some sixteen thousand each year, but we only cleared seven thousand profit. That was before our trouble with Burritt and Graham. Before we met Atkins and his chums. Before we paid off McClennon. How were we going to get what we wanted? I studied that tally book, Mag, and every cent I could wring from it, I wrung.

It was impossible.

We're doomed now. We've always been doomed. We were never big enough to dominate and wring out the world. I might have put my hands out over the horizon, and squeezed a grain or two of sugar from what resembled a sweet future. I was looking west, into the sun as it went down, because it wore the visage of the fire we wanted to become. As the sun set, though, the fire and the horizon receded. They left my hands empty. We have been diminished and defeated by numbers.

The whole world sings itself away, and goes to Hell.

Chapter 4

Wake up, Jim!

Listen as the ghosts and the winds come down to the ground, revealing the channels they ride as they low and blow around, blowing upside down this dark and shaking shack.

Listen to the winds and the ghosts dive down, picking up snow, each curve a circle, all circles spirals and spirals cyclones, and each current turns in toward a channel, a path through this dark and shaken shack.

Listen to the ghosts, the gusts of winds. For this is a shack that Bob made for himself by the railway tracks where the jobbers get off so the shanty boys that put in stakes might take him on from time to time when their trains roll by, roll into Meredith. Except now the trains don't pull into Meredith, so Bob and you and me are left alone with the winds, the ghosts, the gusts that dive down and around, and whistle and groan close to the ground. This dark and shaking shack.

I still remember when you met me at the station in Harrison. The town was empty except for some dives and a butcher shop. The Flint-Marquette line had just gone in, and you took me up to the hotel.

"What will you call it?" I asked.
"The Devil's Ranch," you said.
"Why?"
"They say that Harrison is Hell on Earth. I'm the most powerful man in this town. If Harrison's Hell, then I'm the Devil."
"That's good," I said. "It is good to speak the truth at all times. The

Devil's Ranch. Show me."

You took me through all of the rooms. You showed me the piano and the bar, the fifty stools for fifty shanty boys, the well out back and the bluff overlooking the town.

"You forgot something," I said.
"Forgot what?" you asked.
"Whores don't like to be whores. Whores like to save up a bit and be on their way. How are you going to keep your whores from leaving?"

The next week, when the trains were in town, you got your boys, Oliver and Henry, and the next morning, a pile of rossed timber rested atop the hill.

> "Now choppers, grind your axes,
> And sawyers, file your saws,
> And teamsters, mend your harnesses,
> For these are lumbering laws."

* * * * *

I still remember that first trip down to Bay City. We wrung it, both of us. We understood the adventure in its essentials, but the odd chance, bad luck, quick questions... and all the problems of loading up a wriggling and furious cargo... this was a fresh experience for us. Henry came along, and for a while we stalked the bagnios, but in Bay City the madams understood the need for safekeeping. They closed their doors and bolted them shut, and there was no way that two men and a woman with a red cloth on her face were going to get inside at the same time.

We must have visited every bagnio in town, and at eleven o'clock at night, we were ready to try the Catacombs, those pits of filth and murder. It was then, in the street, that I saw a girl pounding on the doors to the Episcopalian church. She was distressed, and probably pregnant and Italian and thrown out by her family, you said. She was surely Italian, you said. But then we saw her looks, her pale Swedish complexion, and the way she almost danced as she swayed and beat against the door. Such a natural dancer. We separated. I waited five minutes. I approached the girl.

"My dear," I said. "Is this your lodging tonight?"

She didn't answer.

"Where are you headed?" I asked.

She didn't speak English. I pointed at my hand to show her the straits. She knew what I meant and nodded.

"You'll have to take the iron horse," I said, and she followed me to the railway.

We'd almost arrived when you and Henry rushed from an alley, and you grabbed her arms and held them behind her, while Henry wrapped his arms around her legs and hefted her off the ground. Poor fool, Henry, didn't know how to compel her leisure. First he lifted her up and then he set her down, and then he lifted her up again, while the girl kicked and squirmed and screamed. Little Red knows how to deal with squirming girls. A hand, a paper, firm against her mouth, the other hand clenching her nostrils shut. Then she was then much easier to carry. Since we didn't know her name, we called her "Little Casino." After all, finding her then was our pure luck, and you were so sure she was an Italian!

* * * * *

By the time we got back, your hired boys had finished doing their work. One hundred and twenty-two timbers had been driven into the earth, making a pen in back of the Devil's Ranch, a dozen feet high.

"Good," I said. "But what if they climb? Whores have long and strong nails."
"Tomorrow, we strip the bark. Sand the knots."
"Good. But whores are resourceful. What if they find a way?"
"I'm buying some dogs. We'll keep them outside on the perimeter.

Keep them staked there."

"We'll get fighting dogs. They'll bite each others' legs off. We'll give them peg legs so they can beat the whores who try to run."

"We'll sharpen the tops of the fence posts. The girls would have to leave through the front door."

"I think we need a new name. It is the Devil's Ranch, but it's also a bagnio. It's a great plant."

"The hanging gardens of Babylon!" You smiled then. It was a sharp smile. "We'll call it the Devil's Ranch Stockade."

We were truly a great Big Bad, and no minor devil could have trifled with us. We were truly a pair of beastly, gnawing, hungry rats.

> they run and ride across the world
> no rest for their boys or sleep for their girls
> where rain thunders and tornadoes whirl
> and into the sunrise where the world hurls
>
> the only argument they'll hear
> is a pure pork sausage, and a beer
> the only prayer that they'll say
> is that they're not satisfied today

* * * * *

Oh husband, my husband, those early days actually convinced me that we would make speed from death, and even outrun it. I'd lie down beside you at night and look out the window and search the monsters and stars. Some nights I was patient enough. I saw them moving before me. They slowly slipped along the lip of a leaf and sank behind the dark buildings below. When I saw this soft song from such a great distance, it was easy to imagine the speed of the world, tumbling, tumbling and moving, with all of the people and ghosts holding on for themselves. If we didn't hold tight we'd be flung off. We must have had tethers, not gravity, not a pulling down, but a line from our souls into the ground that kept us from falling away. That line was also what kept us from flying.

A couple of our girls came on their own, knowing what the work was.

Frankie Osborn, Daisy Young, Belle Baker. They were the prettiest, because they knew that in a town like Harrison the pickings were slim, and they could ask for more money. Sometimes, you recouped these costs by writing them bad notes. After all, it was easier for them to come than to leave and we hadn't a nickel to spare. Other girls, the girls we picked out in Saginaw and Bay City, were also attractive. Little Casino, Edith Stoll, Hannah Carbine, and Jennie Scott. Why kidnap an ugly girl? It cost too much to keep her if she didn't make her keep. No, the ugly girls were the ones who answered the ads for maids. They outnumbered the others. They were as homely as pine knots, and as wide as horses as often as not. They didn't know the first thing about fucking, but what could we do? We didn't need a maid. "Into the stockade. Into the stockade." We saved a lot of money that way.

We made a lot of money from the red-sashed brigade. Two hundred strong in April and March, those shanty boys lined the bar and drank so many forty rods that they couldn't make it ten. It was during these months that we gave them yellow fever and reaped the rewards. You couldn't give them the fever at any time. The hour must be very late and the stockade very crowded. Who would notice what happened to one son of a cuss in a bagnio filled with a hundred? If they noticed, who would care, with all the boys stumbling home or trying to get with a girl?

This was how we laid our trap: at three or four in the morning, you told the pianist to play *The Tavern in the Town* and sent up one of the prettier girls to dance. That was our signal to infect.

I made the drink, for that was my area of expertise, potioner that I am. All it took was a forty rod with chloral hydrate and Nimrod crumbs to hide the flavor. We put it in a special cup, a yellow clay cup, so that we would all know who to watch. "Yellow fever," yes! You chose the mark, for that was your area of expertise. It was a man who drank freely but came alone. He took his drink while the girl danced. We set metal buckets out on the bar – Casino and Frankie and Belle did the buck-and-wing, but they never stripped completely until the buckets spilled over with cash and time cards. Then, they'd step down and off to their rooms with some lucky customer. An hour later, the bar had emptied and most of the boys who had passed out were carried home by their mates. We took our chummy with the yellow cup out through a different door. Henry carried the enfevered man into the pen and turned his pockets from in to out. Then, when we were sure he'd stopped breathing for good, you and Oliver took him into the wilds, slit his throat for safe measure, and buried him a few feet deep. Some – some – started calling the stockade "Deadman's Hill."

To the ghosts with them now.

* * * * *

Wake up, Jim!

Listen as the snow and the ghosts and the winds dive down and make circles around this slimpsy shack. It's down from the north, from the polar way, where ships and dogs and men vanished for so many ages, searching for a passage. That wind is purple from the aurora and dusted with soot from volcanoes. That wind has come down on us from high above the Earth. That wind is from Antarctica with its sea swirling, its turning currents, its race in gray spray. Wake and listen to that wind. Soon it will be spiced with the perfume of Cashmere and Punjab, that sage, that spice, that thunder of horses' hooves on the Asian plains, circular tents and brightly painted tapestries. Just like you told me.

Wake up, Jim. I'm cold too. I don't like the dark any better than you.

I remember in eighty-two, just one year after you first took me up to the Ranch, I brought you a piece of news in your office.

"Jim," I said. "This is for us."

You leaned over the tally book, your fingers bracing your forehead and your elbows on the desk. You looked up at me. I leaned against the doorway. I had my right arm on the frame of the door. In my left hand I held a newspaper: the *Cleaver*. I handed it to you and you read the words in ink:

MOVE TO MEREDITH!

SAGINAW AND CLARE COUNTY LINE TO EXTEND SERVICE FROM LONG LAKE TO MEREDITH

The article said that Meredith was the staging point for our lumber to bring up the rear. The next decade would see the last of the lumber drives hereabouts; the complete logging off of the lower peninsula! Meredith, that speck, that dot, that knot of a town, was expected to take a sensational bit of lumber.

We didn't speak. But your eyes glinted as dark and sharp as a gang saw. We didn't need to smile. Our happiness was greater than smiles. *I love him*, I thought, *and he knows.*

"Meredith," you said. "It's how far? Ten miles?"
"Ten miles," I said.
"That's just far enough. We don't have to break up here. We can keep the stockade here and open another in Meredith."
"Meredith," I said.

* * * * *

It wasn't long after we opened in Meredith that the fever failed for the first time. A shanty boy named Charles Cobden. I must have mixed his drink too lightly. You must have taken too long rifling his pockets. The sun was coming up as he lay in a heap in the middle of the pen. As you dug through his time cards, he started to groan and said, "fucking pirate, God damn you!" He sat up, then fell against the pen. He clenched his head in his hands. You ran into the ranch. Oliver and Henry had left for the night, and I was wiping down the tables.

"Mag, go fetch me an empty whiskey barrel."

You took a keen axe from behind the counter and ran back into the pen. Charles looked up. One moment. One glance, its wink. With one down move, you chopped Charles' head off his body. You swung so hard that the axe bit an inch into the fence behind him. I came out with the barrel and saw what had happened and started singing.

> "So merry, so merry, so merry are we,
> Not a mortal on Earth is so merry as we.
> Hey-derry! Ho-derry! Hey-derry-down!
> Give a shanty boy whiskey and nothing goes wrong."

"Cheese the racket," you said. "We can't have the johns seeing this. Help me bury him."
"Aren't you going to take him back?"
"I can't carry this alone, and you can't carry it with me. Without the barrel, he'll leave a trail of blood right to the spot."
"Roll the barrel?" I asked. "What do you think, shanty boy?" I asked the corpse.
The corpse bled from its neck.
"You're right," I said. "We'll have to bury him here."

Atoiling together, we dealt with Charles. You put your arms under his own and around his chest and lifted him off the ground. I bent his legs up at the knees and pushed them against his belly. Holding him so, we lowered the body into the barrel. I folded his arms around his head, which peeked out from upon his knees.

"Goodnight, dear," I said.

We bolted the lid on and buried the barrel. The pit was thin and shallow. Just so, deep enough.

"We have blood all over our clothes," I said.

We undressed and stood naked and radiant as the sun rose and started to shine through the cracks in the wall. I looked at you and you watched me. We were magnificent this way – this was the way we were intended to be – envisioned so, we saw each other, and became our Heaven and Hell.

"My God," I said, "there are monsters and there is a great fire there.

That hellish sky. *That* is the source of the mainstream."

"Take that scarf off your face," you said.

"I won't," I said.

In those days, the Devil looked after us.

Chapter 5

He looked after us, Mag, but he did not cleave to us. The Devil is not a loyal man. He divides his affections among the many competing for his attention, and he prefers those with the most to offer. In Clare County, with the bagnios and the shanty boys and the pine kings and the rest, he had more suitors than Penelope. We should have known we couldn't rely on the Devil's good graces. Our expenditures were enormous, and we would only win by crushing our esteemed colleagues.

I remember the day I went to establish matters in Meredith, curse it. The Flint-Marquette had been running the train as far as they could to load up lumber on the way, and in the springtime, in eighty-four, the line finally arrived. I rode it up that day, sweating like blazes, and I sat on the south side of the train. We pulled into Meredith, and there were still stumps all along the old road. No route for a carriage for respectable people to ride. The ground was muddy and wet and lined with ragged planks. At least a hundred sweaty fists held nails and hammers and tacks and wood. I didn't see six finished buildings in there, but it sounded like a plague of woodpeckers.

That day I had business in two houses. Every galoot has heard of the first. The Corrigan House. It was the largest building in town and twice as large as any other, and when I stepped inside, I didn't need to wait for my eyes to adjust. Gas lamps hung from each wall, God damn it, hot and shining even though it was bright as blazes outside. I stepped up to the bar, which was polished mahogany. I could tell it was, God damn it, because of the damn lamps. I counted over a hundred stools, and twenty or thirty shanty boys sat there on a toot. Quite an assembly for a saloon that isn't a bagnio at three in the afternoon, on a Tuesday, in March, in a third-rate town that barely makes the map, God damn it! I called the push, and the push called Tom McClennon. McClennon had an office on the third floor with a balcony that looked over the floors and the bar below. The man took his time going upstairs, and Tom wasn't in any hurry coming down. I thought he was trying to rile me at first, but when I discerned the man I understood why he moved so slowly. McClennon must have been the fattest man I've ever seen.

"Mr. Carr," he said. "Your reputation precedes you."

"Mr. McClennon," I said. "It's a pleasure to finally make your acquaintance. As you know, I do a fair business down in Harrison, but it's an old town, hardly on the way to anything anymore, and I had neither the financial resources nor the foresight to put my stake in at Meredith."

"Running a business in Meredith is like buying a jade for a Chinaman," he said. "You throw your money away. It's a freezing hole in the ground, as cold as Hell is hot and remote as the North Pole. I give Meredith five years. Why would you want to build here? You do a fine business in Harrison."

"Might we speak in private?"

"This is my man Sammy John." He gestured to the lousy grouse. "My old friend from Bay City. He's as reliable as a gold tooth."

Sammy poured me a Red Eye, took his hat in his hands, and looked at the floor, humble as a pig.

"I am certain that Sammy is a perfect gentleman," I said. "But as you know, I do not run a gentleman's business in Harrison. One cannot be a perfect judge of character at all times. It is better to have to judge as few characters as possible."

"A fellow after my own heart, and advice that ought to be of application to any Christian in intercourse with the world. Come to the table with me."

McClennon and I sat down, and he looked like a wise man, a grandfather, fresh shaven with bright red cheeks. Besides Burritt and Graham, that viper was the only man I never got my hook around.

"Now we have privacy," he said. "How can I be of assistance to the famous Jim Carr?"

"I want to buy into the Meredith business."

"So you've heard the whisperers, by Holy Moses. You've have made up your mind and are disregarding my prior advice. You are, in fact, correct. Some *are* going to make a lot of money in Meredith very soon. I congratulate you on your acumen. I am not, however, myself, an arbiter of character, and the magistrates to whom we entrust such inimitable funds have elected to build no jail in this county. It is easiest to prosper and continue from day to day through objectivity and sweet impartiality. I own all the land in Meredith, there are no other landowners except the railway, and I have a uniform offer that I extend to all parties."

"I am aware of your offer."

"Then you must also be aware that I make no exceptions."

"You must understand that when I say 'I want to buy into the Meredith business,' I do not mean to sign a lease from you, Mr. McClennon. Listen. You are a businessman, not a justice of the peace. If you do not make exceptions, it is because it is not in your interest, and it has more to do with time cards than with your safety. In any circumstance, nobody else has been able to make you the offer that I am going to make."

"I am doubtful, but by all means, proceed."

"You have put your stake in for this town at five years. In five years it will be all dried up, correct? You are charging... what... two hundred a year on land? That means that you could make up to one thousand on a lot in the time anyone is willing to pay a red cent for land in Meredith."

"One thousand dollars is a lot of money."

"In silver or in gold? You must hear me, Mr. McClennon, because what I do not understand is how you could possibly expect such a sum. If the town is as crowded with shanty boys as you say it is, are any of these businesses going to last very long? You lease a lot for five years, and then a bartender will be shot, some shanty boys get drugged and buried, some bagnios burn down. When the lumber winds down, when the slashings lay all about, do you expect to be able to lease your properties again? It seems more likely to me that you will let most of these lots for two, maybe three years, probably collect shy of five hundred dollars on a five year lease."

"Five hundred dollars is a lot of money."

"Five hundred dollars is not one thousand."

"Your estimate is low. You know why."

"I don't want to lease land from you, Mr. McClennon. I want to buy land. My land, my deed, my right to run it as I like. My right to sell my whiskey. My right to laugh at the neighbors when you decide to raise the rent. Your gain, because I will pay many years' rent, and you are guaranteed a profit from the deal... a substantial profit... and all up-front."

"Your autoconvivial estimate is drastically low, Mr. Carr. You are a man of more than common intelligence. I am almost affronted to think that you are not more forthright with me. You know why I choose to lease my land. Most people would rather open a saloon than a house of prostitution –"

"I am not one of those people –"

"The money I collect on rent is almost incidental. There is a much higher return on liquor permissions. Three hundred dollars per year, to be specific. Even if I lose a tenant after three years, even if he's only paid for two, I've made twelve hundred dollars. If I sell to you at the price that I would rent out for *six* years, I've only broken even with a two year lease."

"I am not a bartender. I run bagnios. Men want women."

"Men want whiskey more than they want women –"

"And whiskey runs like water in these parts. Your takers will run dry. That is certain. Women are harder to come by. Attractive women, like the women at Harrison's Devil's Ranch, are as rare as gold. I am offering you an up-front sum many times a yearly lease that you may dispose of however you wish. Today, if you like."

McClennon leaned back, and I couldn't see his face. He was silent for moments, thinking.

"What number do you propose?"

"Fifteen hundred dollars."

He laughed. I continued.

"That way it's a gamble on both of our parts. You hope that my place gets a torchjob, you buy it back for a song when I'm ruined and lease it out again for a profit. I hope that my good luck continues on."

"I think you'll last five years. I have no lack of confidence in your ability not to have your place burned down by some... careless shanty boy or jealous competitor," McClennon said. "Let us say two thousand, five hundred dollars."

I stopped to consider this. When we'd combined the purchase of the land with the cost of building and staffing the new ranch, it would easily have amounted to two-thirds of that year's profit. But we knew the man's reputation, and there was no prayer for him taking a stake in the whole shebang. Mr. McClennon waited for my answer.

"Eighteen hundred?" I asked.

"Do I look like a Hebrew, Mr. Carr?" Mr. McClennon peeked into his trousers. "No. When I enunciated the merits of two thousand, five hundred dollars, that was the sum I intended. No loans. No bargains. No back-and-forth on this."

"Then I can pay you two thousand dollars today. But I'll have to stop back in Harrison to secure the last five hundred."

"You are quite sure you won't take out a liquor license and pay the rent... like everyone else in this God-forsaken town?"

"I don't want to own so I can sell liquor, Mr. McClennon. I want to own so I may do what I choose on my own premises. Bagnios are my business."

"And even with that business, you'll need to take out a loan for five hundred dollars. You must not be quite as rich as they say."

* * * * *

I wasn't pleased with the deal I'd made with McClennon. I had known he'd be willing to sell, and he had known I was willing to buy. He'd taken me, though, for every penny he could have asked. He had guessed my limit and put in his stake with great accuracy. You know I hoped, Mag, that he wasn't as accurate when he predicted Meredith's life.

The second house I visited was a tiny shack, a hotel with one story and maybe six rooms, owned by Peter McCarthy. Meredith's only bagnio. I went in and asked the madam to please inform the owner that Jim Carr was here. Peter was a weak looking cur, his eyes full of water and his lips fat and trembling. He met me at the bar and asked what I wanted. I was quite direct with the man. I told him that I planned to open a business in Meredith and didn't care for his competition. I offered him one thousand to buy out his lease with McClennon if he'd peg out in the middle of the night and settle in another county. He shook his head.

"First, no sir. This town is a goldmine. I couldn't make half this much in Saginaw. And second, one thousand wouldn't even put me even. You haven't forgotten that license I have to pay for the liquor. Say two thousand and I'll think about it."

I ordered a whiskey. I had just settled with McClennon, which meant I must already take out a loan of five hundred against our profits later that year. Another two thousand was far too much. We probably wouldn't see profit again until late summer, or autumn even.

"Two thousand is not a reasonable request," I said.

He watched me as I drank.

"Please consider twelve hundred a final offer, and add to it the money you might save on your convalescence in the next year."

"I consider you unwelcome in my saloon," he said. Now two shanty boys had come in from one of the rooms. I smiled at them. They knew how many chums I had in Harrison, a short ride away. The shanty boys understood, even if Mr. McCarthy did not.

"Gentlemen," I said. I put on my hat and left.

It had not been a successful day. On the ride back, I sat on the north side of the train so I could watch the shine of the sun reflected on the waxy pine needles, lighting a fire in the pine woods from behind me. Reminding them of their death sentence. I thought about how to make up the extra thousand dollars the deal with McClennon had cost us. I thought of how to remove McCarthy from Meredith... of whom we could trust with him. Who would be willing to deal with him for a modest sum. *Much less than one thousand dollars*, I thought. The train pulled into Arnold Lake, the only stop between Meredith and Harrison. This time, I saw the lake from the grade, and a ratty two-story hotel was gray and blue in the twilight. Mag, you know I hit the wall with my fist. I saw James Silkworth's bagnio. Just four miles from Meredith and six from Harrison. How had it escaped my notice?

Shanty boys and bagnios, and don't you know, Mag, the Devil is objective and impartial with us all.

Chapter 6

Hear the ghosts. The rats scratching. This dark and shaken shack. For the most part, my husband sweet, you swindled the Devil and made only deals of the first water. We buried enough shanty boys that year to pay off McClennon's extra thousand. You were right; the men preferred their women to whiskey. Will Villeneuve took care of Peter McCarthy, and you took care of James Silkworth. November of eighty-four was more responsible for our troubles than that March.

But our future had already been poisoned. How could you have forgotten them? The muses? The angels? Their grace. What am I saying? It's this damned cold. It squeezes my throat and jams out lies and lies. They were soiled doves and pitted bitches, spots of shit and spunk that ruined us.

I am climbing down a mossy well.

"Down-down-down-down, derry-down."

My fingers and toes clutch for each cranny and hold, and soon I will reach the bottom. Like the hungry rats, I am everywhere.

> they climb the towering mountain peaks
> they swim the crushing ocean deeps
> and if her children die in heaps
> their mother ever onward creeps

The first time I rode out to Meredith with Belle, I wasn't sure what to expect. You'd saved a lot of money by capturing logs, and you got those shanty boys to plant them for free by offering them discounts on whiskey and whores. But I preferred the Harrison Ranch. The Devil's Ranch in Meredith was too small. You supplied it with a dulcimer and a small stage for varieties, but no polished bar, no chairs for sitting, not even stools.

Fine then. I am climbing up a tree into the sky serene. Jim.

> maybe you thought you'd use persuasion
> but that won't work on this occasion
> the hungry rats don't like oration
> Hell and damnation is their destination

That German shanty boy.

* * * * *

It was December of 1884, when Jenny Kinney first arrived. You were out of town, dealing with Silkworth, and we were both angry about the election. The wench hadn't told me that she would be arriving that day, so I didn't send the omnibus to pick her up. I was managing the Harrison Ranch fine by myself, and there must have been sixty shanty boys at the bar when I saw her standing in the doorway. She was in her mid-twenties, maybe, neither the prettiest nor the ugliest girl we've ever seen, although she was quite large. She had wrapped her personal effects in an apron she brought with her. The boys leaned out and stared. I didn't want the girl startled, so I went to her side.

"Are you Jenny Kinney?" I asked.
"I am. This is the Harrison Ranch?"
"Yes."
"It is – not as I expected it."
"You are here for the maid position. My name is Maggie Duncan, and my husband and I will be your chaperones. Oliver, Casino, please help Jenny with her items."

While she was gone, I took bids from the shanty boys. She fetched more than Frankie or Belle that night on account of her tenderfooting, and I'm sure her clear confusion drove up the price as well. She came down and stood at the bottom of the stairs, not understanding her situation.

"You're a maid," I said. "So maid!"

She knelt behind the bar, moving from one empty money bucket to the next, looking for a cloth rag. She found none. She stood up, uncertain. She looked out at all the shanty boys. They laughed at her now. I laughed. We all laughed. She went out from around the bar and, in utter perplexity, began wiping down the table with the hem of her dress.

Later, Lewis said he heard her cry out from inside the room where we'd sent her. "Oh, the bars!" was what she said. "She must mean on the window," said Lewis. I liked to imagine that she'd actually seen a hairy monster in the sky. "Oh, the stars!" was what she'd really said. But I was downstairs, serving whiskey to the shanty boys.

＊ ＊ ＊ ＊ ＊

In most ways, Frankie Osborn was Jenny's opposite, but in other ways, they were one and the same girl. Most of us agreed that Frankie was our prettiest girl. She arrived one afternoon after her lover, Tom Murphy, our Harrison bartender, recommended her.

"I'm as good as any of them at anything they do," she said. "And I dance better than most."

As soon as I saw her I knew that she'd die in Meredith. She had slate-colored eyes and jagged little teeth and the same anger and hunger for life as we did. She climbed into those beds with the ferocity of an April storm, and her speed and warmth warned that she had strength to spare. Yet she, alone, without friends, made too small of a monster to rage forever among the big trees. We watched her. We knew that if we could flank her, we could squeeze her and savor the wet warmth of her living blood. She might think she could overcome us, but life is a trial, even for a Big Bad like us. Predators overtake the little ones who are all alone, vicious as they may be.

We worked Frankie the hardest. She danced and sang and fucked for twelve months without ever leaving the Devil's Ranch. We saw her look with poison at Tom, and we knew that she had directed her fury at him. She wouldn't touch us and barely objected to us. We may be her masters, but he was her Judas. We partook.

Late on busy nights, when we prepared and worked the fever, it was most often Frankie we sent out to dance that last dance. We never told her about the fever, but if she had learned of it, I don't imagine it would have mattered to her. During that dance, she made more money than the other girls might have made in a week. She danced brilliantly, with stomps and spirals and curtseys and courtesies, and she didn't just dance, but she sang. Nobody else could work those shanty boys into a frenzy with such a rasping and whispering voice.

> "Some love to roam o'er the dark sea foam,
> Where the wild winds whistle free;
> But a chosen band in a forest land
> And a life in the woods for me."

Sometimes she ended the song stark naked, but sometimes she kept on a pair of German socks.

* * * * *

Jenny, by comparison, was so ineffective in bed that we kept her wages back. When she worked, we gave her grub and water. She didn't fuck often enough to warrant use of the pan boy, so once a week, we let her take a sponge bath. She climbed to her bedroom in the early morning and slept through the day. She never learned to buck on the thrust, and without that, you'll never raise your rates.

And so, my love, Jenny ran after Frankie danced. For Frankie had stopped dancing in June of eighty-four, and Jenny didn't start running until the next January. You were out in Meredith. I was left in Harrison alone. I think that's why she chose that night. Jenny hadn't made Frankie's mistake. Jenny knew that you and I ran the show, and that we drew our strength from each other. That you had the strong legs and sharp claws, and that I was the muscles in the neck that power the jaws. One of the shanty boys wanted to have a go with her. She declined.

"You can't decline," I said. "This is what you're paid for."

"I do decline. I came here to be a maid, and you haven't paid me a single red cent."

I called Henry, and he gave her a good beating and sent her up to bed.

"Sleep, my dear, sleep," I said as she climbed up the stairs. "When you wake, we'll bind you with twine and put you in the pen until Jim returns."

But Jenny stood her bed on its end. She climbed onto the headboard and used her shoes to punch out the boards on the ceiling. She climbed up through the hole and ran to the front of the ranch. She held onto the lip of the roof and let go. She was so fat that when she dropped, she hit the snow like the log that struck the shanty boy and drove him nine feet into solid granite. If her bed hadn't fallen over with the shock of her impact, we might have lost her right then. As it was, I heard the sound and sent Henry up to investigate. In a moment he made it downstairs and called out that she had escaped.

"Shanty boys!" I cried. "There's a girl on the loose and the first man to bring her back fucks free all night."

She'd run for the forest, but her bare feet left deep prints in the snow, and Jenny was freezing and didn't make it very far. Within minutes, a group of shanty boys carried her, screaming and kicking, through the front door. We poured the boys some Red Eye, and Henry carried Jenny out into the pen.

"Those sons of bitches will fuck ten dollars worth tonight," I told her. "That will be your next month of wages cut. Maybe two months. You don't exactly bring in the cash."

"You've never paid me!" she wailed like a banshee. Oh, Jim, listen to the wind.

"Beat her," I told Henry. He beat her. "More," I said. So he lifted her up by the hair and there was hitting and kicking and stomping, and eventually she was bleeding. "Is that enough?" I asked. She shook her head. She opened her mouth but didn't say anything. "I don't believe you," I said. "I think that you're pretending."

"Henry," I said. "Beat her until she thinks that she is going to die. Don't kill her. Just make her think that you have."

Henry beat her for another five or nine minutes, then went inside.

"You'll stay out here in the snow," I said. "I could tell you something about that, I could you cunny whore! I've been out in the snow myself, and I've learned never to scorn an ally. I am your ally. Without me, who else do you have? But you have scorned me and have repaid my kindness with cruelty. The grub and water and clothing and shelter we have given you. So you'll stay here and freeze with the hungry rats until Jim comes back. If you're lucky he'll kill you. He's done it often. He'll leave your body for the rats to eat." I lifted my scarf and showed her where my nose had been. "It'll start like this, and it'll get worse. Goodnight, love," I said, and shut the door. I was so angry that I wanted to kill two shanty boys that night.

As events made their claim, I had been right about one thing. Jenny had been pretending, and quite well. She took a beating well. When she had fallen back under Henry's fists and his hard nob nails, stiffening her chest and back at just the right moment, she had emptied her eyes and stared off into space. As if she were unaware that there was a world moving among the stars. Henry and I had both believed her. Almost as soon as I had left, Jenny sat up in the snow. She tried climbing the posts, but was unable to. Then she ran around the pen, looking for something to help her up. I know because her footprints told me so. Finally, she wedged her fingers, her actual fingers, in the gaps between the timbers. I know because her flesh and blood, stuck on the wood, told me so. And when she reached the top, the dogs must have howled in rage and hunger, but Jenny didn't jump to the other side, and the noise inside was too great to hear the growls and yelps. Instead, she worked her way along the fence, on hands and feet, climbing from one sharpened timber to the next, until she was on the roof again. She ran across the roof again. She dropped into the snow again. Once again, she ran away.

* * * * *

Frankie and Jenny.

Jenny and Frankie.

Two little creatures trying to vie, to feed, to knead through us. On us. Very sweet and fine of them. But we too had made mistakes. Which of us would have thought that Jenny had the sharper teeth, the faster feet, the stronger arms, the more granite-hard resolve? How did we wrong that cabrilation? It was in her appearance. Her silence and modesty fooled us. Yet, having learned that hard lesson, how did we miss the threat of Frankie, gone, rotted and ruined and torn and trampled? She set her own ghost upon us in rage, to deny us, to take us, to destroy us.

I've never been afraid of you, my husband, though you might have made a noose of your hands and killed me in a moment. You've never feared me, though I could have killed you with any of the ten thousand drinks you've taken since we met, and you think yourself unpoisoned now. Because I love you. Because you love me. Yet I swear against God and Heaven, if I had caught that girl that night, I would have killed her myself before you returned, and you would have raged at me, and then we might have been at odds.

Dangerous odds and happy circumstance kept Jenny from my reach.

Not long after leaving her, I went back to the pen and opened the door and saw the footprints and the blood on the wall, and Jenny was gone. I yelled for Henry and called him a useless bastard, though I knew that I was the fool. I should have bound her; I'd seen how resourceful she could be. So Henry brought me the biggest dog and we set out after the girl. The dog's nose was buried in the snow, though Jenny's tracks were easy to follow. This time, they led into town.

We followed the footprints to the door of a house and Henry went to knock, but I stopped him. I knocked with my soft knock. A man came to the door with his wife. He was a shanty boy from years before, back when the lower Saginaw Valley was logged off. Why he bought a house and made moss up here, I'll never know.

"Pardon us," I said. "I am Maggie Duncan of the Devil's Ranch Stockade."

"What do you want?" asked the man.

"What do we want?" I returned. "Hm. Yes. I think you know what we want. I think you know *who* we want. We are here for a girl, Jenny Kinney. She is in the employ of Devil's Ranch as a maid, and her payment consists of room and board. Now I don't know what Jenny may have told you. We love her very much, but she has an imagination, and it is more than wild sometimes. I cannot deny that I am angry. Jenny's terms of employment states that she should receive room and board from us in exchange for her service. She has the wrong thought that she may end her contract with us at any time, or that by refusing our payment she can discharge her obligation to work for us. No. This contract is our covenant with her. She *is* to receive room and board on our behalf, and she *is* to work for us."

The man thought about this for a moment.

Then he said, "I've known many people, men, women, who would try to shrug off their agreements and responsibilities. I know that this woman is at this moment hiding under our daughter's bed. And I don't believe that whatever you've done to make her want to hide under a stranger's bed is something she's agreed to in any contract. Now we've summoned the deputy sheriff to look into her case, and she'll stay here until he arrives. I suggest you be on your way, unless you want to tell your own part in it."

What could we do, Jim dear?

Now the whole county would know that we were taking girls from the streets and taking them with advertisements for maids. What bagnio of any size doesn't do the same? Jenny Kinney had taken her pound of flesh. The deputy sheriff arrived and escorted her to the Midland jail far away south. Henry and I left and waited for you to return.

* * * * *

But if that was my mistake, if that was one soiled dove's moment of fame, you know that I feel, though I do not blame you, that Frankie Osborn was the greater mistake of the two.

I still dream, sometimes, of the two. Jenny chases Frankie but then Frankie chases Jenny and they both are chasing chasing through the snow. She is upon her. Her fuming breath. Her hot stench. Rotten sausage and wretched red horse the shanty boys leave out at the stockade. Pawing about her and rolling her over. Who is on top of who and all that. Claws and nails, fingers, toes, oh! But then Jenny lashes out like a viper, and Frankie is slain, and dead, and I am slain, and I, and I, and no no no! I wake! I wake! I claw around my face, yes! Because there is a rat there, a rat there. There is a rat there, a rat there. A rat! A rat! There is a rat eating my face!

Oh, Jim.

Jim?

Jim! Wake up, wake up! Listen, Jim! Listen! Listen or I'll drown you and choke you and strangle you and burn and burden you! There is a poison in here! There is a rat! Be silent.

...

...

...

Oh.

...

Jim listen –

...

– to the wind.

...

...

Frankie?

...

Are you there?

...

You are not.

...

Jim. We worked Frankie hard that spring, that summer.

One night, in Meredith – June – we had been making plans all day to work the fever. We happened to know that this son of a bastard had more boodle on him than any of the others. He'd be killed and rolled, that was certain – it was simply a question of who got to him first. He'd been one of the first jobbers up in Seney. He was a river driver, though he admitted he was a punky one, and he'd just finished one of his first jobs. Then he'd come down to Harrison and helped Gerrish push the spring yield through the mills. They were atoiling fast and furious that year, faster than any galoot imagined they could go. Rumors flew about that Meredith might not even last the five years McClennon had pegged it at. We saw that shanty boy, and we listened and overheard, and we knew he must have had sixty, seventy dollars on him that night.

The dark got thicker and thicker, the dancers got tired, and the shanty boys got drunk. I doled out a strong dose in the yellow mug with a sweet forty rod, so we wouldn't repeat our adventure with Charles Cobden. You had told Lewis to play *The Tavern*. Everyone was ready. Then Frankie went out back and puked in a bucket. We met her in the cook room where Daisy held her hair back from her face. James stood in the doorway with Murphy, and Mae and Nettie and Belle all sat on the table. We listened as Frankie said she couldn't, she wouldn't, dance.

"You will dance," you said. You have three voices: one of darkness, that puts candles out; one of destruction, that lights fires; and one of death, that burns forests down. You said this in the third voice, and we all shuddered. Every one of us except Frankie.

"I can't dance," she said. "Get Daisy to dance."

It seemed to get awfully dark and cold in there. I'd seen that you'd taken plenty of whiskey – not wise, Jim, since so much rode on this one night. If we took this boy, we could pay off McClannon for the Meredith purchase. Everything from that moment forward would be our profit.

"Daisy won't dance," you said, in the same voice. "They don't like Daisy like they like you."
"Casino, then."
"Casino already danced three times tonight," you said. "They're sick of her. They see her again, they're as likely to shoot her."
"Get Edith to dance."
"Edith dances like a cow and you know it."
"Well I don't care who you get to dance!" Frankie said. "It isn't going to be me. I'm pitted and I can't dance."

Why waste my time on an argument, you thought, *when I already know how it will resolve? Why not arrive at the station at once?*

You went into the main room and opened the cash drawer under the bar. We heard the drawer slam shut. You returned. In your hand, you held your favorite five. A ring and a ring and a ring and a ring and a ring, fused together. You put them on your hand. Your brass knuckles. Frankie sat up and looked at you, while Daisy backed away.

"What?" Frankie asked. "Are you going to hit me with that?"

You hit her in the stomach.

You hit her and hit her and hit her and hit her, all in the stomach. Her face went shades between pale and green, and she knelt to puke. You hit her in the neck and she fell to the floor, gagging. She got puke on your hand. You wiped it on her dress.

"What?" she asked, her eyes unfocused. "You going to hit me with that?"

You kicked her. You kicked her and kicked her and kicked her. In the ribs, the shoulders, the thighs and hips. In the neck. She seemed to be smiling, but the color had left her face, and she crushed her eyes shut. She lay face down on the floor. She mumbled something. You knelt down to hear her better.

"Judas priest, she's asking the same God damn question!" you laughed.

Frankie lifted her head, and blood ran from her mouth to her chin, and she said, "Jim, if you don't stop, I'll tell them what you did to that shanty boy. How you lopped off his head and buried him out back in the pen." You grasped her hair and lifted her up and kicked and kicked and kicked. In moments like these, I see the hunger, the viciousness, the weakness, and the stupidity that each person carries under their skin. Daisy put her hands in her fists and wept. Lewis stared at the floor. Tom Murphy grinned like a fiend, and his joy seemed great, as if *he* came down with such blows upon her. And me? I felt the lightning that coursed in my veins and sang in my blood, as if I was a star myself. They called it sad, but I knew that it was sharp and startling, my heartbeat, the way I felt sure that it would expand and explode, so great was the exhilaration I felt in such moments. You stomped her on her back. You stomped on her bottom. You stomped on her back. You kicked her again. You were exhausted. The beating had taken all of the energy out of you.

> "Once Frankie had an employer,
> But he don't have her now.
> He kissed her when he left her,
> And it broke her lower jaw."

"He patted her back gently,
And it broke her ribs in two.
They call him Howling Jim,
Because he's the Big Bag Wolf."

Frankie lay on the floor, her mouth wide with the smile that would send us to Hell for good.

"'Hell,' he said, 'is all a humbug.'
And he showed as clear as day
That the Bible was a fable,
And I 'lowed it looked that way."

"She cost us seventy dollars tonight, God damn her," you said. "Tom, you finish her off. Kill her."
"I will," he said.

We left as he began.

A moment later, when you closed the bedroom door, I was amazed by its motion as it swung shut. The darkness of the surrounding space was clean, a sharply defined blackness. I saw the open shape of the door, an orange-gray rectangle lit by the candle on the lamp stand outside. *How fast the shapes change*, I thought, as the door swung shut. A moment before, my world had brimmed over with light and violence. Now, darkness and calm.

I lay down in our bed.

I rolled over onto my side.

Outside, the stars, the snow, the trees waited.

They weren't burning yet.

Chapter 7

Sweet Mag, I've been awake and asleep, and the whole time you've been speaking. You've told me of our downfall predicted, providenced, perhaps acknowledged early on by those who knew our indiscretions. But Maggie, Margaret, Mara, Mag, we were outflanked and outmaneuvered by a sanctimonious army of pursuers. While we took shots at their infantry, they sent in their cavalry. It is a fact that if we had not quickly made up the money we lost to McClennon, we would have failed. Early in the vestry. Burned heretics. If we had not removed McCarthy and Silkworth from our path, we would have drowned. Deep waters. If we had let Frankie and Jenny get an upper hand, all the girls would have left us. Fires. We had no better option. We met our adversaries head first, teeth locked, fingers forward, and for several years, we triumphed.

Maggie, there were other hounds at our heels. We weren't prepared. My only thought was of obtaining money with speed. To move on by the time the barons had logged off and cored the county. Why suspect that the county itself would change in the logging off? I should have seen this. Farwell and Clare in the south, with their courthouses and jails and one-day coaches to Midland. They had already put down their stake to become something different. Something "respectable." They cut off the bagnios, they rejected the shanty boys, their pinewoods were scoot, their fields were for farmers. Eunomia. Those homesteaders and churchgoers and bankers hated us. Mossbacks. I should have seen that each felled tree allowed them a single step further. With so many trees falling each day, soon the forest would be gone, and the world wouldn't care about the shanty boys and their soiled doves. All their bars and bagnios. I should have acted on this.

Instead, I wrung over Silkworth. I was wrought for finding enough girls. I didn't even think of the election. I was correct in my estimation of the money materials, of that woody money coursing in from Muskegon and Saginaw, Flint and Detroit. "Bring us lumber!" bellowed those savage, noble, swaddled Americans. "Bring us lumber, and don't trouble yourself with worry for the welfare of those shanty boys, whether they bleed or breed, live or die, or whether they work an honest day or lop the ends off logs. The only thing is wood, wood, and bring it fast." The trains ran in and out, carrying thousands and millions and billions of board feet each year. The forests vanished. The mossbacks became enraged with us because they were a poor folk living in a country of stumps, while we took in our hundreds of dollars. Yet we paid out hundreds of dollars, and "we knew not to what measure day by day and in the watches of the night fate had written that we should run."

Sheriff Cramer understood the tug of the tides in the rails and sawdust. "Let Jim and Maggie be," he said, "because they bring the red-sashed brigade into Harrison and Meredith when they've got cash in their pockets." And those mossbacks in Clare, those fools from Farwell, they listened to Burritt when he said, "I'll not tolerate a den of ill repute. It's known that they steal girls from their families to work in that place. It's a known fact they're never seen again, those girls. It's a known fact that some shanty boys go up there for a drink, and many of them disappear. It's a known fact, sure as that hill is named Deadman's Hill, that they don't call it the Devil's Ranch Stockade for no reason."

God damn him.

I want, I want to devour him.

Doesn't he know that we built this county, Mag, you and I? Shanty boys cut wood, but before we were there, they took their money to Bay City and Saginaw. We kept them in Harrison and took and took. And we took even more in Meredith. We may be a monster, but from one monster to another: these towns are monsters themselves. They fester in the swamps and steam. Smoke and stink. God never meant for towns to sprout here. This land belonged to the forest. To the mud and the marsh. We made these towns into towns, and we held them against their destiny of dissolution. We are the only ones deserving the thanks of the farmers.

Lumber.

In eighty-four, the Democrats ran in Clare, saying that we were fiends and demons. They won and we lost because we missed the significance of the moment. Graham, who couldn't tell a donkey for an elephant and probably fucked them both, edged out Cramer for sheriff, and that fat walrus Burritt became prosecutor. I should have killed them both. I should have pinned them down in their bedrooms and put corkscrews in their eyes. I should have used my thumbs upon them. I should have bit off their tongues. We could have survived if we'd seen the threat. We could have made it by if we'd only seen the threat. We could have —

Such expenditures. Frankie and Jenny and Daisy and Lewis and Henry, and I don't know how many besides. I carry them all on my back and it is broken. Now it's dark and I'm a wreck. Mag, I've been wrecked. You asked me if I heard the wind blowing, and I hear it. So let us turn our eyes, too... I cannot see a thing. Will it never be morning? We were making ten thousand, seven thousand, five thousand, three thousand a year. And less.

God damn it.

Chapter 8

If you'll stay awake for just a little longer, I will promise you some whiskey, Jim. If you'll stay awake for just a little longer, you will see the sky turn gray. It cannot stay dark out forever. It cannot, cannot. Besides, we must remember our triumphs. Even our temporary triumphs. Do you remember what happened with Silkworth?

Every bastard who lay down with one of his girls could have lay down with ours. That was why you called on John Ryan and Sammy Johns. They were that breed of drifting floating shanty boy, the kind who is never alone because he carries a whole city of lice wherever he goes. You were as sweet to them as sugar syrup. You met them in the Corrigan House, with its gas lamps and mahogany bar, and there you bought them the finest whiskey brought in from Tennessee, and you smoked Peerless, and drank, and discussed what to do with your competition.

Not too long before, Peter McCarthy had refused to pay his ten cent fee on a mug of beer, so the bartender jabbed a pool cue against the man's temple and that was that. All the boodle you'd been saving to get rid of McCarthy was suddenly available for Silkworth. Once Silkworth was gone, we'd own the largest bagnio between Harrison and Gladwin Counties.

"Dis be some fine spensif' wiskee'," Sammy said.
"This is only a glass of whiskey," you said. "For two-hundred-and-fifty dollars, you can get a quite a bit more."
"What we gotta do?" they asked.
"Give James Silkworth's place a torchjob. I'll be in Harrison tonight. I'll be gone, you understand. They won't be able to say, 'Jim Carr burned it down.'"

I was proud of my Little Blue, and you embraced your Little Red. We really were the world's wolves and hungry rats.

> they've got a villain's narrow snout
> and eyes so dry from hunger's droughts
> and voices red from all their shouts
> they're barking for their whereabouts
>
> from your vantage point on high
> you see their numbers multiply,
> and as you see the hordes divide
> you know you won't get out alive

The next week, you took the train back to Meredith, and you sat on the north side. As Arnold Lake rolled by, you expected ruin, you smiled for it. But you saw no bleak space of snow and blackened timber. Silkworth's was unscathed. Untouched. When you arrived in Meredith, you headed straight to the Corrigan House, and there you found Sammy and John tooting the finest whiskey with your money.

"Dont's attack yer wrath on us, oh Mr. Jim Carr, Sir," they said, shaking.

You frowned. Then you grinned. Sammy and John almost shat their seats, crying and begging to explain what had happened.

"See, chummy," they said, "we soaked da girl in oil. We ran it all round da bilding," they said. "An' at night, we were just outsida da town, awatch for all dose folks to go inside afollowed der peregrinations." "But while we awaited, a man come up." "Looked at da building." "Looked at us." "So we couldn' setta fire." "He look at all dat oil spot." "We couldn' setta fire or ev'ryone would know it happen on purpose."

"I should kill you," you said. "Listen, you cusses, Arnold Lake is an unknown dot, a speck on the map, with forests all around. It is an easy thing, a simple thing, to set a building alight without getting caught. A torchjob doesn't get any easier than the job I gave you. I've already overpaid you, you cowardly curs. I'm not getting my fair day's work from you two."

You sat down. You thought. You took Sammy's whiskey. You drank it. You took John's whiskey and drank it.

"Here is what we will do," you said. "Tonight I will take the train to Harrison. I will pass Silkworth's and when I do, I will look for the oil on the building. If I see it, I will telegraph you and we will wait a few months and make another go of it. If I don't see anything, you will come back tonight and we'll try again."

You saw no oil on the ride back. You had trusted this very important task to fools, my husband. You had underestimated the expense needed for the task, and so doing, put both of our necks on the line. That evening, Sammy and John rode the train into Harrison, and I brought them round after round of Red Eye while the girls danced for them. For winter, it was a busy night at the stockade. Sammy and John left. You waited a halfhour, then left. I stayed in and paid the girls. You led the erring bastards along the back trails until you got to Arnold Lake. Did the forests ring with their English-Irish noises or did you stuff the words tight down their throats? I can almost imagine it, that creeping, wending, and winding about brown paths amid blue trunks in that winter darkness. As you reached the sticks, as you crept up outside, a piano banged away in a Laconian key – all the blacks were missing – beneath the laughter of the shanty boys. Silkworth had painted his hotel. You wondered if the white paint would color the smoke as it lifted into the sky. You watched as Sammy and John lay the wood and poured out the headlight oil. You gave each man a pistol and kept two for yourself. As the men banged their flintstones together, you aimed at the windows and the building's corner. You had decided there would be no witnesses except those graybacks. The flames started. I suppose even a fool becomes something of a wolf when helped along by a Big Bad, a Little Blue. You ran and hid in the forest. The flames grew. Someone screamed inside. Bubbles of girls bounced out wearing bedsheets, their breasts shaking back and forth. It was a cold night, and the snow had started to fall. Now the shanty boys burst out from the heat, and as the wind hit them, their swinging cocks curled up and went to sleep. You thought they must have forgotten why they'd come forth in the first place, what, so afraid of the ice and the burning? Finally, Silkworth emerged with his assistant, lugging a heavy wooden chest and dropping it into the snow. He swore. You laughed and left them there in the smoke.

* * * * *

We've managed fools, my husband sweet, but others dove upon us. By the time we realized the danger, it was already too late.

After November of eighty-four.

I knew at once that the game had changed. I've always had a keener eye, a better sense of judgment, than you, my husband sweet. Sheriff Cramer was gone. No more stretching space as a gift from the Long Arm of the Law. Now it was Sheriff Graham, trying for all the world to look like that President Lincoln, who summoned and arrested you. The word was out that Prosecutor Burritt had put a stake on you. They said he wanted you out of the county for good, and the ghost of Frankie Osborn was going to do it for him. Do you believe in ghosts, my husband sweet?

I tried to warn you. I tried to –

They began the contest with a tiny discretion. That March, they raided the Harrison Ranch. We'd been raided before, but this siege stank with a different flavor, another taste, something smoky and brown. Isn't the purpose of a raid on a bagnio to arrest the whores and make them pay a fine to line the county's pockets? Yet they only arrested one of our pretty waiter girls. Georgie Williams. She was a homely girl, one who had answered a call for the maid service. She was vain and sent us to blow all of her money on expensive clothes, and we all knew that she hated you. Did she feel like a prisoner here? Was she worried, perhaps, of being beaten if she asked us to let her go? Did she think, perhaps, that if she went to jail, she could peg out of her bondage as well? Had some virtuous shanty boy, maybe, taken this message to Sheriff Graham, as the cause of a raid that would take her into his custody?

Some of this must have been true. That very night I saw Graham and asked if I could pay the girl's fine to have her released. He said she'd already been transferred to a jail for holding. A jail for holding? On the same night as a raid? For prostitution? Why, he must have commissioned a coach for her! The train didn't run so late. Curious. And where had they sent her? Gladwin perhaps? No. They sent Georgie to the Midland jail, where she doubtless shared the very same cell as Jenny Kinney. "How providential," I said, and left.

I met you at the stockade.

"It doesn't mean anything," you said. "They're trying to cause me a headache. They want me to put them on the payroll, same as Cramer."

"It means a great deal, husband," I said. "The *County Press* wrote about Frankie Osborn last week. They're taking you to trial, Jim. Those two are going to be their witnesses."

"How could they be witnesses? Georgie was in Harrison, and Jenny hadn't even arrived last March. They neither know a jot about Frankie."

"They're witnesses that you abducted their virginal souls. They're witnesses that will make the jury despise you. Burritt doesn't have to prove that you killed Frankie if he can make the jury hate you."

"What would you have me do for it?"

"Georgie was wearing that dress that she bought on our credit. She can't possibly afford it. I want to ask her to give it back. She will take it as a threat. She will know, and she will be correct, that it is a threat."

"That's good. You know, Mag, how women's minds read statements. Let's go to Midland."

"If we go to Midland to talk to a witness before a grand jury convenes, they'll know what you're up to. We should send a deputy."

"Who should we send?"

"I believe," I said, "my Little Blue, that a journalist is worth more than any judge or sheriff. They dress fine, as you know, and they are quick of wit, sharp minded, flabbergasting in their speech. They calm people because they carry pencils instead of pistols. Now listen. We pay out thousands of dollars to the Corrigan Club. The *Cleaver* is part of that club, correct, and the *Cleaver* has given us favorable editorials. Do you think, husband, that an editorial in the *Cleaver and Standard* is worth the sorts of sums that we've given them? I would say that the editors owe us more of a favor than that."

You laughed. "Mag, my dear, what does an editor know about jails and whores?"

"They know more than you think. They are the only people allowed to interview them in the jail."

You agreed to my plan. We moved our first pawn forward to meet Burritt's move. A.J. Canfield, the *Cleaver's* editor, knew the chief of the *Midland Sun,* who himself happened to know that the Midland sheriff was out of town on a call. When the two writers arrived at the jail with only the sheriff's wife in attendance, it was an easy thing to get inside. Yet our stratagem had not been unanticipated. Burritt had coached the girls for such an encounter.

Canfield asked for the dress. Georgie lied, the cunt, and said that I'd told her to take the dress for the trial. As if she didn't know that her appearance was spoiled beyond tinkering. Yet we had not unanticipated *her* stratagem. Canfield expressed that I was insistent, and had even sent her a new dress to wear. Georgie refused. Canfield told the girls that Burritt was a real devil of a man, as if Satan himself had put on forty pounds and grew his mustache a little thick and shaggy on the sides. "Best not to answer too many questions," he said. "You never know what your answers will get you." The girls sent him away. Those first moves seemed a draw.

Burritt may not have known of the bribes in our tally book, but he knew how we'd kept Sheriff Cramer on our side. He thought if he cut off our cash flow, he could get more witnesses to cooperate. The day after we sent Canfield to Midland, Sheriff Graham raided the Meredith ranch. They arrested all seven of us there at the time. Myself, Daisy, Belle, and Mate Trainor, Cory Keith, Hannah Carbine, and Minnie Ledlow. Belle and I went free, of course. The charge was "disorderly conduct," which meant prostitution. Belle was strictly our madam in Meredith, and I hadn't tricked since I first met up with you.

We took a pawn, then. I offered to pay the girls' fines, and most accepted, but Daisy declined. Daisy had seen you beating Frankie. Now we knew who would take the stand as Burritt's star witness.

Then, they took a pawn. You spoke to Justice Levanworth in Meredith about the "disorderly conduct" charges against our girls. You lined his pockets a little, and the county conferred. They determined that Levanworth was in it on our side, and Circuit Judge Hart removed him from the case.

On the day before the trial, Burritt brought Georgie and Jenny up to Harrison. He figured you wouldn't do anything to them the day before the grand jury convened, but he meant to tempt you, tempt you. You resisted. You *had* started to learn a little, my husband. You were famous now, and the next day, the county interviewed more than fifty jurors before they found an impartial dozen.

Judge Hart summoned you to court to read you your indictment for the murder of one Frankie Osborn.

"Is that all?" you said. You put on your hat and gloves. "Your Honor," you said, "I am an innocent man and a *business* man. Since you must contest neither of these facts, we can act for each other's expedience. How much do you think it would take to make this insulting bit of slander go away?"

Judge Hart shook his face, and his little black beard shook as well. "Sir, you insult this court," he said. "You will kindly remove your hat in the court of law. You are accused of murder, and your case will be determined not by whatever sums you may offer, but with evidence and witnesses and a jury of your peers. You will now be jailed on the contempt of court. No bail. Good day to you, sir."

You were not learning quickly enough.

In jail, you thought and thought and remembered the night when you and Tom Murphy killed Frankie. What had Daisy seen? What had she heard? Frankie had said, "if you don't stop, I'll tell them what you did to that shanty boy. How you lopped off his head and buried him out back." Daisy heard this.

When I visited you the next day, you told me to return to Harrison at once, and to resolve the problem of Charles Cobden. We must their bishop with our knight. I called Henry and we waited until nightfall. We went out to the pen and found the spot where we'd buried the shanty boy. We unearthed the whiskey barrel and slid it from the earth with skids. We pried off the lid with a peavey.

"Oh God," said Henry.
"Hoof it!" I said.
"Oh Lord Jesus in Heaven above," he said.

The whiskey barrel had not sunk, and so had not collapsed. It had, however, cracked enough for the worms and grubs to get inside, and the moisture of the soil sped along Charles' decay. In the year that had passed, our shanty boy had nearly been reduced to a skeleton, and only a few shreds of skin and muscle had clung to his greasy bones. I reached out and plucked his severed head from his hands and carried it inside. I put it in the furnace and fired the wood up.

"Oh God above," Henry said.
"We cannot fit him in the fire whole," I said, and dragged the man from the barrel. "We must chop him up."

I started chopping. Henry carried the arms and legs to the furnace, his own shaking, and set them inside. By early the next morning, with the fire raging, I didn't expect there'd be much left of Charles Cobden for the county to examine. To err on the side of caution, Henry and I burned the barrel as well. We filled in the deeper parts of the hole and widened the shallower parts. We killed a Cayuse we'd bought a few months back and put her in the hole, and buried her.

A few days later, Sheriff Graham showed up with his men and orders to dig up the pen in search of Charles Cobden's body. It seemed Daisy Young had said we'd buried a shanty boy out back.

"Daisy wishes to be famous," I told Graham. "She's a sweet girl, and we love her, but someone ought to cut her tongue out, to help against the slanders and the lies she tells."

After digging for hours and finding nothing but the Cayuse, the sheriff laughed and agreed with me. He scratched his Abraham Lincoln beard.

"My husband always wanted to slit rebel throats," I said.

...

A couple days after these events, I called the turn and advanced our bishop. I knew that the defense would call on Tom Murphy as the other man who waxed Frankie Osborn. They could have charged him, but we were the ones they wanted to destroy. That night, when Tom came up to the ranch, I took him aside and poured him a cup of our finest whiskey. I poured him a cup and another cup. As often as I poured, he drank and drank. I told him that the defense would try to work the angle that his beating had killed Frankie, not yours. I explained that we must discover a solution that would make it seem that someone else – a third party – had committed the crime. Maybe someone in the county government, or Burritt himself. We all knew by now that the prosecutor wanted our stockades gone for good.

I poured him another cup. He may have caught the fever.

When Murphy had fallen asleep, Nettie and I carried him out to the railway and laid his body on the tracks with the bottle of Red Eye in his hand. I stayed at the edge of the woods with the gun in case he moved. He didn't. The iron horse came galloping through.

> "Whiskey, dear whiskey, from the hour of my birth
> Is dearer to me than what else on Earth.
> For days I have labored and days have I toiled
> And many a dollar for you have I spoiled."

* * * * *

I've become convinced that our lawyers were more trouble than our laws. The lawyers could keep the law away, but they didn't work for pennies. Green and Gallup were the local fellows accustomed to whiskey provisos and lumber pirates. They took their payment in time cards, which we'd been stashing for years, and they knew how to counterfeit cash. And yet, their skills were not sufficient to address murder charges, not when the muscle of the government was arrayed against us. We called on Draper from Saginaw. We summoned Atkins from Flint. They asked for payment in government-validated bills stable against a gold standard. I'd never heard of such a thing in all my life!

On the first day of the trial, the real trial, the parade of witnesses began.

Prosecutor Burritt smoothed back his slick black mustache, and Graham stroked his impressive beard. They both sat in the back. The county had appointed assistants to conduct the interviews and argue the case. Potts and Perry. Judge Hart shook his head and squinted at you as if still waking up. Dr. Scott, our dear friend Dr. Scott, took the stand.

"I knew James Carr from Meredith," he said. "I knew where his house was, and Maggie called on me to visit Frankie Osborn on June eleventh, 1884. I visited her five times that week. I visited her the first time on the eleventh and the last time on the sixteenth. The first time, she seemed to have a chill, but the next time she seemed depressed and in shock. I asked the poor girl what happened. She told me she was beaten, and I examined her and found... injury on her body. Her injuries ran from her neck to her toes. She told me her man Murphy kicked her."

"And what wounds did you find?" Mr. Potts asked.

"She was covered with bruises on her arms, chest, abdomen, legs, and she was hemorrhaging."

"Could the bruises have been caused by brass knuckles?"

Dr. Scott thought for a moment.

"There is no way to determine that."

"The court will note that Frankie's assassin, by Dr. Scott's testimony, was struck by a train the same month that Mr. Carr was indicted."

"Objection!" said your lawyers, stepping to their feet.

Mr. Atkins continued the complaint. "Misleading, Your Honor, the prosecution seeks to poison the jury with baseless speculation about a known drunkard who was found clutching a bottle of liquor at the scene of his accident, –"

"Sustained," said Judge Hart.

Atkins continued. "– which might easily have been the effects of alcohol, or the foolishness of youth, or even the cries of a guilty conscience, –"

"Sustained," said Judge Hart.

Atkins continued. "– at an hour when my client was in the Midland jail. Surely, Prosecutor Burritt must do better than this, if he thinks that county facilities are an insufficient alibi!"

"Sustained," said Judge Hart. "Mr. Atkins, please be seated."

A few moments later, Mr. Atkins interrogated Dr. Scott himself. He kept his questions short.

"Dr. Scott," Mr. Atkins asked, "will you please describe your last meeting with Miss Osborn?"

"By that time," Dr. Scott answered, "Frankie had been in her bed for five days. She had gotten up a little the day following her examination, but she felt lightheaded and returned to bed. Her fever got worse each day –"

"Please answer the question, Dr. Scott."

"By the time of the last visit, it was apparent to me that she was not going to live for long. She asked me, 'Doctor, am I going to die from this?' AndI told her that the chances were against her. She seemed to be very much agitated to think she had to die. I told her that the chances were that before morning she would be dead, and she laid there and cried a few minutes. I says 'who did it?' and she either made a remark like this, 'Tom did it, or Murphy did it,' I don't recall just which way."

"Tom did it. Murphy did it. Neither possibility, the court will note, did the victim call out 'Jim' or 'James' or 'Carr' as her assailant. Let us make this perfectly clear. Dr. Scott, did at any point Frankie identify Mr. Carr as her assassin?"

"No, she did not."

"One final question, Dr. Scott. What is your opinion of Miss Daisy Young?"

"Objection," said Burritt from his seat. "Misleading. The defense seeks to 'poison the jury with baseless speculation.'"

Mr. Atkins smiled.

"Overruled," said Judge Hart. "The credibility of the county's witness is of consequence to the case."

"Pardon me, Mr. Burritt," said Mr. Atkins, "allow me to rephrase my question to your satisfaction. As a *medical professional*, what is your impression of Miss Young?"

Dr. Scott smiled. "We all love Miss Daisy Young, sir. She tells stories of her homeland that –"

"To the point, Dr. Scott. We can't have you poisoning the jury–"

The jury chuckled.

"She is imaginative sometimes. If I may say so, the girl is very much enfeebled in the mind and body – I believe in consequence of the hardships of her life of late, and also due to some social evil she may have chanced upon – in consequence of – well, her own profession, to be quite frank."

"No further questions."

Fine. The doctor put the blame on Murphy. Now Daisy Young took the stand.

* * * * *

"Is Daisy Young your birth name?" asked Mr. Perry.

"Beg a pardon, sir?"

"Is that the name you were given when born?"

"Oh. No, sir."

"What would that be?"

"Dolores."

"Dolores. That is a Spanish name?"

"Ah, yes, Your Honor. I'm originally from Spain myself. From the south of Spain. But a couple years ago, I took the trip over to Canada and did a maid service there. I lived and worked in —"

"Quite unnecessary, Miss Young."

"But after a few years going by the way I was starving. I moved to East Saginaw, and there I went in at a bagnio there. Carlotta's. One night there I met Thomas McClennon. Who is up in Meredith. That was later last year. Around Christmas time. He told me about the work with Mr. Carr in Clare County. Then I moved up to the county here, and Mr. Carr put me to work in his ranch."

"Which ranch?"

"Which ranch — it depended. I started up at Meredith, but sometimes when they were short in Harrison they sent me over there."

"And when did you come to know Miss Frankie Osborn?"

"I met Miss Frankie at the Harrison ranch. I remember because for a little while after I got there, Mr. Carr kept his best girls at the Harrison ranch because it was still making more money. He sent us new ones out to Meredith. Then Meredith started making more money, so he would make a switch. I met Frankie once, when we were both in Harrison. I remember that night because it was the night when Mr. Carr and Miss Maggie killed that shanty boy and chopped off —"

"Objection!" said your lawyers, standing at once.

Mr. Atkins continued. "Irrelevant and misleading, Your Honor. The witness invokes an alleged crime disproven in recent investigation. My client cannot be held accountable for one murder because in an unrelated incident an errant lumberman wandered into the wilds and got himself lost."

"Overruled," Judge Hart said with a rumble. "The defense cannot interrupt or object to witness testimony, and he knows it. Miss Young."

Daisy had been flustered by the interruption, and Mr. Atkins continued to glower at her.

"Frankie had seen, you see –" she murmured. She stood.

"Miss Young, please be seated," said the judge.

Daisy sat.

"Miss Young," said Mr. Perry. "Tell us about the night when Mr. Carr beat Miss Osborn."

"Well, sir, we all know that Jim Carr beats the girls often," she said. She stared at you as she said it. I wished to cross that room and dig her eyes from her head. "Not Frankie. She was his prize girl after Miss Maggie. He was usually civil to her, and he didn't kick her very often. Still, Mr. Carr gave Miss Frankie a few beatings. The last one was a week or two before she fell down like a stone. It was so bad, it laid her up. She was complaining of being pitted that night, but still the boys wanted her to dance. She was beat up because she couldn't dance."

"Do you mean to tell me," Perry asked, "that Miss Osborn was physically unable to dance that night, and because of this, Mr. Carr beat her?"

"That was what he said. 'You will dance,' he said. But she said she wouldn't. All the girls were there when he hit her. They'll tell you. Belle, Nettie Evans, Mae Harvey, and myself. Morrison and O'Brien saw it also. Jim took out his brass knuckles and hit her. He pulled her up by the hair and kicked her. Then he turned to Tom Murphy, the bouncer, and said 'finish her.'"

"What did Miss Osborn do when Mr. Carr had finished beating her?"

"She didn't do anything. She was out in a swoon." Daisy bit down on her lower lip, then said, "Frankie died that night."

Mr. Perry paused, sighed, and said. "No further questions, Your Honor."

But Mr. Atkins stood at once and strode up to Daisy's chair.

"Miss Young, you have just stated a moment ago that Frankie died the night she was beaten."

"I did, but I meant –"

"Do you mean to impugn the reputation of Dr. Scott who, a half hour ago, stated that he attended to Frankie not once, not twice, but five times during the course of a week as her health declined?"

"No. I meant that she was senseless after that —"

"I see. Then do you mean to impugn the honesty of Dr. Scott who so recently described the heart rending conversation he had with Frankie on her deathbed?"

"No! No! I only meant that *I* didn't speak to her after that. And... I meant that I had to carry her up to her room. She wasn't well, sir. It didn't seem to matter."

"You may think, Miss Young, that it doesn't matter. But it does matter. To you this may be a flight of fancy, an adventure like a boat trip across the Atlantic or an idle month in the company of shanty boys at a bagnio. But a man's life, his reputation, hangs in the balance —"

"Objection!" called out Mr. Potts. "The defense is harassing the witness."

"Sustained," said the judge.

"Earlier, in your conversation with Mr. Perry, the honorable assistant to the prosecution, you started to tell us about your residence in Canada, when he cut you off. I wonder why this was?"

"I couldn't tell you to be sure."

"I might speculate myself, perhaps. You resided in Kingston, Ontario from July 1883 until September 1884, during which time you assisted a Mr. McClennon in the receipt of time cards." Mr. Atkins produced one of the yellow cards with the red stamp from his vest pocket. "These cards were stolen from lumber jobbers in bagnios in a dozen towns throughout the Upper Peninsula: Seney, Manistique, Shingleton, Newberry. Gentlemen of the jury, each of these time cards from six different lumber companies represents between a week and a month of jobbers' wages. Their confiscation is an act of piracy worth thousands of dollars per year. For this reason, they were routed through Canada to escape detection when they were bought out in the Catacombs of Bay City, and redeemed at banks further south. This time card in my hand arrived in Flint by such a method. When Miss Young arrived in East Saginaw almost a year ago, her connection to Mr. McClennon provided her with employment at Carlotta's brothel. It was later *his* decision to move her up to Meredith, where she would be less likely to expose his operation. We've already seen Miss Young's propensity for gossip – would a time card pirate be inclined to leave her free to work among his victims?"

"Objection!" called out Mr. Potts. "Can the defense actually prove any of this?"

"The defense cannot prove it," said Mr. Atkins. "It turns out that Mr. McClennon is a resourceful man. I ask the witness if she denies it."

For a moment, nobody spoke.

"What?" asked Daisy. "I don't understand."
"No further questions."

Mr. Atkins had, in fact, invented the story of the time cards. In Clare County, however, they'll hate any woman who takes both the banks and the shanty boys for a roll.

"Miss Young, you may step down," said the judge.
"But," Daisy said, "she did speak once. After Mr. Carr struck her. Murphy was kicking her by then. But she didn't know it was him. 'Don't kick so, Mr. Carr,' she said. 'Don't kick so.' And it wasn't Murphy whose name she said, but Mr. Carr's. She named Mr. Carr."

* * * * *

Gamepieces moved quickly. The prosecution called upon Jenny Kinney, who told of her imprisonment, her rape, and her two escapes. The prosecution called upon Georgie Williams, who spoke of her own abduction and Canfield's threats at the Midland jail. The Court broke for lunch and reconvened in the afternoon.

* * * * *

The morning had matched three prosecuting witnesses against one for the defense. But Burritt had only produced Michigan Crumbs while Atkins had called upon a doctor. After lunch, you almost smiled as John Dewey took the stand, a slim young man with red eyes and an unhealthy pallor. You'd met this man, a fiddler, in the Midland jail, and for forty dollars he'd agreed to have "been" at the Devil's Ranch in Harrison the night of the murder, helping you clear up after a busy night.

"I was work't at the Harrison Devil Ranch 'at whole month, June, because 'at was when it was real busy, and I can, do, testify 'at Mr. Carr was previous 'at whole time, 'at whole week. I never knew nor saw any man so previous as Mr. Carr was. Pukin' an' moanin' all day, all night. So on 'at night the 'at died, Mr. Carr calls me into his room, where he was layin', an' he says 'at he got 'his telegram sayin' 'at one of 'is girls died b'cause a man hit her. And he asked if I could give his wife a ride to a undertaker in town and 'hey could pick out a coffin and ride with it to Meredith to bury a poor girl. And we went to Meredith, took't a body and put it in a coffin, 'an 'en we rode with it back to Harrison where Mr. Carr met us, even 'o he was sick. Bully fellow. We buried her 'at night. But he was in Harrison 'at whole time."

"Do you recall whether Frankie died on the fifteenth, or the sixteenth, or the eleventh?" Mr. Potts asked.

"No sir, I don't recall 'at sir."

"What if I told you that the eleventh was a Wednesday, the fifteenth was Sunday, and the sixteenth was Monday. Does that help you recall?"

"No, I can't say 'at it does. I'm sorry, honor –"

"'Your Honor' refers to the judge. I am Mr. Potts."

"No, I don't recall. See, I drank a lot in 'ose days."

"No doubt."

* * * * *

Mae Harvey came up to the stand. She wouldn't commit to one account or the other. She hadn't seen you wax Frankie, she claimed, but she couldn't prove that you hadn't. As for Murphy, she said, every galoot knew he had it in for Frankie, since his own girl had become a prostitute.

"What about Miss Young's testimony that it was Mr. Murphy who actually introduced Miss Osborn to Mr. Carr?" Mr. Perry asked.

"I can't answer for that," Mae answered. "But Frankie didn't die for a whole week after she was beaten."

* * * * *

The prosecution called Nettie Evans to the stand. A clever little rook. I'd promised her that when we pulled up stakes in Harrison and Meredith and opened a third Devil's Ranch in Seney, she could be the madam. She had sought out Burritt and volunteered to testify.

"Miss Evans," said Mr. Perry. "Was Mr. Carr in Meredith on June eleventh, 1884, or the week following?"

"I don't know what all these people are saying," she said. "I've known both Mr. Carr and Mr. Murphy for several years and they always treated us all fine. There are some bagnios where girls go in, and you never hear from them again. But Murphy, he was my man. Sometimes, after all the shanty boys went home, he'd play the piano for us a little. So I don't know what they're saying. And Mr. Carr was always kind and he treated all the girls with respect and kindness, and I always went out to see him when he came to Meredith."

"Miss Evans, please answer the question."

"Mr. Carr wasn't in Meredith for several days before Frankie died. He was sick in Harrison. We all knew it."

Then Mr. Atkins questioned her.

"What is your opinion, as a coworker, of Miss Daisy Young?"

"She is a sweet girl, I suppose – for someone who lies so often. She would tell us the most fantastic stories, of dragons back in Spain, and that she took a tour of China and they had her feet bound. But they only do that to little boys. Or her name. Dolores, Daisy, Deirdre when she wants to be Irish, Agatha, Ada. She has so many names I can't even remember them all!"

* * * * *

The defense called Lewis Schramm. His testimony seemed to render any other account impossible, since it featured Murphy beating Frankie on the fourteenth, then making her square dance. You looked at me then. "He forgot the story," I mouthed, but I wasn't sure you understood.

* * * * *

Finally, husband, as the sun went down, you took your turn at the stand, and Atkins interviewed you himself.

"Where were you on Wednesday, June eleventh, 1884, Mr. Carr?"

"As these fine people have told you, Mr. Atkins, I was laid up at home, at my saloon in Harrison, with an influenza that didn't diminish until almost two weeks later."

"And where were you on Monday, June sixteenth?"

"As they have told you, when I received word on the sixteenth, which *was* a Monday, that Frankie had passed on, I sent a helper, Dewey, and Maggie Duncan, and George Tracy, the undertaker."

"Who purchased this casket?"

"I did."

"Who paid for Frankie's funeral?"

"I did."

"Who was in attendance at the funeral?"

"I don't recall his name, but I remembered that Frankie was a Presbyterian, so I brought in a Presbyterian minister from downstate to preside. Not many people came to the funeral, though. Some shanty boys she knew. All of us who worked with her at the ranch were there."

"From Harrison?"

"Yes. Everybody from Meredith came too. I gave everybody the day off. I closed up for the night."

"That must have cost you a lot of money, Mr. Carr."

"We loved our little Frankie very much."

"And how did you deal with Tom Murphy after hearing of his role in her death?"

"Originally, I thought that Frankie had died of an influenza much the same as my own affliction. Everybody left it to Maggie Duncan to tell me what had really happened. She didn't, however, because she knew if she did, I might kill him. And to speak honestly, if I had known right away, I might have killed him. Then Prosecutor Burritt would have me here for a murder I actually did commit."

The jury chuckled.

"As it was, Maggie kept me from finding out for another month, and then, figuring that reason would prevail in me, she finally let me know. I rode to Meredith that night, not knowing what I would do when I got there. I didn't know if I would just yell and curse at him. I fired him that night, for 'poverty compels free men to do many mean and servile acts, for which they deserve rather to be pitied than to be broken on top of everything else.' I left the trouble between him and his conscience."

"You didn't turn him over to the county?"

"With all due respect, Mr. Atkins," you said, bowing your head. "That would be the prosecutor's and the sheriff's responsibility. As you've seen, they have plenty of witnesses to what he did to her in Meredith that night. As you've seen, I'm the one they chose to put up for murder. I suppose the government here is more concerned with keeping a businessman of the county from making his way under their watch than giving a criminal and a fiend his just desserts."

"Tell us, Mr. Carr, how Frankie's death affected you personally."

"It is a mysterious thing, death, and terrifying. Frankie was a young woman. She was a beautiful woman, and nobody would have denied that she was a woman who loved life in its music and song, in the nature, the trees, the grass. I think that's why she stayed up here. She could have moved to Detroit or Chicago or Flint, Mr. Atkins. But she stayed up in Harrison and Meredith. With the wind and the snow and the axes and the lumber and timber and all of the shanty boys. Her death struck me as death strikes death. It struck me hard, for 'to all mankind the end of life is death.' When her casket came back on that train, on Tuesday the seventeenth, she had a Certificate of Death pinned to her coffin. It was the first time I'd seen such a thing. It just chases you, death, wherever you go, I suppose. Oh, Frankie, 'Death's cruel angels have stole you away.'"

"And what did this certificate list as the cause of death?" asked Mr. Atkins.

"I believe it was 'Inflammation of the Bowels.' It had been signed by Dr. Scott."

$$* * * * *$$

The jury was hung. Nine for conviction, three for acquittal.

Judge Hart dismissed the jury and set a new trial for December in Ithaca.

"I thought you promised me better than this!" you said to Mr. Atkins after the trial.

"And you saw the show we put on, Mr. Carr. This town must have come to hate you, or else it wouldn't have been so difficult. The more liberties you take, the more you must pay your lawyers. We'll triumph in the end. I suggest you go home, rest in your own warm bed, drink your own whiskey, and avoid putting your name in the papers from now until December."

You had to move. You had to move fast, my husband. You had to learn to dodge or die. We were learning, husband, but slowly.

There was more than enough to learn.

Chapter 9

What is this blood on me? What is this darkness? Shouldn't it be light out by now? There was never a night as long as this night. Give us a sky serene. Where is the whiskey?

I moved as soon as I was out and had some boys speak some words to Daisy on the street. Then she disappeared, and while some said that she ran off on her own, to Farwell or Hubbarston, I've always thought that Graham took her himself, and not by way of the Midland jail. Then Burritt passed papers on me for the Silkworth torchjob. Passed papers on me and Joe Silverstein. Joe knew about it but didn't set the fire and didn't carry a pistol. But Burritt tore up the papers on me, saying it was a mistake. Instead, they found Silverstein guilty. How is that? They arrested me twice for abduction and assault and "keeping a house of ill fame," but after Daisy disappeared, Burritt was having a hard time finding witnesses to testify.

Our situation seemed to be improving a bit. Ascending. We always had, my dear, the most willful ambitions. We started, once again, to dare to hope. Yet as you've said so often, passions, pleasures, they all hang in the air, suspended. Such suspension is dangerous. When we slip, we fall down to a place that is dark and miserable. Underground. A small shack by an abandoned track where the ghosts roost outside the empty town of Meredith. Oh, Maggie.

They arrested Dewey for rolling a fellow and he called me to jail, where he said that he had agreed to my earlier offer without knowing that I was "Jim Carr, the great desperado." Now he wanted me to pay his bail and a thousand dollars besides. After paying off the lawyers, we didn't have that money anymore, for "a man overwhelmed by poverty can neither say nor do anything: his tongue is fast bound."

I told him "no."

They arrested Henry and took him to jail. It seems his conscience had been plaguing him over some matter, and he told a chum and his chum told Graham, and Graham had our man arrested. He had invented some story, a nightmare, maybe, about when Jim Carr was in jail, and Jim's wife dug up a barrel with a headless shanty boy inside, and Henry helped her burn the corpse. There was no evidence to convict us of the crime. Graham sifted through the cinders and found some teeth and bones, but you told him it was a dog and he couldn't prove otherwise.

Still, the stories went around, and went as far as Ithaca and further.

In August, some landlookers found an old shanty boy starving in the wilds of Wexford County. It was John Ryan, and when they brought him back, they charged me again in the torchjob to Silkworth's. I paid the bail, five thousand, but that almost broke us. They called me the Devil, but you know that a Big Bad can't collect souls or government guaranteed bills from a jail cell. They acquitted me. "No cause for action." Now we had a couple months to build up our profits to pay off Atkins and the rest. Their hundreds in fees had become thousands.

Lawyers and "reformers" and cranks, God damn them all! John Cramer went to trial and he told them about our tally book as part of his own "not guilty." Our payments to the Corrigan Club, and the Long Arm of the Law. The jury found him not guilty. We burned the tally book before Graham arrived at our gates, but now the county had secured a millage and was building a jailhouse in Harrison.

What is this blood?

And where were Atkin's questions at the second trial? He seemed exhausted by then. We found witnesses... over a dozen... but they faltered and failed and contradicted each other. Burritt arrived with Daisy, and she *had* been hiding from me. This time she stood and pointed at me with her finger and said, "I watched him, I watched him. I watched Jim Carr, with my eyes, lift Frankie by the hair and kick her in her side. I watched him hit her with his brass knuckles."

The prosecution brought in Dewey. James Silkworth had paid his bail. Now Dewey explained that he'd never known me before we were in jail together. He said that I'd bribed him with forty dollars and told him to pin the murder on Murphy. He said that I'd told him, "they can't hang a dead man."

The prosecution brought in a statement from Henry Jones, claiming his innocence, but bearing witness to the burial of Charles Cobden and his dismemberment and disposal in the furnace.

Burritt stood and delivered the closing argument, using Potts' words and his own deep and trembling voice:

"If guilty, he deserves the severest punishment that human law can inflict on Earth. And if there be a God who resides over the affairs and destinies of men, James Carr and his Maggie Duncan will feel the hand of a righteous judgment resting in vengeance on their blood-stained and guilty souls."

* * * * *

Very well, Mr. Burritt. Very well.

It may be that I feel the weight of that hand upon my back in this shack right now, and it is sufficiently heavy to keep me from standing, to run the blood down my chin now. But don't think it is the hand of God. There is no God. The eternal monsters press down upon me, perhaps, but it is only in consequence of their pursuit of a fuller nourishment. Warm blood. Runs to cold. Oh, Mr. Burritt, I have been a Shanty Boy Blue and my wife is a girl with a little red scarf, and we combine, and our hungry teeth will tear some flesh before we go. Oh, yes, we will. My, the chestnut.

* * * * *

Oh.

* * * * *

Christmas Eve.

They found me guilty, that jury, God damn them. Half of them said murder in the first, and half said manslaughter, and so they settled on murder in the second. Fifteen years in Jackson, they said. At the sentencing, I told Atkins, "I've paid your team close on ten thousand now. You will have to do better than this."

"We will," he assured me.

Graham raided the Meredith ranch and charged you with keeping a house of ill fame. They sent you to prison in Detroit for a year. And in your own fool's move, my imperfect wife, you put fifteen hundred in your socks, as if they wouldn't search there first. No money, no money. The other hungry rats closed in around us. They closed. We drew blood. They drew blood. Why is there blood on my chest? Who has cut me? Where is the morning? I am here and you are there and I cannot fathom the cause or occasion of this blood on me. It is, it is —

Where is the damned whiskey?

A year went by, went by. Atkins and his boys managed to make the Michigan Supreme Court hear my case. They called me a "very depraved man," those snakes, but they also decreed that the evidence was inconclusive. It hadn't been proven, they said, that I was the cause of dear Frankie's death. They ordered a new trial.

In response, Burritt dropped the charges.

On the day they released me from prison, though, he delivered a third round of charges of arson against Silkworth's. I paid out another five thousand on bond, and you finished out your sentence. Now we paid out another four thousand to Atkins and the vampire lawyers that year. Mag, it kept falling so quickly. We put out our arms and put our hands and fingers around the structure, but the shards and pieces of wood and sawdust kept coming down around us. A raid. A raid. I told Atkins I'd be able to pay him the next year. A raid on the Meredith stockade. I told Atkins I'd pay him as soon as I was able. He assured me of no legal aid until I paid. A raid.

I sold the Harrison stockade.

Late summer, 1887.

We'd paid our debts, but by this late date, Meredith itself was starting to wither and wilt and the stockade itself seemed ready to fade and blow away. The stream of lumber, the seam of timber through the politeia was slackened. We'd only held on to to two of our girls. Nettie Evans and Belle Baker. The rest had bought their way to freedom or slipped away. Two sharp knocks upon the door. Sheriff Graham opened it and smiled in.

"Good evening, Miss Duncan" he told you. "You and your husband are hereby charged with running a house of ill fame. Miss Duncan, you are also charged with assisting in rape. Please summon Miss Evans and Miss Baker. They are charged with unlawful conduct. Your customers will be charged with soliciting prostitution."
"Maggie," I said. "Go get the girls."

On your way through the house, you took the pistol from the desk and slipped out a second story window and dropped to the ground. An officer confronted you. "Now, Miss Duncan, what are you doing there?"
"Shooting you, if I feel like it," you said, and you pointed the gun at

his face.

You made him recede to his knees, facing the ranch. Then, with the pistol against his head, you bound his hands with cord and gagged him with your handkerchief. You left him face down in the dust and ran off into the forest with your noseless face bright wet in the sun.

I thought you'd left me then, Mag, and forgive me, but I cursed you and wished you dead. On the ride back to Harrison, they bound me with the cord you'd used on the officer and put me on my hands and knees on the floor of the train car, my face to the wall. I couldn't see them, but I heard their voices.

"Now that Mr. Carr is fixed, I have a proposition for you, Nettie, Belle," Graham said.
"What?" they asked.
"You understand that there is nothing we hold personally against the two of you. Prosecutor Burritt and myself are simply trying to clean this county up. After the war, when army men became shanty boys and the lumber was moving through the state each day, there was a reason for gambling dens and whiskey saloons and bagnios. But Jim here is an evil man. You know this as I do. He has killed many people, men and women. You know this as I do."

He propped his heels upon my back, the bastard. I couldn't speak.

"My wages," he said. "They aren't astonishing. The people here give me a small amount. But with that small amount, I'm going to go home tonight, and I'll sit down to a fine meal of partridge pie and cod fish with drawn butter, boiled potatoes with onions, prunes and sausage, a beer, a coffee, Hell, even a slice of lemon pie. I'll reckon you didn't know that some small wages could purchase such a feast, but that is how it is in this country, for those of us who aren't slaves to sin and devilry."

He coughed and cleared his throat.

"Now," he said. "We have it out for Jim Carr, Prosecutor Burritt and myself. We'll have him starving and cold in another county for our wages. We would not like to see any more trouble for the two of you. All of Carr's other girls left, all under reasonable suppositions. You know it's him and that nogood woman of his that are no end of trouble for you. Prosecutor Burritt has a suggestion, and I find it agreeable. I will tell you now. There is no room in Clare County for the bagnios any longer. Promise to peg out of this county. You can go to Gladwin or Midland and find honest work. Or... if you truly wish to keep on as you are, you can easily find work in Saginaw or Bay City. There are enough bagnios there that you should be able to find one with better treatment, and certainly better pay, than Carr's. I happen to know that Jim Carr isn't paying anyone very well these days."

When we arrived in Harrison, the girls agreed to Graham's suggestion. The sheriff paid a man to jerk the hash, then bought the girls two tickets to Saginaw and sent them on their way.

During the two days in jail, Mag, when you had left me, when everyone had left me, I thought of taking my own life. The lumber was drying up. Meredith had yet a year or two of life. Three at most. McClennon's place was fast and fresh enough to keep the men in liquor as often as not, while independent whores tricked out of railside shanty shacks. I had run out of funds to keep the county off my back. There was no chance to build a ranch in Seney. There was no chance, even, of returning to the pinewoods. All I wanted was my whiskey. All I wanted was my sharp woody drink, and maybe a noose around my neck.

That was when a very young shanty boy came in and paid my bail. He told me that a woman missing her nose had found his shanty camp and promised him money, favors – the whole shebang! – if he'd bail me out and lead me where to meet her. She had plans, he said. So I bought a bright red scarf and took the dinky locomotive up to Roscommon County, and there in the forest, when we'd killed the boy and cashed in his time cards, we made our final play in the game. It was a desperate move. We'd lost all of our pieces, except for our queen: the Devil's Ranch Stockade in Meredith. We'd play that one piece against their whole board, their vast array. If we lost this move, we'd lose the game.

"Do you remember, Jim," you said, "that night, as we lay on our backs in the warm forest snow and our eyes cut apart all the branches overhead?" We lay under leaves, green and shivering. The ground gave off its earth-scented warmth. "You found me. You joined me. We built a bagnio under the stars. In the last six years we've been dragged down and almost destroyed, but those monsters up there haven't changed. They still run the show. They aren't going anywhere. Just circles and circles."

"Circles and circles."

"Every circle a sprial."

"Each spiral a cyclone."

"I see a rat."

"I see a hungry rat! And a noseless wench. And a whole lot of shuffling and moving about."

For a week we passed word of a time and place among the shanty camps. At dusk on the thirtieth, one month after Graham arrested me in Meredith, we met a couple dozen shanty boys on the grade just outside of town. They'd brought axes, and long flat skids. We ran into the town and out to the stockade, and cut away the building from the pen and hewed away the supports at the base. By midnight, we'd cut the building into two parts. One part was just the stockade pen, but the second part was the building itself. We slid the skids under the wall, and with twelve shanty boys pulling with ropes, and the rest pushing at the back, we started to slide the ranch out and onto State Street.

Sheriff Graham arrived on the scene around dawn. The building was touching the far side of the road and continued to slide on into a cleared spot.

"What in the name of Heaven and Hell are you doing, Jim?" he asked.

"Monumental delineations!" I said. "You are the sheriff of Clare County. As you can see, my business is located in Gladwin County."

Mag, it was magnificent. A magnificent hour! Beautiful, a powerful hour! If it weren't for that new jail in Harrison, I might have put a bullet in Graham's head right then. Instead, we went into our bagnio and fucked in our room for an hour with the shanty boys cheering and drinking outside.

"Ah, Jim," you said. "There are no more ends upon us. This is the beginning of our bright new day. It couldn't be night-time forever."

"I think we need a change of name," I said. "Something more respectable. Let's call it the State Road Hotel."

Chapter 10

It wasn't a new beginning, Jim.

The past never trailed us so near.

Just one week later, a new crowd congregated in the night. Not shanty boys. Farmers. Homesteaders. Mossbacks. Not Clare County. Gladwin. They burned our bagnio down. At least you hadn't paid out to McClennon yet. We rented out a little house in Meredith, and I went back to turning tricks myself. It was the only way, Jim. Two months later, when you went before the court over Jim Silkworth's torchjob, you lay down the last of our money to put yourself off the docket for good. It worked. "No cause for action," the jury decided. Burritt and Graham never brought charges against us again. They knew we were finished. Harrison was too far away from us. Meredith was ready to blow away from us. We sold the house to pay our debts. We came to this shack, to catch the last of the shanty boys as they leapt from the track for a trick. We were lost. We had lost. We had nothing, and –

"Z is for Zero, that makes us all think."

You're sleeping, dear?

Sleep, dear, sleep, yes.

It is almost time for you to sleep.

* * * * *

Meredith lasted longer than we thought. It lasted even longer than the five years that McClennon had pegged it at. The Reardon brothers built their general store, and Frank Whitmore founded a shingle mill and hired out ex-shanty boys to run the old stumps through his machines. Cedar savages. Just as with Clare and Farwell, and just as with Harrison, they were trying to build a respectable town out there. But Meredith, Meredith was simply, beautifully, elegantly, too small. Too alone. Too stuck in the swamps and the slashings. Their efforts bought the town a year or two, at most.

In ninety, there was a train wreck, and fire and coal and smoke showered into the sky. Explosion after explosion. The flames spread to Meredith and half of the town burnt down. In ninety-one, there was lightning and hailstones. Snakes stuck up along the railway, catching the cars that rolled in time to time, thick with chips from the slashings and underbrush. All was reduced to lumber stumps.

In ninety again, McClennon sold the Corrigan House to Black for a song, and Black let it sit for two years before reopening. In ninety-one again, the villagers finished building and furnishing the Town Hall, but by ninety-one the red-sashed brigade had left for good. By ninety-two, the villagers were leaving.

Meredith was all but empty.

Now the ghosts crouched tight around us. They waited. They sat and waited for their final rush. For us to die and leave them some scraps for feeding.

We, my husband, we've waited in and around our little shack with Bob. During the day I slept and drank and ate the huckleberries. During the night I tricked. During the day you picked raspberries and during the night you drank your whiskey and slept. Each week, Bob came by, and sometimes he brought us bread and beans, and every time, he took our liquor. The bastard. I don't need beans like I need whiskey.

Husband, let us curse Meredith, but let us remember Meredith.

We were Meredith, with our cryings and strivings, and Meredith was the sharpening stone for our own teeth. We were a pair of hungry rats, and Meredith was our Devil's Ranch. Meredith was our tomorrow.

> they call to God with voices raw
> submit their souls to Satan's claw
> and if the rat men kill to a draw
> the rat women eat them after all

Shanty boys. Shanty boys.

> you swing your axe, you fire guns
> the village died, yes every one
> the army's lost and overrun
> the rats are hot and hungry as the sun

Do you sleep, my husband? Sleep, sweet, sleep.

Chapter 11

No. No sleep. This blood. Why? What I mean to ask is, Mag, where is this blood coming from? My mouth. It runs down my chin. You know, don't you? I wish I could move, God damn it. Get some drink in me. Awipe of the bitter breathers. Yet even a good smell of it would do me an endless good. You had to give me all that grief. Had to take in those bugs. I don't blame you for it, but it's a horrid way to go, and a horrid way to make me go, with the crabs at work on me nightlong. Oh, this is not an end. This is a fresh beginning. When that sun comes up, he will get up to the Dante's docket with all the what for will we'll have from him and I'll be blisterburned like the rope necklace I'm wearing right now, today.

I think we may climb up on the last train to roll through Meredith and ride its smoky back to Harrison. At Arnold Lake, we'll stop and burn down Silkworth's and, what else, that effigy that stands there now. Torch it down for the twice time. At Harrison we'll disembark and climb inside and maybe I'll buy two bullets, one for Graham. We'll peg him in the head so he looks like Lincoln in more than a beard. One for Burritt. Kick his teeth in. Maybe kill him with a gun without shooting him. Just put the barrel so far in his mouth it cuts out the back of his throat like all those cocks he's been gumming up on the state Supreme Court. Because they should say that "punishment" ... "not inflicted by a rational man for the sakes of those crimes that has been committed." What is dead is dead, God damn it! "But for preventing the same man or, by his punishment spectacle, some other man, from doing evil again." Dig it up... pour it out... catch a train... ride it on up to Seney.

In Seney, where punishment is punishment, all known and told, we'll go in with Dunn on a Devil's Ranch Stockade. We'll hunt down McClennon and befunnel his fat gullet with pride and pennies, and string him up for a liquor tax. We'll ride down to Bay City and fill the Catacombs to the brim with blood. We'll find McCarthy and split his skull in two with a billiard cue. Maggie. We can. We will. Where is the whiskey? We will go, oh, we'll go, we'll go ago, we will always go. Out of here, never to Meredith, curse Meredith and neither remember nor thank it. Damnation on it, Mag. To the north, the jewels and the stars, the pearls and gemstones and gold and silver and diadems and daisies given from this monster to that one.

The Blue to the Red.

The true to the true.

Oh Red, I will give you a blue blood, a bright moth, a birthright, a blood, a bloody and a bloody handkerchief to tuck about the simpler eddies, the starken philosophers that wade with brick shoes through that thick and crimson mainstream. Aliquid cogatibile. A new scarf to fit on your face, an iron collar around my own neck. To cover up, oh, the shame. It isn't the same as it always was, is it? And tattered streams, tepid torrents, truth, truth, it cannot be. I have not believed it and won't, no, not this, not the boiling water, in truth, of blood? We will eat the Earth, my teeth hurt, they hurt for it now, yes, they do now? Boiled blood. Deaslee and his boiling water. Ha! He makes tea, far out in the forest, instead of his flaggins. Pours it out. A stream upon the soil. Over the rocks. The dirt. It isn't, but it isn't, and it's difficult to move. Difficult to turn the shoulder over, away from the wind, oh. Father Jove, where is the whiskey?

Where is...

...

Mag?

...

Mag.

...

I am going, I think. Are you there, Mag?

...

Oh, this cursed band around my neck.

...

Take it off!

...

Take it off.

Chapter 12

Shh, my dear. Listen to the words.

> the lusting rats, a herd, a mass
> live but to feed, bleed, breed and harass
> they forget their judgment waits at the pass
> their only king is their emptiness

Shh, my darling. Hear our lullaby.

> the rusting rats, a herd, a mass
> live but to feed, breed, bleat and harass
> they forget that a judgment, judgment waits
> the only king is the emptiness

Our song.

> these musting rats, a herd, a mass
> live but to feed, bleed, breed and harass
> they won't ever forget
> their emptiness

Sleep now, Jim. Sleep. Don't go, ghosts, abide. I know you're hovering close. I know you're waiting to rush on me, to take me, and I'll be taken soon. I have been trespassed upon. I may have lost my nose, but I still have my click click teeth. I still have my teeth. My sweet, sweet lips. My click click eyes. My ice.

> and by the way, I think they're here
> can't you listen? don't you hear?

Your fever. Have I enfevered you, husband? Your last draft of whiskey? I admit: I did this. You, my husband, love, dear, I couldn't see you wither for another day. Don't begrudge me, husband. I've also enfevered myself. You'll see me soon, I believe, and I believe that you'll forgive me. You had the teeth of a wolf, my blue husband. You were never meant to starve to death.

> the scrabbling of their feet out there
> the wet of thirst, the sweat of fear?

In a dream, oh husband, I was in this shack, only I was here alone. But let me change the story and tell you what really happened. Daylight. Summertime. I climbed up on the stove and screamed out all of the words.

"Rats and Hell and fire and flame to all of the people of Meredith! As you fucked in on the mainstream, your trains and tracks shot out where the ice and the skids should have done well-enough for an honest God-fearing folk. You looked around and oh dear! You'd logged off the rest of Michigan. Just logged off the whole damn state! Except for this island at the heart of the hand. So you hewed down some lumber to start the creature up and in the middle of those choppy echoes and gang saws, those whirring blades and cutting axes, it was time to build a bagnio. You called on your gut and Little Red Riding Girl and Little Shanty Boy Blue came to you, in from the cold, to keep you in spirits and girls and growth. Hell on you all!"

"But who will climb high, spurs to the trunks? There is a legend in the plat book that tells what penstock to open to the sea, while the coarse of course are too high to climb and you have to use a ladder, to design, to follow beams plank by plank as they rise into the sky. Don't you tell me. You know what the answer is. You have to follow the mainstream upstream if you want to find the fire."

"Don't tell me Meredith."

"Meredith?"

"Where are you going?"

...

Coming here *was* our greatest mistake. The source and summit of our calamity. That is recognized now. You told me that "those in our position are obliged to make certain calculations," but I said, "we cannot say these calculations must result in the conjurations, oh, we anticipate. We cannot always know our success." When I froze and freeze to death, whether in the woods or on a rood shack, there's no choice but to calculate for hunger, and to bite off as much or more than I can chew. Better to bite too much than too little.

So you had a dream, husband, but let me tell you what actually happened. There is a shack, this shack, and it stands in a summer haze where sap ferments in the hardwoods. Pine needles underfoot and the smell of the white pine, fresh and cutting, uncut, untouched, here in Clare County. Beneath the pine needles, in clearings of witch-hazel and hawthorn and honeysuckle, the sun starts to sink, and the lip is steeped in the stench of an amber drip, a film and phlegm, that filters over the sky. Just the sunset, yes?

Is it just the sunset?

Or is it poetry: esemplasy?

And then I hear the wind, but in this dream, the real dream, I recognize the ghosts at once for what they are. Why do you rustle in the branches, ghosts? Are you trying to frighten me? You cannot be frightened of me. I am alive and you are not, and you feed on death. Dear me, ghosts, do you think I am to be your scraps for eating soon? Don't forget who ate who. *Ah,* you breathe, *but we are turning the tables, little dying one.* Dear me, Frankie. Do not kick so, you said. I say to you: "Do not kick so." What did Charles Cobden say? Do not cut so, he said. "Do not cut so." What do we all say to the rats? "Do not bite so." "Do not bite." Look back to the light. What is it? The sunset?

No. It is esemplasy.

And then I run from them, those honeysuckle huckleberry saints, those train tracks running, those gang saws, Gibson girls, shanty boys. They chase me all day, but they cannot catch me. As my husband said once, if I run fast enough while the glades dim around me, I might, at the very last whisper of twilight, fly into the sky and catch those ranches and clusters and diadems. But in the end, when I arrive, I find only Meredith, one street, stump clustered, thrust among the swamps, the trees, the reedy weedies, the wumpty stumps of scoot land. All brittle, dry, and empty. Lost and forgotten. Someday, you see, every town must look just like this.

Nobody lives in Meredith any more except the ghosts. The shanty boys left their ghosts. They crowd heavy on the boundaries and wait for a signal to enter. But wait.

If the hour is late, and if twilight has already passed, then why is the light so bright?

Surely esemplasy is not so powerful and phosphorescent.

I climb onto the Devil's Ranch. I mount the lumber posts as Jenny Kinney did, and let my blood trickle down from the pointed poles. It is a magnificent view. I can see far, far away. Far out over the tops of these thousands of trees. At the horizon I see the most glorious sight. A glance of Heaven and Hell before me. There, where the Earth makes a curve, a slight and a gentle curve, I see a flickering light, and it comes from the Earth. Because a long time ago, the northern lights had frozen. They'd fallen into the dark of the deepest woods. They'd thawed with time and now, fed by billions of frostbitten needles, they stir themselves into a magnificent blaze. The fire is deep and silent and approaching. It is fast and still. It roars with its approach. It will overcome me.

> "And we realized at last
> That every camp that we had passed
> Was ours. Yes, 'twas then we found
> the river we was on was round,
> And though we'd driven many a mile
> We'd driv a circle all the while."

...

It is cold. I never told you, Jim. It is cold. I never told you about my last adventure.

One month ago, I rode down to Farwell with the deed to Lot 8 in Meredith, that you bought so hard from Tom McClennon, because I knew that we were going to die this winter. There is a church there, Methodist, and they have taken in abandoned children. I chose a child, only a year or two old, they called him Joseph, but I said I'd named him little "James." How else are we going to travel around the world, the Arctic and Antarctic, and Cashmere and China and Ethiopia? How else are we going to make ourselves into kings and gods?

"James?" they asked. "Then you know this child?"
"I know this child. He is my child."
"Who are you?"
"My name is Maggie Duncan, and the father is Jim Carr."

They didn't know what to say then, my Jim. So rest.

"I didn't want the child to suffer as a result of my reputation," I said. "We are known in this county as difficult people."

They didn't know what to say, Jim. So rest.

"But I want the child to know I am his mother when he is a little older. You need not tell anyone else. I want to entrust these to your care."

I gave the man our deeds, as proof of our legacy and devotion, of where our Devil's Ranch Stockade had once stood. I know it was the last of what we had, Jim, but as you said, Meredith has blown away, and those lots weren't worth one red cent. Better to plant a seed, even if we'll never see what the sapling brings. This child will grow, and believe he is of us, and in that way – we bring something into this world, my husband.

> these raging creatures, these hungry rats
> do not fear Hell or angry cats
> they feed on flesh and leave it ash
> and hope to make the world crash

if you think they're far away
they could come in your house today
a single one could name you prey
and their multitudes block your way

It is quite cold now. Coldest, usually, in the last hour before dawn. Unless that isn't the sound of the wind, or the ghosts, but of sound of soot falling like snow and covering up the sun. Is this what it's like to be in the midst of a fire? I thought I would be gone before it came to pass. Yes, we went away, and far upstream, and built a Devil's Ranch Stockade. A Little Blue and Red made a Big Bad. But should we have?

"Some love to roam o'er the dark sea foam,
Where the wild winds whistle free.
But a chosen band in a forest land
And a life in the woods for me."

And a life in the woods for me – among the stars – among the monsters – moving along the lips of the leaves. Oh, Jim. Oh, God. Oh, Jim. I can't move a hand to help you, Jim.

I am so weak.

The whiskey... is all gone.

That damned heathen found the bottle and swilled it all down his damned throat.

...

Oh, Jim. I'm so weak. I'm dying too. I know I am.

...

Oh, Jim, can't we pray? God help us. We've been all wrong. Give us a show. Give us a chance. Oh, help me.

Somebody.

Help.

PART THREE:
HUNGRY RATS, ADRIFT IN THE MAINSTREAM

Chapter 1

Imagine your eyes, Margaret, your eyes. They're xes. They're all xed and empty. Imagine your nose. Your nostrils. You have lips, yeah, lips, I guess, just like dots, like ellipses, with pointy ts and vs and ws because your teeth got all broke up no matter how you tried to hide it from us bad. And you got a neck, I guess, yeah, like two capital Is and one lower-case i in between because that dot is your Eve's apple you ugly bitch, bumping like a bob in the water, all those pork rinds, pigs feet, ham hocks you ate all the time fuck you. And you got two ovaries right, 'cause that's inside, that was one thing didn't get ruined on that farm, but hell you must have damaged them up yourself, because all you wanted to do was cut out on the world, kill them kill them, well that's fine, but there's easier ways to get by than by cutting people up. You got two hands too, you x-ey bitch. Two hands. Stigmata. Stigmata mama you filthy aunt, don't tell me I don't remember.

I know you.

I know you.

Mom gave you stigmata once.

Maybe you forgot, maybe you decided to make yourself forget, but a long time back you brought Rodney, me, both of us to a pumpkin carving party at your house. We cut jack-o-lanterns, evil faces, ghosts, monsters, goblins, and I told you how I'd got my scars. You know, dog bites, cat scratches, cigarette burns, acne, kids' stuff, right? But you had a lesson to teach me and you were gonna put my stories right out of the water! You told me how when you were thirteen, you decided to prove to yourself and everyone else you loved God more than anyone and you wanted to pay the price for all the sins of everyone in your family. That's a lot of sin, Margaret! So you went out back and leaned against a big tree and told your sister to stick nails through your hands and feet.

You only got through one nail.

It went straight through your right hand and deep into the tree, and you screamed and Mom jumped back and laughed like she was surprised, like it was funny but she didn't know why, you all stuck to that tree and all. You thought she looked like a Roman there, but anyway, she didn't leave you, and you didn't thank her for the favor. She put that hammer claw right around the nail's head and pulled hard 'til the nail came out. She went off to play her games. You put alcohol on the hole and wrapped it up in cotton with your other hand. You put yourself to the test and proved once and for all that you only loved Jesus one-fifth as much as He loved you.

That serves you right. You are the sick esemplastist adrift in the mainstream. Oh, yeah! Esemplasy. Esemplasy. I haven't forgotten that word.

You were born in Buttfuckegypt, Michigan above the scars of your punctured right palm you know. Where your pinky hits your hand. You lived way off the 14¾ Road, and the nearest town an esemplasy in the gray. They named it after an Indian right but you thought they named it after a car. Not like you ever saw a car like that no, not even a used one, you all broke ass. You lived in the house from *The Evil Dead*. You lived in the house from *The Blair Witch Project*! I haven't seen it but I know. It made Maryland look like heaven. It makes Flint look like Paradise but fuck it was the Manistee National Forest. I know. Mom told me. She told me lots of things while she was alive before you killed her.

When you were born, your parents hated you.

Yeah. It was just your turn in a great tradition in our family, passed on up to me from down there. From the the Devil's Ranch Stockade. Jim and Maggie died in Meredith, the ghost town. Meredith, the ghost town that burned down in a forest fire. Then the Carrs from Clare County became the Carrs from Osceola County. The Carrs from Roscommon and Wexford Counties! Ha! Yeah! In the end they all came up the same, Mammy Ada and Pappy James still horny swine, still trapped with daughters they hated. You're right. Mom did tell me that she hated her kids. 'Cause they sucked the life away. They devoured. So you would devour. You wanted to. Not your own kids, no, you never had any. Someone else's and the parents too right? They hated you, Grams and Gramps did. They kept you alone in that dry and bendy farmhouse, way out on that swamp, that forest with the reeds and weeds and cattails.

I guess you never saw anything bright but the flash of the sun.

I guess you never heard anything but that loud wind out there. No human voice all day long. Definitely no one who cared.

You... disgusting –

You disgust me!

When you were little you went through the yard and picked your nose and fell and scraped your knees and cried and shit your pants and picked up pine cones and pine needles and wet your pants and Papa took you out to the barn to show you the door. Mommy yelled at your stinky clothes, stinky wet, and Pops took you out to the barn. Your Mams said "fuck fuck fuck fuck," and Gramps swung his cleaver down on his pigs.

I guess you never heard anything but those noisy pigs. Honk honk? Blow blow!

You disgusting –

You got older. Fed the pigs, slaughtered pigs, cleaned up pig blood and pig shit. You played and ran and dreamed and climbed up the branches of those old dead trees. You walked through the woods and the cattails and menstruated and didn't know what it meant but it must mean something bad, nothing good could come out like that and your parents didn't contradict your ass on that. And you read every book in that fucking house. Not many books though; it wasn't hard. Your sister read the *Old Farmer's Almanac*, fifty-eight fifty-eight, over and over. She memorized the seeding times and the wrinkled bends in cotton dresses to cinch up around your waist that you neither of you would ever own. She predicted weather for a year that had already passed and just went further and further away. You found and read the Bible and Coleridge just like great-great-whatever-Uncle Jim did.

Coleridge: Esemplastic.
The Bible...

...

But your family was doing things all wrong!

They'd neglected grain and sin offerings and you cried and cried, and
Gammy Ada started missing the farm's cats and rabbits. Reading 2
Chronicles you fell asleep, and you punished yourself by staying
awake for three days straight. You spent the last day on your knees in
front of that ugly green clock with the cracked face. You told me.
And at thirteen, you read the Gospels again and went out back with
your sister, and stigmatad in the sun. You screwed it all up. You
screwed everything up, everything up, from the very moment you
tried. That's what your mom and dad told you.

Six years later Mark Malady came. He was a dropout from the other
side. He'd flunked out in Seney and sold Bibles all the way to waxy
Wexford, wifty woowoo, weewee, putting the pee pee, looking for
life, cheap thrills, esemplasy. One out of three is better than none.
How'd he find you, anyway? Was there even a road that reached all
the way back? I've never seen your drive on any map. How did Gamp
and Gams drive their pigs to the market?

Mr. Malady needed a place to stay so he paid your folks to sleep in
the shed, and he'd get their bed, and that irritated them. Then he
started screwing your sister, and that really got on your parents'
nerves. Nineteen seventy-nine! The New Year passed, Dad started
killing pigs and my mom got all knocked up with the twins, and shit!
Gawpa Gawpa said he'd kill you all. You knew he meant it because
you heard him sharpening his big axe again out in the shed that night.
It was a weird sight, how he kept the beat, his foot pumping up and
down, the granite wheel spinning spinning its sparks all flying flying.
You stood out the door and watched and heard.

You never heard nothing – anything – but that spinning wheel.

"I hate my kids," he said. "I hate they don't got no prospective for going an be stuck here make me me me less happy I'm already not not happy for I've got no reason for happy. I better kill that one that would be easier than to raise another of them now right? I should kill that girl them girls too much noise they make and they stink up it all. That is sound logic, my logic."

The wheel squeaked. The pigs honked. The wind blew. The ghosts?

So you ran back into the house and grabbed Mark and Mara and ran up the road into the dark. You cut through the woods so you wouldn't be followed. Near morning, you got to 55 and caught a ride to Grayling. Mom married Dad and the three of you hopped a train to Flint. You were nineteen. Eighteen? Twenty. Mr. Malady was twenty-two. The new Mrs. Malady? Seventeen. My age today. In those days my dad had a spine and hunger. He squeezed in at Buick and held on as long as he could. After that he worked in a junk yard. After that he worked at a strip club. After that he didn't work.

Mom and Dad had four kids. Bitty and Betty, then four years passed, then Rodney, then three years passed, then me. Then fourteen years and we moved onto Maryland Ave. Bitty died and Betty cried. You kidnapped Rodney... to protect him from us? Me? What about me? A miserable lot with a miserable lot. A pretty miserable parking lot! Bad roots in good soil always grow into self-pruning family trees.

...

I know you lived with my parents for a while, but in the eighties you got work as a secretary and bought a pickup and moved out to the suburbs. To Flushing on the Flint River. You had all the time and privacy you wanted and you could think of Hell and the End of the World, morning, noon, and night. It was weird, you thought, it hadn't happened yet. Yeah Jesus was weird and ambitious and sneaky about all sorts of things but here he was so so clear. His esemplastic ambitions had to be met with us admitting that we really are failures through and through and our sins are a cinder block that drops from trapdoors through the cobwebs of our good intentions to break on the basement floor. But we've got to meet his sneakiness with a pledge to take cinder blocks and mallets and sledge hammers to each others' heads until we smash them into understanding. But Jesus' clearness – his clarity – we've got to just... accept it, right? That's what you said you thought, you bitch. "This Generation Shall Not Pass Away Until These Things Have Taken Place." Nothing sneaky about that!

...

But it didn't happen like that, did it?

So you dug around in your attic thinking "how can this be?" 'cause you didn't doubt a single line or sentence in this superauthority, and this problem, this contradiction, was like a nail in your hand. "How can this be?"

It must of have been one of those late night when you finally found the answer. I like to think it was winter at like 3 AM, and it was as cold and dark and numb as a hole up there. *I understand*, you thought. *I've been reading around the Book, against the Book. I need to read under it.*

And then things started to make sense to you very quickly.

The Devil, you figured, wrecked God's plan that Man should live in harmony forever in the Garden of Eden, by becoming the Serpent and persuading Eve to ho herself out for a rotten apple. You knew how that worked. Stories you heard about your great-great-grandparents. They chose to give up being humans on Earth for a shot at being a monster in the sky. And the Devil wrecked God's plan for Men to live in faith by making them build a tower like they thought they were God, and then the Devil wrecked God's plan for Men to live in peace by making them so nasty and sick that God had to wipe them out with a flood. So you realized that whenever the Devil goes up against God's plans, God wins, but only after everything gets spoiled and disgusting. Without sickness, no punishment.So the cure only comes after the sickness. Well, okay, so you got your answer you stupid bitch, I hate you.

"Just," you said, "as every defiance of the words, 'I will be your God and you will be my people,' forestalls, but doesn't diminish God's promise, Satan always works to bring Men to the very brink of ruin, the only point from which they understand their awful sins and beg for reunion. Moving on math and strong logic, Satan *must* be God's ally. How could he not be? Men are the real Enemies, the real Adversaries, the fat rats aspiring only to languish in slothful pools of their own vomit and shit without any awareness of their profound degradation. Satan shoves the pendulum in fury toward blasphemy, murder, hate, and prostitution. The pendulum always swings back harder."

"Therefore," you said, "even *if* Satan's true allies were not God's true allies, they nevertheless served His purpose."

This idea swung around in your head awhile.

When it settled, you realized you were important yourself. No false prophet. You'd stick like sharp pine needles in the direction of winter, and would... force... something awful! To crawl...

...

To crawl like a spider up the lightning and web the stormy sky with your kind of change.

It couldn't be just anyone after all. It had to be someone who knew awful. You knew awful pee, trapdoors and water chestnuts and...

Every night, when those deaddying factory flames spread their glow from the city toward the suburbs, you looked at that wall of pine trees and farm fields six miles thick and you remembered the stories that every man and woman has told their sons and daughters from the beginning of time.

A vast fire moves out in all directions.
It is bigger than the people and the trees of the world.
It is bright enough to blot out stars and monsters.
It is a roving sunset, a moving mountain.
It is an aurora from the Earth.
It is silent in its distance.
It is fast and unstoppable.

The hungry rats run ahead and prepare the way.

Feeding rats. Hungry rats. Filthy hungry rats.

You started working out your plan. You found two friends that you trusted. You met them. They trusted you too. They thought you were onto something with your sound logic and knowledge of God. They weren't sure about that fire, though. They thought you were just into eugenics, or a white supremacist looking for an excuse. You weren't that, you told them. You were less. And a whole lot more! You knew they wouldn't agree to murder until you showed them the fire.

But how could you show them the fire when it wasn't visible yet? When it hadn't all thawed? When the idea was still down in Hell?

Then Dad told you about Warren Dunes State Park on Lake Michigan, where he was planning a trip for the family. You asked him where it was and he said, "across from Chicago. It's down there!" You borrowed some geometry books and did the math and figured out, yeah, you could see Chicago across the lake, just a little. On a night with low clouds it might even look like a distant fire. A huge fire. You might even see the expanding flames as they moved across the blackness of the world.

And so, when the right night came with the right weather, you went out with your friends. And wouldn't you know, but your stupid family had made their trip the very same week. You didn't want them to see you or to guess "the depths of the drains you plumbed by then," so you got a room in a motel up the lake and waited until the sun had set. Then, you and your friends dressed in black clothes and carried black blankets to hide your features. You found a stretch of beach, big on every side. Empty for miles. You waded in hip-deep and looked out into the water darkness. You waited and waited, your eyes adjusted, and the darkness became filled with fire.

What did you say?

Oh yeah.

We're raging creatures.
We're hungry rats.
We fear not Hell.
We fear not cats.
We haven't thoughts.
We haven't cash.
We hope to make the world crash.

Will you come in this direction, fire?

Because they think we're far away.
Because we're in their homes today.
Because we take them as our prey.
Because we outnumber them anyway.

Will you come in this direction, now?

Some try to choke you in the sea
Where the wild winds whistle free,
But you can feed on forest trees,
And you can take your breath from me.

We're hungry rats, adrift in the mainstream.

Esemplasy.

The fog got thick to the west. The waves ran like rats up the shore. They rushed around your body and you knew that Vast Deeds were possible. Horrible yeah, but still. Oh God. Possible! Then, out of the corner of your eye, you saw me standing at the edge, looking at you with the widest little eyes you'd ever seen. Meredith, your niece. You even thought I thought of coming in with you for a second, before I turned and ran away. I looked so lonely and cold, tender toes wet as you said, yeah, like a starving rat, adrift in the mainstream.

Chapter 2

I should have started in the beginning. We didn't begin with you and me at the edge of Lake Michigan. You didn't start when Mom nailed you to a tree in Wexford County. It's been running down our nasty blood for more than a hundred years. Nasty branches, nasty roots. You told me. Little Boy Blue. Little Red Riding Hood. They woke in the middle of an awful forest surrounded by lakes. Red grew hot out there and she poured herself out for all those lumberjacks and destroyers. Blue came in from out of town, and he snuffled along for the scent of sawdusty blood. His nose led him to her noselessness. They met at the center of it all, where steel rails crossed like swastikas on the pine needles. How could you think I'd forget?

"Each trunk rang out like big bells as they drove it into the earth and hammered it down, hammered it firm. The bark wrinkled on impact, like Michigan girls' dresses did when they waded into ponds to espy the fish. Girls carefully clasping their hems in their hands and lifting from the ankles to the calves. To avoid the dresses' soaking and wrinkling. Soon the faces of the girls wrinkled. Their pale hands wore slack skin. They died. They all died. After all, they'd served lumberjacks by the hundreds. They'd been slaves."

Oh well, Aunt Margaret.

Oh well.

Red made potions of whiskey and poison that smelled like mushrooms from the basement, and after a few shots, the lumberjacks died. Then Blue stripped them and robbed them and beat them with sticks. He broke their ribs and snapped the teeth from their mouths and tossed them on the nearest train and rode them all the way back to Saginaw.

Red looked after her ladies, ringing them between her roost and roosters, an old bitch learning new tricks. Get it? The girls tossed against their will, and if they tried to get away, and Red caught them before they made the train, then Red and Blue and all their wolves grabbed them. They stripped them and robbed them and beat them with sticks and brass knuckles. They cracked their ribs and cracked their teeth and peeled the skin from their flesh.

Don't pretend your reasons came from the Bible!

The Bible was only your crutch. I know better. When our Great Carr discovered our Great Duncan in the snow, they knew each other because they had the same religion, and it wasn't the kind you find in a book. It was all written in the sky for them. The sky and the forest. You'd say, you'd say, Aunt Margaret, you'd say you were doing God's work, but I know where you come from. I know what you come from. I know: Amen. Let it be!

You never heard nothing but that river, right?

Don't pretend that I've forgotten this, either. You know I remember the story!

When you were twelve, you wet your pants. Your momma held your stinking shorts up. Your dadda took you by the wrist. He took you through the back, through the weedy reedies because no one cut a path through there. He took you out to the barn and led you into a room in the back. It was a weird room, small, with brick walls and a stone floor, bottles of preserves stacked on shelves. And a small wood door in the middle of the floor. He made you stand on this door. He took several steps back and looked at you with his arms crossed. He was sweating, smiling. Your legs stuck. He turned and took a cinder block off a shelf and gave it to you. The door squeaked beneath you. He took a step back.

"Don't wet you pants no more," he said, "you know what I keep down there."

Several minutes passed and your arms hurt. He gave you another block off the shelf. Now you heard the wood started to groan loud. You held a block in each hand. He took a step back.

"Don't pee urine no more," he said, "you know who I have down there."

Time didn't pass but you know it did, Margaret. Now your arms started to shake. You were sweating. So was he! But your hands burned burned! Oh God how it hurt! You kept changing your grip on the blocks so they wouldn't slip... what would happen if you dropped one? A crack, a smash, a fall into dark. Your dad turned and took a third cinder block off the wall, and acted like he was going to throw it at you. You screamed at him, showing your teeth, and he laughed at you.

"Don't fuck it, don't," he said. "You know about the ratties down there!"

"Jesus, Jesus, Jesus," you said. Did you cry? You sure did! And you never heard nothing but that trapdoor creaking from that day on.

Later on you told me that your throat hurt too. I know, Margaret. My throat hurts too. I don't like the trapdoors any better than you. You never heard... anything – but the chestnut in your throat.

You never heard anything but...

What?

* * * * *

I don't think you hated what happened to you. I think you loved it. It was the best excuse, the only thing you needed, some horrible wound, some humiliation to cut, to sharpen your teeth on. The way you say it, your parents murdered your soul. The Bible gave you a reason for it all. Jim and Mag told you how murder goes. The eighteen-eighties were a prediction and the nineteen-nineties, a prelude. When you stood in the lake looking out at the fire, the future seemed fat with rats and prostitutes, didn't it? The world all happy and wrecked, all "crack assed among the reedy weedies."

As for your friends, to hell with them! They asked to *see* the fire, and they were disappointed with what you showed them. But when you saw *me* looking out, you *knew* that I saw what you saw, even though I never said so. Your blood, my blood, a pool of fire. You'd get support from your family or from no one. You'd spent all those years reading the Bible. Now was time to plan what was coming on next.

You drove back to Flushing and went down to the basement. You brought up the boxes of your life up north. *The Old Farmers Almanac* and the Bibles, but these ones had the notes you needed, the notes you scribbled in the margins decades ago. The stories of your family, your past. You went to work during the day. You dressed in your sharp skirts and smart blouses and drove to your office and you looked so normal. You went back home. You recited and edited and memorized your parents' stories all night. During the day you went to work and you looked just like the wise worker. But when you went home, you rooted for a photo of Maggie. You found it.

Her nose was missing, hidden behind her handkerchief. But her face was beautiful and her eyes cold. Perfect for a callous killer. You look like her, Margaret. You say that *she* was the one who put the poison in your veins? Well look at *me*, Margaret. *These* are your eyes. *These*, your nostrils. *These*, your lips. Now you can tell me how you made up this shit about redemptive sin, but I know, I know that you just wanted to murder us all.

...

You waited.

You had to leave it all a while, to think about what you wanted to do and how you were going to do it. It was a big thing this thing and you wanted to make it perfect. You bought a house in the desert of southern California. There, on land as empty as Wexford County, you waited for a sign.

"A trapdoor opened." Bitty died. Beautiful. You went back to Michigan for the funeral, and when you left you tried to take me with you, but you couldn't pull me away from Mom. She knew about you. She suspected you and much as she hated me, she wouldn't send me to *"that thing"* she called you. On the other hand, nobody cared about my brother, and to you he seemed like a blank page you could write on. So you took him instead.

At first he couldn't speak and drooled in front of the TV all day. We did him wrong I know. Mom and Dad were too harsh, Bitty and Betty too mean... and I ignored him. I had enough! But I fucked it up here. I was wrong. Back in your wilderness out there you just held on. You held him to you. You refused to return him. Rodney at your side. Rodney day and night. "Rodney, I'll never leave you," you said. He stopped drooling and started to talk. You'd gotten a partner in prayer. Someone you could trust. Someone you could prepare for to do some amazing things in your plan.

Outside, the world rolled on. A struggle for the presidency. Terrorist attacks. The economy fell apart. It was pretty quiet in southern California.

Then, one day, two signs.

First, a small voice. A man's voice. Mark called. "Mom... er... Mara's got out of the asylum. I'm picking her up soon enough."
"She'll shriek about it plenty. She won't even want to leave," you said. "She's my sister, but I've always thought she had a few screws loose and rolling around inside her."

Second, a loud voice. A fire's voice. Southern California burned down. Windows melted in San Diego. At night, you turned out the lights and watched from your deck. The fire was a long way off, but it was brighter than the light over the lake. It was the most beautiful thing you'd ever seen.

"Rodney!" you called. "We're going to Michigan."

Chapter 3

Okay okay. I'm a bit calmer now. I'm wrong, I guess, to think just from this that you're the Rat Man. But what were you thinking, pointing a gun on me? You said, "let there be light," but you didn't think you could kill me in it, did you? No. If you are the Rat Man then you killed with knives and poison and never learned about guns. You have to turn the safety off, Margaret. It's sad for you to lose because you fucked up something so simple. If I'm the Rat Man, like you said, it doesn't look real good for you now, does it? 'Cause there's definitely a connection. This isn't like the end of *Summer of Sam*. Someone knows shit about shit. And our story got around. I told my "best friend," and she told others... that's my fault. Another bit of my part in it.

Anyhow there's something I just can't figure out. If you are the killer, then you killed to kill and leave the rats. To say that you pushed the world toward a fire. What about Maria? Where does she fit in? For me, she was what got this whole thing going. Answers that leave her out aren't even answers to me.

So what about it?

And what about Amalee? Who did they draw? It wasn't you, or you'd be long gone by now. It wasn't me, but you must know that won't matter after the popo drop in.

What are you going to say when they get here?

I know I know. You'll say something like this:

A few days after you got back to Michigan, you were still too scared to get on the phone and call Mark. If you called, you'd have to tell him that you brought Rodney. You'd say it had been too much: how hard it got taking care of a man-who-was-a-child. The medicine, the money, the long nights without sleep. You'd say you were at the end of your sanity and savings. You'd say you were wrong. Who never admits she's wrong! You'd end up having to ask for help from a man who hated to help anyone. You couldn't do it. You couldn't pick up that phone and call.

You checked in at a boarding house on the South End and a week went by. On the seventh day, Rodney stormed around the room for hours and hours. Your neighbors bitched and the manager said something like "I'll throw you out," but you brought up Jesus and he relaxed. Finally, Rodney fell asleep on the bed. You said a quick prayer and, knowing it was a risk, you wrote him a note saying you'd be back. You left it on the night stand. You just wanted to get away for a cup of coffee.

I know how Rodney sleeps twenty hours at a time between his storms. You thought you'd by okay if you got back by dark. You drove downtown, up and down each block, but everywhere you went was either boarded up or packed with those "welfare types" you hated sitting out on the curb. Oh, they reminded you of your parents! But you finally found a coffee shop and went inside and saw a tall man there.

"What can I get you?" he asked.
"Something fancy," you said.

Let me guess. A cappuccino?

You sat and read the newspaper about the Rat Man who killed people all over Flint. You looked out the window at the sun setting in a fire, and you thought all about poor Flint, abandoned Flint, *nobody notices you except when you writhe, with your ghosts and your humble weeds in the mainstream, a victim to motion just like Meredith.* You thought of me, and you wondered if I might be the Rat Man. After all, I'm a strange girl, a freak, and I wet my bed, and don't a lot of serial killers wet their beds as teenagers?

The whole time, the sun kept falling.

You liked its look. It was hot like a furnace. Like an aurora from the Earth. It lit and surrounded all those factories and clouds like it was going to eat them all up. "The Timbers of Hell," the Lumberjack's

Apocalypse told by your dad while he made you stand on a trapdoor. You scared yourself, sitting there, thinking about your family. *Who gets born into a family like that? Who gets born?* That's what I want to know, all my life. My whole life! But you went back to the hotel and Rodney was still asleep. You lay in your bed awake all night and tried to beat your fear.

The next morning you booked a new room at a Christian hotel downtown. It had a huge lobby and a big stuffed bear and other animals in its trophy room. You watched some religious shows with Rodney and thought about getting on the phone.

You'd been a sinner, you knew. You had *judged* your family. Mara so desperate. Mark so angry. Your parents bathing in pigs' blood so they could look young. Rodney so stupid. Betty so mean. Bitty so dead. Meredith so quiet and miserable. Well I'm not quiet now! You *judged* us. Oh, why did you have to end up with people like that? Now, now, these awful people, these awful shits, what would you say? What *could* you say? What would you say when you got them on the phone?

Instead of calling, you lay on your bed, and watched TV. You fell asleep, and another couple weeks went by in Flint. You took Rodney to the museums but he screamed and hit his sides with his fists. Your hotel bill grew and so did the number of murders. You shook and remembered the fairy tales you told us all to scare us into being good. You wondered if I was the killer. You thought of this killer, this crazy creature. You thought of the power he had when he decided: he killed victims who knew they were being killed, but you couldn't even make a phone call.

At night, after the sun set, you found a window near the ice machine. You stood there, twelve stories up, and looked out toward your old home in the suburbs. Almost half of the people in Flint had left, and when they tore down the factories, they tore down their lights. Thousands of houses were empty and abandoned... no light there! Even street lights flashed and died. Now, the suburbs fought back with *their* lights, brighter than Flint's. It walled you in. It locked you up.

You stood there and you shook. You shook and shivered. You saw a fire, wild, bright, and it moved in and ate everything in its way. It was coming for you.

Chapter 4

So thinking about this, I have to ask: What if Amalee drew Rodney?

My big brother an evil Buddha. My big brother a Gein. Maybe he's the Rat Man, after all. A little boy in his big shoes, twenty years old, and the smartest mind in Flint. It makes sense. Growing up, he drew pictures of rats and people and put the paper in his mouth and chewed it. Retarded with ADHD and the worst temper in the world. Rodney, the squirrel stomper. Rodney, the cat scraper. Rodney, who stole dad's car sometimes, to drive in the wild looking for stray dogs to hit. That's what he mumbled about when he got home. He gave Bitty the pork that killed her, and three years later the Rat Man killed with poison.

If so, he kept the act up for so long. So long! What with his glands and his dumb "hellos," but at the end of the night there was blood on the knife. How did he get you to bring him home? How much did you know? How much do you know? How much do you know and think is okay? How much do I know? Does he know what he's done? Did he watch his parents too closely all those years?

I should tell you, Margaret... Rodney wet his bed too. Bitty was the only one of us who didn't wet her bed. She stopped when she was seven. Did we all know? You can't ungut entrails. The harder you pull, the thread knots and the mess gets even tighter. What if it happened like this:

You brought Rodney back a month ago. You'd told him about the mainstream and the fire, and you'd read to him from the Bible, but never the Golden Rule. Now, while you were out getting coffee —

we'll say before the Rat Man murders happened – Rodney woke up. He left the hotel. He walked along the river. He went under the expressway where it's dark and all of the houses are abandoned. He found a girl there, walking home alone at night. She looked like his sister, like his aunt, like his great-great-great-grandma with a red scarf on her face. That was the moment that turned him for good. He ran at her and raged at her. She pulled a knife on him. He took her knife and stabbed her. He thought it was delicious. When she was dead, he put her in a garbage bag and threw it in the street. He walked back to the hotel. He washed up and waited for you to come back.

This is fun, he decided.

You had told him your stories of the rats and the apocalypse, and that became his M.O. You became his alibi. He'd slip out when the rain put you to sleep, go down by the river which ran under your hotel, and pick up the dead rats with a rag. He'd poison in the mornings and wait for the juices to start working. Then, when his victims were sick, he'd knock on their doors. They hoped for help and answered. He pushed his way in and stabbed a little, and after some practice, he stabbed a lot.

He saved his biggest stabbing for his own family, and he left his aunt to discover his mess. He knew his aunt would blame her niece. And she has.

Chapter 5

Or... what if Amalee drew Ashley?

She seemed to get interested when I told her I could figure it out. It's kind of crazy to assume it's my family just because my family is crazy. She wanted to make her weird family seem normal so she, herself, could make it weirder than it was. Why would she lie about her parents being divorced? Because it's romantic? It isn't romantic! Not in that house. Not when she and her mom lied about her dad going to London. Where was she when Mr. Catgut was murdered?

Where was she when Mrs. Helmet died?

Where was she when Maria...

Oh. She was with me.

Except I was asleep. How long did I sleep? If she could kill with poison, then she could make me sleep for as long as she wanted. She came back in time to wake me up. But why did she want to kill Maria? Even if she did want to kill her, how did she know where to find her and when?

And so we arrive at Brian. A Brian is a Brian and a dangerous beast at best. It made her crazy insane that he had been with Maria before he'd been with her. She didn't act jealous on the outside, but she could have been rotten and persuasive on the inside.

While she drove with me to Clio to give herself an alibi, making a scene at the movie so those old mothers noticed, Brian waited outside that bar in his truck and watched for Maria to leave. When she left alone he crept along, following her along the unpaved roads by the river. She walked under the expressway. He pulled a knife and Maria fell, wearing her scarf that looked like mine. Maybe she reached out with her arms as she fell, like she could break them through the overpass and up to the invisible moon. But I don't know. Then it was still and dark under the expressway, except for the flowing of the river and Brian's panting breath.

He could've tied some rocks to her feet and rolled her into the river. It was just a few feet away. But Ashley wouldn't trust disappearance; it's too easy to make up "proof," like a rat's heart instead of the princess' and all that. "Run away to Grand Rapids, Maria, and leave me your coat to stain with pig's blood!" So he dropped the body on the road. He texted Ashley to say it was done, then went to his mom's to comb his hair and wait for his girl to call.

She woke me up when she heard the news. She made me "convince" her to take me home, knowing I'd ask because the buses weren't running anymore. We drove back on the path she chose, because Lewis isn't the fastest way to go... something she didn't know I knew. She saw the body where she expected, and screamed, and we went for help.

Was her shock real?

"Oh my god!" she screamed.

It sure sounded real to me! But people are predators. I don't think she had to fake it. That sound could have been an excitement that clawed up and jumped right out her mouth.

Ashley had an excuse for the next murder. She was worried that the police might link Maria to Brian. But she also knew there weren't enough police in Flint, so if she killed again, more perfectly and randomly, Maria's case might fall to the side. I accidentally helped out, by telling her about our family's rats and pigs and bloody noselessness.

After the Eastside Autoworker was dead, murder became a game. Ashley arrived on some porch, looking scared, and these people, these men from Flint and women from the suburbs, they pulled her inside. "Come in, we'll call your parents." Mr. Catgut, protecting his student in his Victorian home, and Candi Grim with her children running 'round. It was easy. Too easy. They were too sick to move by the time Brian got there.

But soon it seemed like I was catching up. Because I knew about the rats. So they entered my house and murdered my family. They knew the blame would have to fall on either you or me.

Chapter 6

Then again...

Maybe my mom was the Rat Man.

We know she knew the whole myth! She'd got enough cruelty at ten to put a nail in her sister's hand, and now she was forty-two. You can't say, you can't say, her life wasn't full of hurt and hate. She poisoned and stabbed and xed and left rats and the horror got to be too much. After she killed her oldest daughter and husband she poisoned herself and with her dying breath arranged for the knife to fall on her stomach. When she killed Maria, maybe she thought she was killing me. But she was locked up for the first murders. Hm...

Maybe my dad was the Rat Man.

We know he knew about my fucked up grandparents. Maybe he caught their insanity. He did help them with the pigs. He groped and strangled and dropped and slashed and the horror got to be too much. After killing his oldest daughter and wife he poisoned himself and when he lay in the dark ready to die, he carved out his tummy with a knife.

Maybe Betty was the Rat Man.

She *did* smoke up all the time. She *was* pretty mean. She *had* seen her mirror image dead at a young age.

Maybe Bitty was the Rat Man. Hungry for pork was her take on the hungry rats. She was a hungry pig.

Maybe Mr. Catgut was the Rat Man.

He *was* always quoting *The Iliad* at us.

...

Maybe the ghosts of Jim and Maggie are the Rat Man.

"There is hunger, oh, there is a hungry question, oh, oh."

"There is hunger, my Jim, my dear, my Mag, there is a great vast feeding hunger here. This is for us. A three-chime rhythm. I like it. The chimes." The rhythm:

Do. Be do. Be da.
Do. Be do. Be da.
Do. Be do. Be do do do.
Do. Be do. Be da.

...

"You know, Aunt Margaret," I told you once, "we wish that Mom would just die and that you could be our mom instead."

"Meredith, Meredith," you answered. "I know that your mom is unkind before you. I understand that it doesn't seem fair. You have to *appreciate* your mom because she's the only mom God gave you, and God isn't accidental or arbitrary about lines of descent. Everything he chooses, he chooses for a reason. You were chosen for your mom in particular in Heaven. Meredith Malady. Believe me."

"Anything," you said, "that either of you do that is correct will be rewarded. Any infraction that you commit will be punished."

"Now," you said, "I know that you're thinking, 'Aunt Margaret, it's very easy for you to say all this... you have it easy. You live out in the suburbs and don't have to deal with this craziness.' But don't forget that I lived with your mom for most of my life, and your dad for many years, and that I myself will be rewarded and punished."

"You should also know," you said, "that every person is a kind of rat. Just like there are two kinds of people, those who are going to

Heaven, and those who are going to Hell, there are also two kinds of rats. There are hungry rats and fat rats, and they all abide in the mainstream that rolls toward the end of the world. The mainstream, the flood, the motion of movement, the tide of ghosts. It rolls from the fire, through the forest, to the fire. The mainstream."

"Now the fat rats are not hungry," you said. "They once devoured but they don't anymore. They are useless and bloated things, not worth the air they breathe. Because while they don't destroy what is good around them, neither do they destroy what is evil inside themselves."

"But some of the hungry rats," you said, "never get filled up. They're always hungry, and to ask whether they are good or evil is quite beside the point. These hungry rats cause all of the motion in the world. They are predators. They are not ghosts. They move on the mainstream, individually insignificant, but together, they become great currents."

"And when you're miserable, Meredith," you said, "when your feet shake because you stand on a trapdoor and your throat aches with a water chestnut... when you hate your life and everything about it, you know you're not fat but hungry."

"Now," you said, "since God finds glorification in all things that happen... since God turns all events in His favor... and since the fat rats, 'good' and 'evil,' do not bring about change... and since the hungry rats, 'good' and 'evil,' *do* bring about change... motion and movement... and since we *do* start out so very evil... tell me, Meredith... tell me what kind of rat do *you* think will be let into Heaven?"

"You talk about so many things," I said. "What do they mean?"

"Esemplasy."

...

A long time before you told me all this, my mom held a hammer tight in her fist. She put a nail in your hand.

Maybe you are the Rat Man.

How would that go, I wonder...

Chapter 7

Rodney grinned, and the spit on his lips shimmered in the gloom. There was blood on the knife. The blood had dried like a crisp and crinkled ketchup stain. The man licked blood from his teeth. There was blood on the knife. She turned on her foot. Pivoted. Like a ballerina shrugging off the demands of gravity. He blinked his eyes fast; he was trying hard not to cry. There was blood on the knife. You've told me so many stories. What time is the time? Is it getting light out? It can't be night forever.

Lamp posts stood outside St. Joseph Hospital. Milk-white ovals squatted on their poles. They looked like spaceships. Bright and pale flying saucers. They threw their light against the maple leaves and made them seem to wrinkle and wilt in the summer gloamy.

Okay.

The lights *were* flying saucers. For centuries the Martians and the rats have communed in symbiotic bonds. We threaten the Martians with our empires and wars. They know that, one day, when the sun expands, we'll push our Earth out of its orbit and move in on their kingdom. The hungry rats, on the other hand, they don't give two shits about interplanetary expansion or approaching fires and gases and death. They just want to eat and they don't want to wait. And so... the Martians make the raw materials of disease and plague and discord and poverty for the rats to seed around the world. The Martian spaceships docked as lamps at St. Joseph, and the rats took the goods. That's why Flint is ruined and collapsed.

...

Do you hear me?

Once, in Flint, a woman washed her baby in a thin tin tub. She scrubbed and scrubbed and washed and washed and the baby squealed because he was happy. The woman cried because she was sad. They'd lost their money in a mutual fund. The father ran off with the milkman and took the Chevy too. The house was devoured by scarabs. The septic tank exploded and the pilot light turned pink, and all the woman had left were twelve cans of lima bean soup, thirteen votive candles, three bars of soap, and an old tin tub for the bathing of babies. The mother wept and her tears fell in the tub and mingled with the suds. But the baby knew nothing about any of this. He giggled in his sacred joy and sacred contentment and his sacred happiness rose to heaven as a sacred prayer, and the Sacred Powers had compassion. Then the mother got a lot of money.

But most dollar bills have blood and cocaine in trace amounts.

It happened in August. August 121st. August 122nd, 2099.

Do you understand?

The man licked blood from his teeth. He kept his eyes on the knife. "What?" he asked.

Rodney smiled. He smiled sweet. Babies arrive by stork.

Once, in America, the storks all worked freelance and didn't require an official pay program. They didn't ask for health care or benefits, or food, or clothing, or shelter. They did what they did because they loved the job, the joy of bringing new life.

One day, a stork with wicked intentions was swept into power and he unionized all of the others. They named themselves the United Storkers United... the USU... and demanded a seven percent raise. From then on, the storks went on strike from time to time causing global infertility. When they *did* make deliveries, the storks bumped the babies' heads against smokestacks, causing retardation and mercury poisoning. Worse, they'd get all mixed up and leave black babies with white mothers, and white babies with black mothers, and that led to all kinds of predictable problems. That's why babies are so horrible and unwholesome today.

You began your work at midnight, and Rodney complained about the rain. You found your target. A lonely house at the end of Lewis on the Eastside. An enclosed exterior stairway climbed from an alley to the second floor.

"Stand to the side of the door, Rodney," you said. He pressed back against the house. "No, the other side." He moved out of the way. You put a steak knife into his hands. "Remember all that I told you," you said. You wrapped your purse strap around your wrist and knocked.

...

Minutes passed.

...

"Who is it?" said a man on the other side. His throat sounded wet and raw. The door had been dead-bolted shut, but it seemed to lean against you, just a little. The man must be slumping against it.
"I'm from the church fundraiser," you said. "I called you a few minutes ago."
"I told you to call an ambulance."
"Just let me in --"
"I told you to call --"
"I thought I'd better come over. I called them. They'll be here in a minute. Open the door and I'll help you lie down."

You were proud of the calm and authenticity in your voice. The best ones always are.

Metal scraped on metal. The deadbolt slid back.

"Rodney," you said.

Rodney put his palm on the door as the knob turned. He shoved in and the door swung back and hit the man in the forehead. He fell onto his back, against the stairs. His eyes were tight with pain. *From being struck? Or from the poison?* No matter. Rodney stepped in like Quasimodo lunging for a bell pull. With a wild slash his arm moved down and stuck the knife deep in the man's belly. The man coughed. He vomited onto his chest. Bits of corn and liquid surrounded the blade. Rodney smiled, sweet.

The man pulled in his splayed limbs and propped himself up, spiderlike. You stepped through the door and closed it behind you. The man began crawling on palms and toes, up the stairs. You put your purse on your shoulder. Together, you and Rodney followed the man, never more than four feet away, never looking to the right or left.

You said: "Precious Blood of Jesus, unending buyer of our redemption and both the whiskey and the sausage of our souls, You continually plead the case of the people before the turkey of infinite indulgence."

Inside, you moved from window to window, drawing the shades tight. The man had fallen on his living room floor, eyes hungry, fixed on the phone. You disconnected it. *Better safe than sorry*, you thought. Then you realized that your action made no sense; a disconnected line was *more* of a risk. You plugged the phone back in. You turned the ringer off. Rodney sat in a chair and watched.

"Wh," the man said. "Wh."

"What?" you asked him. "Or who? Or why?"

He breathed in. He stared at you. He breathed out. His Adam's apple moved up and down.

"Oh," you said. "Water."

You went into the kitchen and came back with a full glass and a wet rag. You poured the water into the man's mouth and he tried to swallow, but it spilled out and made a mess around his face. You used the rag to wipe the vomit from his chest, but he winced whenever the rag got close to the wound. You'd meant to tell him about your plans for him, about the work he'd accomplished simply by dying that night. Now, however, with his perplexed and exhausted eyes following you around the room, straining to stay open, with his labored breathing, you thought that a sermon might violate the sanctity of the moment.

"Hungry rats eat fat rats," you said.

You knelt beside the man. The knife handle was flush against his skin. You wondered if you could turn the blade. You knew you could, but you wondered if it would turn with ease or difficulty. "I wish that this didn't have to happen to you," you said. You turned the blade. It wasn't hard. The man's eyes opened again, wide, and he banged his head against the carpeted floor. He tensed, strangling on his own breath. He stopped. He shuddered. "I'm sorry," you said. You pulled the blade out. His blood began to move again. "I wish it didn't..." you started to say, but his eyes didn't focus. You stood.

"Rodney," you said, handing him the knife, "go wash this. And put on your gloves!" Rodney left and you took a long nail from your purse. You'd saved this nail since you were thirteen.

You xed the man's hands.

He breathed in. He breathed out. He breathed in. He breathed out. He did not breathe in.

Flood of Jesus, mill pond of all virtues, have mercy on us.

Here is what lies beneath: esemplasy.

November. Something. 2003.

"Maria Puerta."

...

When you realized that the man had died, you stood and walked to the window. Victory rushed in on you like a flood, a flame, and you threw caution to the wind and opened the curtains wide. A fire burned, right before you. You still had time to feed it. It was still far away. But you didn't have forever. It approached, noiseless in the moment, but at night you dreamt you heard it. It cracked and slapped and the timber it burned hissed and snapped like a thousand hands clapping. It ate all. Sinful. Snow pure. The forests. The eyes. A moving mountain. An ocean of oil. A pillar of fire. A starbitten salt. Aurora. Redemption. Destruction. Annihilation. Resurrection. The rats ran among it and before it. The mainstream flowed from it and into it. All those corpses. All those rats.

You took the dead rats from your purse. They were still wet, but you'd sealed them in a plastic bag. You tucked them in the man's socks and placed them at the back of his chest of drawers. You didn't want them to be found right away. Only after a day or two. Part of your planned evolution of murder. You took off the man's messy shirt and put it in a plastic bag. You cleaned him up and put a clean shirt on him, making sure to cut it in the right spots so that it wouldn't be stained with his blood. Then, you made his bed. You washed his dishes. You turned off the lights and his muted television.

"What are you doing, Rodney?" you asked.

He didn't answer. He stood over the man's body. He blinked his eyes fast; he was trying hard not to cry. A touch of drool hung in the corner of his mouth and his hands clutched the knife like a vise and the knife was black with blood. There was blood on the knife. The blood had dried like a crisp and crinkled ketchup stain.

"I know it hurt, Rodney," you said. You pried the knife from his fingers and carried it to the sink. You scrubbed and scrubbed and washed and washed. "But sometimes you've got to hurt people in order to help them. Now let's get going. The longer we stay here, we're more likely to get caught."

Don't boast about tomorrow, for you don't know what a day might bring.

Let's see what we've got to read.

Fishermen at Sea confronts us with a most desolate

scene. Ocularily inquiring regarding a brief redoubt in the looms and shadows and furrows of a mounting range of black clouds, the pale Luna shines out, a plaintive beacon, distant, cut off and ultimately vulnerable, and yet never so vulnerable as the desperate flicker that licks out from the precariously hung lantern above the seizing maw of the Sea. Between our immanence and an umber-or-silver inked haze of horizon, huge, ambiguous shapes merge and loom. Are they rocks engorged upon the shallows? Or are they immense seagoing vessels forged in the Abyss perhaps by an alien race of beings? And from such an intrepid distance, the tranquility, the stillness of the water and the waves is deceptive.

Bowls and plateaus in ponderous succession rock the tiny black frame upon which we make out by the mooncast silhouettes against a backdrop of chaos and foam five or six humans, small, inconsequential, only hoping that they may escape with their lives, but all bound and hypnotized by the oblivion chains bound to pounce as soon as the clouds tumble in around the moon. Extinguish their pendulum lantern.

Jesus, Mary, Joseph, I give you my ax and my peavey.
Jesus, Mary, Joseph, assist me in my last toot.
Jesus, Mary, Joseph, may I sleep and rest in peace with you.

November. Something. Two thousand plus three.

Have you actually been reading this shit?

Less than a week after the first event, after it rained and you got rats, you performed your penance again. This time, it wasn't as raw and powerful as your first merry-go-round, but you thought you made up this loss with greater composure and clinical precision.

It was a blind date. A classified ad. You met the man at a bar downtown, and in the Thursday dark the booth where you both sat was tucked away where no one would notice. At one point, the man said something about the watery beer and went to the bathroom. *It couldn't have been too watery*, you thought, *or he would have noticed the antifreeze.* Next time, though, you figured you'd make the victim order a stout. *That ought to hide the taste. And don't go too heavy on that poison*, you thought. You needed the police to think it was the knifing that killed them. If it even bought you a week, you could kill once or twice more without getting caught, and hopefully slip back home to California, to retire or prepare the next installments, and only time would tell.

You left the bar before the man came back. You left a note that you'd meet him at his house. Later, late, when the riot in his veins left him still and comatose, you let Rodney in through the side door.

"Quiet, Rodney," you said.

Rodney sat on the man's chest, asphyxiating him, and stabbed him three times with the knife. You xed the man and left rats.

Whoever wanders from the way of getting things will sit and rest with the rest of the dead.

...

Angry eyes and a proud heart – the lamp of the wicked – are sin.

The lamp of the wicked?

Like fishermen smoothly dragged away from the regular undulations of the deep sea to the intersecting waves of the perilous shoals and shores. Like moons soldered shut behind hostile clouds. Like a heaving pendulum, your only light was that lamp.

When your two Flint events hadn't drawn much press, you decided to try the suburbs. Your judgments were universal. Everyone must suffer and suffer alike. You chose a small ranch house at the center of a cornfield. Each year, developers ripped out some of the corn and put in a new house. The houses, however, stood a quarter-mile apart.

During the day you broke in and spiked her coffee and orange juice with antifreeze. After sunset, you returned with Rodney. He climbed the telephone pole, cut the phone wires, and together you approached the house.

"Go to the back, Rodney," you said. "Wait until I let you in." You wrapped your purse around your wrist. To hold the lip shut and hide the rats inside.

You knocked. A moment. No sound of footsteps. The woman crossed a gray shag carpet. Her door opened a crack.
"May I help you?" she asked. You didn't hear any pain in her voice.
"Ah, yes," you said, thinking fast. "My car has broken down. Can I use your phone?" You put your hand on the door and tried to push it open, but it had been chained.
"Apologies," you said.

The woman's brow creased.

"May I please borrow your phone?" you repeated.

"I'll get it," she said.

No, you thought, *open the door.*

Instead, she walked away into the house. You heard her phone taken from its cradle, and now the woman returned. As she approached, she put the phone to her ear and pressed the TALK button for a dial tone. Her face changed. She stopped. You must have winced. She flinched. She tried to kick the door shut, but you stopped it with your fist. She noticed you were wearing gloves. She turned and ran into the house.

"Rodney!" you screamed. From the kitchen, where she ran, a discordant chiming roar. A vast sheet of glass had shattered. You jammed your hand into the crack in the door, searching for the end of the chain. The woman had almost reached an exit. Then, at the edge of your vision, she turned on her foot. Pivoted. Like a ballerina shrugging off the demands of gravity, ready to fly away or lock herself in the bathroom. But Rodney's young hands emerged from the dark doorway and fastened upon her ankle. You caught your wrist on the chain latch and sliced your skin open. The woman stumbled and fell. She clawed at the carpet, screaming vowel sounds. Rodney's hands dragged her back.

"Rodney!" you yelled.

The screaming became mangled shrieks, then slackened, then stopped.

You pulled your arm from the door, taking care to press your bleeding wrist against your jacket and not the wall itself.

"Rodney, let me in!"

Silence. Then, the sound of a metal edge against something thickly solid but ultimately hollow. A gasping. Air, as if from a bellows. Sticky liquid sounds. You hurried around the house. In the distance, yellow squares showed the neighbors' houses, and the air felt cold and crisp. Through the corn sheaves, glittering Christmas lights, early in waiting. Before Advent. The wind moved.

Behind the house, you stepped through what had been a sliding glass door. Rodney had shattered it with a huge rock. Inside, he had stabbed the woman in the kitchen, first with your steak knife, and then evidently with every other knife he could find. His cuts upon her throat and abdomen had almost separated her in several places, and he'd dragged what still clung together, a mass of red ribbons, to the living room to let you in.

"Rodney!" you said, exasperated. "Bad Rodney. But I forgive you. We don't do it this way, remember."

He'd left her face down on the floor. You knelt and turned her over to x her, and felt a catch in your throat. You never studied anatomy, but here you found a human, beautifully arrayed. She glistened and shimmered as if she'd just come in from swimming. Humans are mostly water. Our organs are packed very tight and efficient. All of our parts and pieces. Here you saw that a treasure chest had been flung wide open for you to see. Her lips. Her eyes. Her dense and fist-sized jewels.

"Thank you, Rodney," you said.

x and x.

Hurriedly, you scrawled the word 'RAT' in the woman's blood across the house and left your rats on the floor. You vaguely remembered that someone had spelled something in blood before, but there was no time to work out something subtler. Better. You ran to the shower and scrubbed and scrubbed. Sent Rodney to the shower and told him to wash. You hurried around the house and wiped down the doorknobs. You wiped off your blood from the chain latch, and when you were afraid that some blood had maybe dried on the inside of the groove, you found some screwdrivers and removed the lock entirely. You put it in your purse. You opened the woman's fridge. The orange juice was as full as you'd found it that morning. Her coffee pot sat untouched. You poured the drinks down the drain, then scrubbed the sink with Comet to hide the traces.

You worried about the amount of time you spent in that house, under that soot-gray sky. Everything had gone wrong. Still, when you left, only an hour had passed since you'd arrived.

We have to pay better attention, you thought, *so that we do not drift away from the mission. For the message... declared through... valid... and... every transgression... or disobedience... it all receives a just penalty.*

> At first, to the unfamiliar eye *Shade and darkness – the evening of the Deluge* evokes a child's errant paint mistake, the colors butter-churned soot gray and Christmas glow yellow. An understanding of the lines quoted from *Fallacies of Hope* is absolutely essential. We need not discuss them here.

Maggie and Jim would have understood.

We of become of the arc of movement of the work,

flung of firmament of firmament, of angles among angles, of and there appears to be an empty space, left, the primary occupant of which is the tossed and churning air. Already sheets of pale rain pile from the sky, and the blackish, brackish clouds stack heavenward, churn and grow. Another churning, however, occurs below, where multitudes of scraps tumble and scumble. Looking more closely, we make out horses and oxen, a man on his back, rabbits and unicorns and hippopotomi and dragons and hyenas, all moving along and through some vast structure that thunderously climbs up, into, and through the storm.

Ada and Jim.

And of however. Of however! A bitch and her offspring, standing in the lower register, a point of clarity among these vague, indistinct and tremulously nervous figures looks straight out at us, the audience, as if they were iphigenias.

Maria Puerta.

They are hurt and scared and a little wounded amid these monstrosities. They just came along for the ride, but now, unknowingly, they ride for their bare survival. In their fear, they are fortunate. Others did not fear, and in the absence of defiant, defining terror, perished.

Have you actually been reading this?

Once upon a time there was a little rabbit who loved to dress up in a navy blue turtleneck embroidered with the image of a little pink hare wearing an olive green turtleneck bearing the image of a little rabbit upon it.

They're all watching us.

At home in Wexford County, you rarely saw a mirror.

After killing Mrs. Helmet, you finally began to pick up some national press. These were moments to celebrate. The first two murders had been an effort to break even. To claw your way out of the blood and into the ink. From now on, everything counted pure profit of the heart.

...

You thought you should take on a whole family, where one effort, one night's work, might double or triple the count of your first three events. Your first three actions. Your first three effects. You were particularly excited to kill children. In America, and throughout the world, you supposed, children received unfair sympathy. There was a paradox here that you both engaged and indulged. In Joshua, the children of Jericho met their slaughter head on. And they, the children, were the evil ones. Later, the same might be said of the youth of the Philistines. You supposed a single idolic sacrifice was worse than most of today's more conspicuous sins, but then, you weren't really a fair arbiter and, let's be frank, everyone killed everyone back then, right? Yet Christ set the children aside as privileged members of His kingdom. They sat on Michael's shoulder and rested their feet on their parents' backs.

It all moves toward effect. Event. From this nest of contradiction, a new effect. An ethical effect broke forth!

You wanted your victims caught in seeming apprehension of the world. To inflict their witnesses with the eyes and rendings. With them. The surest spurs are always the sharpest, and the most able cowboys... well, we live in a world of plastic rocking horses, if you know what I mean. Before there was plastic, we were surrounded not by plastic, but by great big woods. The virgin forest of Arthurian Michigan all burned and fell. Kings and warriors, millennia in the making, didn't give a shit about the Gypsy moths, after all, but about the growing pains of this young and rifting good Christian nation. Now, southern California burned. The lumberjack ghosts had arrived, and with them, the mainstream.

You have always claimed that God singled out all of His Children for Singular Punishment because His Expectations for Them were Singularly High. The problem that you discovered in your long absence is that humans constantly discover anesthesia.

Okay. Sure. No prob.

You could make them feel every barb and nettle. Deanesthetization.

Hell is a burning forest.

Anesthesia is the end of survival.

You never meant to hurt anyone.

You're a very empathetic person.

You... love... everyone.

Your love winds itself round and round in circles, much like that river once did.

That mainstream.

Anywho, some say, Aunt Margaret, some say, in their scrubbed clean email forwards, that the closest thing to love is hate.

You loved them all enough to make them bleed.

But no. You're wrong.

There *is* a difference between putting your arms around me, giving me comfort and affection, and telling me that life isn't a road I must travel alone... and putting antifreeze in my drink, then cutting me to death when I get sick.

There is a difference between these things.

There is a vast distance between love and hate.

But you disagree. Because *you* owed penance for a dozen generations. *You* owed penance for the brothers and sisters. *You* have repented. They? Never.

You helped repair the damage.

Them? Never.

The Maladys, Carrs, and Duncans, the whole filthy shitscrubbed clan, have gone on riots over a hundred years, with never a sense of direction and purpose.

How appropriate.

How perfect.

Your premeditated but reluctant riot has succeeded over and over and broken headlines with the New York Times.

Their riot, the debased prostitution and violence of illiterate masses of leering half-Christians, has locked itself in a single heretical hereditary cycle. Cut itself under. Floated itself away. Finally and ultimately debased itself.

You opened the doors to the fires and cleansing.

They decayed, and decaying, affected nobody and no one.

You ascended through your own descent.

...

I've said it before: you exactly resemble Maggie Duncan, Margaret Carr. I know because I have the photo. When you moved away with Rodney, Dad must have found it with your other things and packed it away in the attic. You did guess that I had found it. You thought that I wouldn't guess its significance. Well, I guessed. Do you want to see it? You haven't seen it in years. Her broad and beautiful face. Her perfect icy lips. Her tangled, ratty hair. Her hidden non-nose. Her eyes.

She *sees* you.

She looks out through the picture paper, and sees our automobiles and televisions and coffee pots and dishwashers, one hundred years after she died, turning tricks in the snow. Oh, Maggie. You can see us now, can't you? I know. Because these are your eyes, these, these. Because I can see you too.

February 303rd, 1930 + sixty + ten plus three.

Boom!

And an ice knife.

...

After you killed the Grims, Rodney sat and smiled as he sawed and sawed. They sat together. You thought you'd measured the doses well this time, giving enough antifreeze that they were incapacitated, almost comatose, and could not move. Yet you still had time to explain to most of them, to lay the quilt over their legs and place within the mother's inexplicably jerking hands her tender photo album. Amalee was already asleep. She might have seen Rodney before she went, but that was just your own good luck. So what I wonder, Margaret, is if I went up to the attic... if I went up there now, alone, would I find Rodney in his bedroom? And did you just poison him to death, or did you bother with the rats after all?

Anyhow. Candi Grim seemed too shaken and upset to accept your kindness, but you were happy to have offered it in the first place. You knew that you were a murderer and in light of this you took pains to extend an extra dose of empathy in consideration of your painful relationship with your victims. Two tearful hours passed before there was even any mention of knives.

By morning, the Grims stared out, the opposite of Maggie Duncan, present but not seeing. Rodney grinned, and the spit on his lips shimmered through the gloom. He cut and cut and sawed and sawed and there was blood on the knife.

Jesus did so much. So much. I suppose if everything was written down, I suppose... I suppose... that the world itself could not contain the books that would be written.

"O Father Jove, yet kill us in the light," said Mr. Catgut.

Maria Puerta.

ESEMPLASY

"Jim," Maggie says. "This is for us."

Jim leans over the tally book, his fingers bracing his forehead and his elbows on the desk. He looks up at her. She leans against the doorway. She has her right arm on the frame of the door. In her left hand she holds a newspaper: the *Cleaver*. She hands it to him and he reads the words in ink:

MOVE TO MEREDITH!
SAGINAW AND CLARE COUNTY LINE TO EXTEND SERVICE FROM LONG LAKE TO MEREDITH

After Jim reads the article he doesn't speak. His eyes glint as dark and sharp as a gang saw. Neither Jim nor Maggie smiles. Their happiness is greater than smiles. They love each other, and they know it.

* * * * *

Bitty lies out on the beach.

"Hey, Betty," she says. "I'm gonna get the most sunburned ever."

"What?" asks Betty, wrinkling up her face, incredulous, confused.

"I'm not afraid of the sun! I love the sun, Betty. Watch me lay out here in the sun. Watch me. Watch me do it all day. They said in school you get three kinds of burn, the first where you turn red and sore, the second where your skin splits, and the third where it burns black and wide open and falls off. But I'm going to come up with a more way for that! You watch, Betty! I'm gonna sit in the sun 'til I got the greatest sunburn ever! I'm not afraid of the sun. I'm gonna sit in the sun 'til I get all burned up."

"Bitty, you're a dumb bitch," Betty says.

Betty plays in the water.

* * * * *

Mara slices her thumb open while cutting a tomato in the kitchen of the house on Maryland Avenue.

"What the fuck!" she says, blood spilling onto the cutting board.

"What's wrong?" calls Mark from the other room.

"Just sliced my fuckin' finger with the fuckin' knife!"

"So put on a bandage," he answers.

Mara storms toward the bathroom. She slams the door so hard that the windows rattle in their rickety frames, and an empty plastic cup falls from the sill to the floor.

* * * * *

Rodney sits in the television room, the smallest room in the house.

He's watching TV by himself. A fuzzy hip-pop ditty buzzes through the strained frequency, but a pink ball bounces from word to word, and Rodney composes his own song:

"Itz... zittig... ot... tigair... zodake... awful... loze... azittig... zo ot... abada dake... badozov."

One room away, at a heavy oak table, Margaret is intent on the medical bills before her. Weeks overdue, months overdue, and she hasn't filled some prescriptions in almost a year. It affects Rodney's behavior, it really does. Margaret usually feels more composed than she does tonight, but the bright track light shines too directly into her eyes and she rubs and squints harder at the numbers under her thumb.

"I can't do this," she says to herself. "That damn medication. That drive." She runs her fingers through her hair, smoothing out her brow.

She breathes in slowly, hoping to calm herself.

She exhales.

She slams her fist against the table, but immediately recovers. She takes a quick sip from her cup of chamomile tea.

* * * * *

Mr. Catgut sits in his favorite chair, the one his father had threatened to throw away decades ago. When his mother had passed on, Mr. Catgut had found the chair in the attic, covered with mothballs. Now, with the relic restored to a place of honor in his study, the teacher grades essays on the American Revolution, jotting quick slashes and hieroglyphics in the margins.

Occasionally, he pauses to write more thoughtful, complete notes.

Finally, he finishes the last paper, and with an excitement that makes him shake, unable not to smile, he pulls an old edition of Hobbes' translation of *The Iliad* from the shelf. He quickly finds his favorite passage and reads aloud in a booming, stage voice:

> *O Jove, give us once more a sky serene;*
> *Remove this mist that we may see to fight.*
> *Or if to kill the Argives all you mean,*
> *O Father Jove, yet kill us in the light.*

He shivers and sets the book aside.

* * * * *

Ashley lay in the bed of Brian's pickup. They are under a blanket, under the stars, and Brian has fallen asleep. Ashley shivers in the cold. She has developed a rash on her shoulder from an allergy. Instead of curling into his arms, she lies flat on her back to let her eyes fully acclimate. To see the dim stars behind bright ones, and even fainter objects hiding like ghosts against the deeper ink.

She breathes out and sees her breath before her.

"Hello? Are you out there, life?" she asks. "And if so, do you know how miserable we all are down here?"

* * * * *

Meredith has just left the library at the U of M campus in downtown Flint. She has finished her first shift shelving books, and while she likes her new job, she has decided that it won't keep her from transferring. To Ann Arbor. To Lansing or Detroit or... who knows? Anywhere. She can go anywhere.

At the moment, however, she is happy where she is. Happy at home. Happy at night.

She may call Ashley, or drop in on Amalee, or reply to Ms. Leavings' worried email. She may even write her Aunt Margaret in prison, though they'll never meet face-to-face. Or maybe Meredith will stay in tonight, at home in her apartment on Nebraska Avenue – you never leave the Eastside – drinking Mountain Dew and watching pirated movies.

But this is all for the minutes and hours to come. Right now, she stands astride the river on a bridge that once linked two stretches of road. They've been torn out and replaced by a rolling green, by night autumnal gray, that fades away to the north and south, the campus on both sides.

The surface of the river is mirror-still. The businesses and mid-rises downtown, neon signs and fiery globes shine out and reflect off the water. It seems to be a pure plane of crystal. The reflection, a fire. The horizon, a darker gray. It fades. In the approaching darkness, the wilted grass seems almost to become green again. In the moving dusk, the chill wind seems almost to describe the lonely contours of a soul passing through space. A lonely soul lost. Yet content somehow.

Wounded but bypassed by the worst of the flames. Above and beyond the mainstream. Feeding on the scraps like a good true ghost.

Turn your face up, she thinks. *Turn your face back down.*

Water chestnuts and tea, she thinks.

Esemplasy, she thinks.

* * * * *

For you:
To send you on your way:

> "Some love to roam o'er the dark sea foam,
> Where the wild winds whistle free;
> But a chosen band in a forest land
> And a life in the woods for me."

> And a life in the woods for me.

DISCUSSION QUESTIONS

1. Meredith Malady grew up in an abusive household. To what extent to you think Meredith's attitudes and actions are explained by her own upbringing? What about Mara? What about Margaret? What about Bitty and Betty and Rodney, or Mark, Maggie, and Jim?

2. All of the murderers in *Hungry Rats* thrive in relation to communities that exist for a single economic purpose, and then are abandoned. How do economic problems create social dilemmas for Flint and Meredith, Michigan? What other cities have had similar problems? How have they coped?

3. Meredith, Margaret, Maggie, Ashley, and most of the other main characters of *Hungry Rats* are women. How do men and women relate to one another in the novel, and how do the women in the story adapt to social, cultural, and economic expectations?

4. *Hungry Rats* is written primarily in conditional second-person, in which the main character is "you," but the speaker is also important. How does this affect the understanding of objective "facts" of the story? At the end of the novel, did you feel that you knew who the Rat Man really was?

This novel did begin with a body of sorts, but it happened in August 2003.

One night, in Flint, my girlfriend and I were out for a drive on the Eastside of Flint, Michigan. Late at night, we saw a human lying in fetal position at the corner of Belle and Lewis, and we drove back to our home on Maryland Ave, and called the police. The next day, I scoured the papers for a report, but found none. I figured that the woman had probably passed out; she would've been taken to the hospital and presumably recovered. But the seed was planted, and later that year I wrote a draft that later become *Hungry Rats*. I have worked at it for seven years, and it's been a provocative, difficult task for me. *Hungry Rats* is about running away, about serial killers, about everything that is dirty and dark in the world, and it has been difficult to keep upbeat working on it, even while it has gotten a better reception than any of the other writing I have done. After submitting it to many publishers and agents, I hatched a plan to self-publish. I spent months raising money, and a few weeks ago I finished the final edit. In one week the novel will be sent out to the printer. It is my official entrance onto the literary scene. It is a major "moment" of my life, somewhere below getting married and having a child, and above graduating from high school. I have worked toward this moment for decades.

Unfortunately, Flint has had a moment of its own lately, and one that makes my little book seem incidental. While I have spent seven years writing about an imaginary serial killer, a real one has taken aim at my hometown, killing five people and attacking another eight. It is despicable, disgusting, and it breaks my heart because this place has already been through so much -- has already suffered greatly. A fourteenth, hypothetical, victim ran to the hospital yesterday from the intersection of Sunset and Ballenger. My best friend and I had taken many walks there in the middle of the night. It was a "safe" neighborhood. The city at night was still, warm, comfortable, musical. There was little to fear, or so it seemed, when we walked down a busy road in the darkness on a hot summer night.

So what do I do?

I didn't write this novel to capitalize on the work of a murderer; to turn a profit from the pain he has caused. I wrote a book that was supposed to look at murder, at violence, and also at independence and freedom and courage and the struggle for a clear perspective. At unrealistic but necessary hope. Like most serious writers, I don't think my work is "mere" entertainment. It is a homily, a sermon, an argument, a plea for its readers to scrutinize their lives more closely.

I have asked many people for advice this week: friends, family, Flint residents and diaspora, law-enforcement and journalists and old and young. It has been a source of great anxiety for me. I've lost sleep. I've had bad dreams. To my surprise, not one person has suggested I abandon publication. Not one person has even suggested I delay publication, since a delay would imply that I had responded to this event, instead of writing a book ahead of the crime. And so I have decided to move ahead with the publication of *Hungry Rats* on schedule.

I am proud of this work, I will be hopeful and mindful that it does not cause unnecessary hurt, but I also hope that it will be a respite, a consideration, maybe even a small catharsis for a community that has been jammed through yet another horrible trial. Above all, I hope that it speaks well of me, because next year I will be moving back to Flint, my hometown.

With all of this in mind, I would like to make an announcement now that I had hoped to hold until the release of the novel:

I will be donating all of my profits through 12/31/2010 to the Food Bank of Eastern Michigan.

From the beginning, this novel has been about my career, not about some slim profit, and I would like to do something small to help my state and hometown this hard year.

Many of you have supported me greatly so far. I ask for your continued help, when *Hungry Rats* comes out in a few weeks. I hope that you will take the book out into the world, with an understanding that our fictions, light and dark, our stories, are how we teach each other, how we understand and relate to one another. I wrote about a killer and now: there is a killer. It's a frightening thought. We don't predict these things, and we cannot prophesy them. But we do know, intuitively, what we fear, and what we imagine that can become real. God help Flint. And thank you for listening and understanding.

Connor Coyne

ACKNOWLEDGMENTS

After seven years, there are many thanks to be given. I'd like to start off by thanking God for holding close to me through this project, in both its adventures and its ordeals. Without my wife, true love, and best friend Jessica, none of this would have been possible. My dear little Mary has kept me up (awake and alert) during the difficulties of the last few months; this novel is for her as much as anyone. My wonderful supportive family, those Coynes and Jalbrzikowskis and Fultons, Mom and Dad, Grandma, Aunt Georgia, Caitlin and Cody, Catherine, Bill, Becky, Jeff, Julie, Chelsea, you keep me going every day. You have been beyond patient with this weird career of mine, and I am grateful for you every moment of every day. Paul is a cornerstone; he is wise and he teaches me how to live and enjoy life. Also, Elisabeth Blair has been an incredible editor, and Sam Perkins-Harbin an incredible designer; I could not have done it without them. Jeffery Renard Allen at New School was my advisor, but he has supported this novel since I graduated three years ago; thank you Jeff.

Also at the New School, my peer group of Hosanna Patience, Sarah Grant, Erica Ciccarone, and David Odegard have given wonderful advice and insight. I must also thank Reinhardt Suarez, Scott Larner, Marco Rafalà, Amy Lawless, Alex Smith, Maggie Kast, Mark Bibbins, David Gates, Shelley Jackson, Darcey Steinke, Sharon Mesmer, and Helen Schulman for their invaluable feedback. Gemma Cooper-Novack read the whole thing back when it was rough and raw; without her it would be still be ugly, and presumably unpublished. Thanks to Emily Perkins-Harbin and Amber Staab for their hard work on the promo videos. The Gothic Funk Nation provided support and a home throughout this process: thanks to Hallie Palladino for reading opportunities at Tuesday Funk, and Skylar Moran for helping with virtually any problem that came up. Thanks to Richard Whaling, Elisabeth Blair, Nova Moturba, Electro Feel, and Mr. Automatic for providing original music to promote the novel. I have to shout out to Alan Gandelman and Gary Neul for coming through for me in my hour of need. Leila Sales, and Arlene Malinowski came through for me with awesome blurbs; you're the best!

My Kickstarter Backers funded this publication; without them it would never have happened. I want to thank Jen Kennedy, Elisabeth Blair, Katie Call, Amber Staab, Marco Rafala, Camellia, Paul Lathrop, Irene Hodes, Matt Reading, Mary Cole, Joe Anderson, Amy Lamboley, chocolatedinosaur, Richard Whaling, Austin Robison, Patrick Augustine, Matt Fink, Meridith Halsey, Joe Bolte, Maggie Kast, H. Joseph Blair, Victor Galea, Hosanna Patience, the Michigan Coyne Family, Jessica, Hannah, the Original Perkins-Harbins, Armand Ryden, Sarah Nerboso, Barbara Swem, Skylar Moran, Cambria Moran, Sarah Grant, Nick Carone, Ben Golden, Emily Taylor, Tana Tymeson, Jacob Saenz, Stephanie Anderson, Sheila Miller-Lathrop, Caron Mosey, Kaury Eisenman, Dawn, Mercedes Gilliom, Jonathan Williams, Aashish Mewada, Allie, Cate Tolzmann, and Lisa.

Uncovering the inspiring and infamous details of lumber-era Michigan was a long and complicated task. I could not have done this without the help of Tom Sellers of Harrison, or Lynn McGlothlin Emerick and Ann McGlothlin Weller. The writings of Tom Powers, Stuart Gross, and William S. Crowe expressed opposite perspectives of the lumber frontier, equally valuable for writing Part II. John Fitzmaurice and E.C. Beck offered powerful accounts of life in the lumber camps of Northern Michigan. The poetry of their long labors appear in these pages (uncited, but such is the nature of subtle allusion) and they have done much to preserve an important era of American history. Ditto Heinrich Heine. Of course Ann Lethbridge is a known name among Flint-area historians, but the Flint Journal Centennial Picture History was also essential.

Noir and the black novel is a rich tradition. Many thanks to Robert Polito for giving of his time and pointing me toward some superb novels. For a more precise look at serial homicide, I have to thank Veronica Howard and Nick Carone for their insiders perspective (and great patience with my unending stream of questions), and the very thorough analysis of former Chief of Police Devon Stavrowsky and Kris Anderson; without their help, the procedural aspects would have beem much less compelling.

In Flint, I am most indebted to Ken VanWagoner and the Good Beans Cafe, and the Perkins-Harbins and Crawford Families. Sumara

Brown, Caron Mosey, Mary Ann Chick Whiteside, Thad Domick, Greg Nicolai, Marcy Sheldon, and Melodee Hagensen gave me valuable insights at critical junctures. And I have many old friends there, some going way far back; I am grateful to all of you. Even after this long list, I'm sure I've left many people off. Thanks to you as well. Add on Harrison and Meredith, Michigan, for striving and sometimes thriving; for their incredible stories and histories.

Finally, I want to thank the city of Flint for being its magnificent self, and especially the Eastside. Remember it for its anger, its rage, its desire, and for its past beauty despite hunger, its present diversity despite want, and God willing, its promise and hope for the future. State Streets forever!

ABOUT THE AUTHOR

Connor Coyne grew up in Flint, Michigan, and has lived in Chicago and New York City. He received his BA from the University of Chicago and his MFA from the New School. He has written plays, poetry, essays, short stories, and novels, and his work has been published in *Santa Clara Review*, *Moria Poetry Zine*, *Dick Pig Review*, *The Saturnine Detractor*, and the Flint *Broadside*. He maintains a website at connorcoyne.com. *Hungry Rats* is his first published novel, but he is even more excited about the recent birth of his daughter, Mary Adelina.

Photograph © 2009 Lisa Marie Ogle